Quest

Quest

Steve Whittington

Copyright © 2018 Steve Whittington
The moral right of the author has been asserted.

Apart from any fair dealing for the purposes of research or private study, or criticism or review, as permitted under the Copyright, Designs and Patents Act 1988, this publication may only be reproduced, stored or transmitted, in any form or by any means, with the prior permission in writing of the publishers, or in the case of reprographic reproduction in accordance with the terms of licences issued by the Copyright Licensing Agency. Enquiries concerning reproduction outside those terms should be sent to the publishers.

This is a work of fiction. Names, characters, businesses, places, events and incidents are either the products of the author's imagination or used in a fictitious manner. Any resemblance to actual persons, living or dead, or actual events is purely coincidental.

Matador
9 Priory Business Park,
Wistow Road, Kibworth Beauchamp,
Leicestershire. LE8 0RX
Tel: 0116 279 2299
Email: books@troubador.co.uk
Web: www.troubador.co.uk/matador
Twitter: @matadorbooks

ISBN 978 1789013 245

British Library Cataloguing in Publication Data.
A catalogue record for this book is available from the British Library.

Printed and bound in Great Britain by 4edge Limited
Typeset in 11pt Minion Pro by Troubador Publishing Ltd, Leicester, UK

Matador is an imprint of Troubador Publishing Ltd

To Alan with all my love

Contents

Prologue	ix
Part I – Beziers	1
Part II – Rome	107
Part III – Palestine	169
Part IV – Coming Home	257

Prologue: January 1208

It was more than an hour after nightfall when the dejected little straggle of men finally reached the banks of the Rhone. A pale moon revealed the swirling eddies of the great river glinting and rippling, but the last few miles had been wearisome, even without the constant fear of attack. Pierre de Castelnau, legate of His Holiness Pope Innocent III, swung his tired and aching legs down from his horse, winced at the pain in his hip and almost slipped on the muddy shore. He could not have been described as a cheery man at the best of times, but the failure of his mission and the growing evidence of physical decline combined to darken his mood on this particular evening.

'Prepare food!' he snapped at no-one in particular.

'Sir, there is nothing. We… left so suddenly,' replied the nearest of his entourage, a youngish man named Elmo with a pock-marked face which seemed to be frozen in a permanent sneer.

'Didn't you see the cottages we passed along the track? Surely there must be one devout Christian left in this benighted land to offer sustenance to a legate of His Holiness!'

Elmo bowed silently, perhaps a touch sarcastically, and backed off. Fearful of riding back alone, he hastily persuaded another of the servants to come with him and they remounted their mules and disappeared into the darkness.

'Damned fools!' Pierre muttered. He glared round at the

other men who were making sure they looked busy, lighting a fire, setting up their master's tent, unpacking pots, pans and blankets.

Once the fire was lit and starting to give off a little circle of warmth he huddled before it, shrouded in his cloak, and gazed into the flames with blank eyes. The day had been a disaster, of that there could be no doubt. He saw now that the meeting with Count Raymond and the public debate had been futile from the start, maybe even a trap. The villain had never had the slightest intention of denouncing the heretic faith. Indeed heresy was clearly being allowed to flourish right across the lands under the sway of Toulouse, like weeds in an untended field. Raymond himself might still more or less follow the dictates of the Holy Church, but he had evidently taken a decision that the only way to prevent a complete breakdown of the feudal order – and his own power – was to turn a blind eye to even the most heretical of practices.

Pierre stretched out his aching legs towards the fire in the vain hope that the warmth would ease the pain, and tried to clear his mind to think. Without help from the Count there could be little hope of fulfilling his mission. His own men had picked up enough tittle-tattle from drinking companions along the road to suggest that maybe half the people of the Languedoc sought spiritual advice from shadowy leaders of the foul heresy rather than from their duly appointed priests. They believed in reincarnation, they believed the world was ruled by the devil, they denied the sacrament of the body and blood of Christ! What blasphemous poppycock wouldn't they believe!

The question was, what to do now? There seemed to be no sense in further parleying, even if Raymond would receive him again. His parting words could be read two ways. What was it he had said exactly? "Take care on your journey, Excellency, there may be dangers on the road for a traveller of your standing. I cannot answer for your safety in these days…" No, he must get out of these parts as quickly as possible. They would charter a boat in the morning to take them down to Marseille from where they could return to Rome in their own ship, and the sooner the better.

Pierre shuddered as he foresaw the inevitable reaction of His Holiness. He would be furious at first, of course. He would rail against the unruly princes, the devious peddlers of false creeds, and the godless fools who gave them the time of day when they should be praying to save their own souls. But Innocent was not just the representative of God on earth; he was no innocent in the ways of the world! He calculated like a prince and would move on swiftly to weighing up his next step. Pierre sighed, knowing what that step would be. Surely now His Holiness would launch the crusade against the heretics that he had wanted all along? The wrath of Rome would be turned not on infidels from the east, not on barbarian despoilers of Jerusalem. Instead it would be turned on men and women from within the realm of Christendom, men and women who only a couple of generations ago had been loyal to Rome.

Pierre might well despise the heretics, and he did. But he kept returning to the words of one of those who had spoken up in the public debate earlier that day. The young man had been a powerful speaker, and brazen in his defence of the heresy. But he had gone on to criticise priests of the Holy Church who railed against adultery from the pulpit, but who were known to engage in carnal acts – with men and women alike! The young man had spoken of the extravagant lifestyle of the priesthood, their rich raiment and groaning tables funded by the tithes of the poor.

Well, of course, there were rotten apples in every sack. But Pierre knew that there was more than a grain of truth in the young man's words, and that many in the church had grown lax. Might it not be partly true that the heresy had grown strong in soil made fertile by that laxity? Should he not advise His Holiness that some edict against priestly excesses should be sent out before the ultimate step was taken? But how would Innocent react to such advice?

Pierre looked up as Elmo and the other man returned from their foraging.

'Well, what have the people provided?'

'Sir, we found the home of a peasant farmer and his wife half a league back along the track. They seemed fearful and at first they said they had no supplies beyond the bread and thin gruel we found them dining on, but we soon found a good reserve of salted pork in an outhouse. They said they couldn't spare any, so we agreed we would only take half. There should be enough here for a goodly supper, and there's a flagon of wine too!'

The man looked at Pierre, evidently hoping for praise.

'And what did you give these poor people for their assistance?'

'Give them, sir?'

Pierre sighed. 'Go back, man, and give them this. Tell them that the legate of the Holy Church is grateful for their kindness. Are you trying to turn decent people into heretics?' He looked up with tired eyes and held out a couple of coins.

Elmo was half-minded to refuse, but he saw the glint in Pierre's eye and took the coins. He had the feeling that there might not be much salted pork left by the time he returned unless he hurried.

'And if you're tempted to pocket the money, remember that God is watching you! Go, now!'

'Yes, Excellency!' Elmo replied, remounting and backing away nervously before turning and disappearing once more into the darkness. He could not understand why Pierre had suddenly developed such scruples.

'Well, what are the rest of you staring at? Stoke the fire and get this meal ready!'

***

Next morning the men were up and prepared for departure soon after dawn. Nobody had slept well, nobody spoke much and nobody wanted to delay any more than was necessary. The supper the evening before had been a tense and irritable business, conducted as quickly as possible. Elmo had got back just in time to chew at the fatty scraps and had sullenly told Pierre that the couple had appreciated his generosity.

The group broke camp, set off and made its way downstream through dense mist and gnawing cold, each man sunk in his own thoughts, towards the tiny settlement where the ferries crossed to Arles. The men's spirits were kept up only by the thought that the city was barely a half-day's journey distant, but in the event disaster was to strike long before they reached it. They had travelled for little more than a league when they were alarmed by the sound of hooves approaching them fast from behind. A man riding a noble stallion, but wearing dark clothing and with his face masked, emerged from the gloom. He came level with the party and wheeled around. The horse steamed and whinnied and for a moment no-one moved. Then came the glint of steel and a great spurt of crimson blood as the long-sword was thrust deep into Pierre's unprotected flank.

Most of the legate's party were armed, but few of them were trained soldiers and all of them were bleary-eyed from lack of sleep and the early hour. On their return to Rome they would report that they had had no chance to prevent the brutal murder, or to kill or apprehend the assassin. They would agree that the mysterious rider had clearly been an expert swordsman. Pierre de Castelnau – God bless his eternal soul! – had bled profusely and died instantly. They would say that it had all happened too fast for anyone to react, and that the killer had swung round and ridden off the way he had come as swiftly as he had arrived. He was never identified, though no-one who had been present at the fractious meeting of Count Raymond and Pierre was in any doubt as to who had ordered the assassination.

Whatever the legate might have said to the Pope on his return to Rome about priestly excesses would now remain unsaid, and anyway who could say whether it would have made a difference? Innocent would not have welcomed whining talk of failings by the priesthood when the work of the devil was sweeping across the land. When His Holiness received the news of the failure of Pierre's mission he railed against the heresy of the people and the treachery of the Count alike. As far as the Pope was concerned, the people were condemned by their heresy, and the bloody murder of his legate had settled the matter. The time for talking was past.

Innocent swiftly proclaimed a crusade against the heretics of the Languedoc and called upon the kings of all Christendom to unite against the poison in their midst. Those kings would in turn call on their nobles to raise armies. Tens of thousands of men would respond to the call, obliged by feudal ties and lured by the promise of glory and of the remission of sins, as well as by the expectation of rich plunder. A campaign of terror, destruction and killing would be unleashed upon the land.

***

Elmo of course had no conception that morning of the consequences which would flow from the events he had witnessed on the misty banks of the Rhone, though he was as shocked as any of the other men present at the suddenness of the murder. But he also felt a secret sense of relief that his own little deception would now go undetected – in this world at least – as he checked once more on the two silver coins, safely hidden in the inner lining of his jacket.

Part I – Beziers

Arrival: March 1209

William stepped out of the woods and the vastness of the sky swept over him. The hammer-blow of light blinded him and he shaded his eyes for a few seconds, then almost laughed for joy. The sight he had been imagining, willing into being with every step over the last wearisome days emerged like a vision from the glare: the sea, glittering like silver. It was still far below him and some twenty or thirty leagues distant, but wider and more beautiful than anything he could have imagined in his cold, faraway homeland. He was filled now with an almost physical longing to reach the shore, strip off his ragged clothes, and wash away in the warm waters the grime and sweat of ninety days. This was the Middle Sea which reached all the way to the Holy Land!

He lowered his pack to the ground and scanned the baking plain which still lay between him and the sea. Shimmering in the heat of the plain, an ochre-walled city huddled for protection around the stubby tower of its fortress-like cathedral. That must be Beziers, the greatest settlement of the Languedoc coast. Much further away towards the south-west faint shadows glittered on the rim of the sky. He had never seen snow-capped mountains before and did not yet realise what they were.

Over the past weeks William had become used to the bare uplands, becoming warmer as the days grew longer. These were ancient lands where shepherds eked out a living tending their scraggy sheep and the villages were few and far between, where woods of beech and holm-oak alternated with the closely cropped pasture, and a man could walk all day without meeting another living soul, watched only by the lazily circling buzzards. As he walked, the only sounds were his own footfalls on the stony track, the whistling of the upland wind in his ears, and the endlessly changing patterns of the birdsong. In some ways he had enjoyed the solitude; it gave him time to think. But here everything was strange and new and full of promise. He shouldered his pack and set off down the steep incline with renewed vigour.

As he descended slowly into the fertile plain he realised that it was not deserted like the country he had passed through but was a scene of considerable activity. He began to pick out huts built of wicker or reeds daubed with mud which blended into their surroundings and were not easy to see at first, and men and women hard at work, harvesting early wheat or planting out long rows of seeds. There were fields of vines too, bare and stumpy at this season, waiting for the warmer days to bring forth their pale green foliage. He had seen vines before, of course, along the valley of the great river which he had followed south for many weeks and indeed in his homeland, where they were said to have been grown in the more sheltered valleys since Roman times.

During the afternoon the track gradually levelled out and towards the end of the day William was at last on the plain which stretched all the way to the sea. The horizons flattened and the land was criss-crossed with narrow waterways, for irrigation he supposed. The coastal plain was certainly fertile and he identified winter cabbages being cultivated, alongside other plants which he did not recognise. Here the women worked mainly on the vegetable plots, whilst the men tended their nets or mended their boats alongside the wider inlets which stretched across the land like moist, twisting tentacles. The men and women bent to their work in the same way that his own people in far-away England bent to their hops and barley, in the unquestioning way that people everywhere had always worked, and surely always would.

William's height and flaxen hair marked him out as a stranger, and those people who looked up from their labours as he passed eyed him with suspicion. One or two granted him a barely audible greeting to which the stranger responded cheerily, but even they did not meet his eye and most managed no more than a nod before turning their backs again. He had encountered suspicion before but had relied on his open nature and facility on the wooden flutes which he whittled in odd moments to disarm it. He intended to stay in Beziers for a month or so, perhaps to find work and build up his funds for his passage to the east, and he hoped the people of the city would be more forthcoming.

The heavily fortified gateway, the Porte de Carcassonne, formed a bottle-neck where the late afternoon flow of herders and pilgrims and men and women from outlying settlements converged in an ill-tempered scrum, eager to get into the city before the gates closed at nightfall. Some carried a few scrawny chickens, slaughtered and tied in a bundle at the neck and slung over the shoulder, or still flapping and clucking in wicker cages barely big enough to hold them. A beggar had set up his pitch right under the gate and would no doubt have been cleared out of the way by a few well-aimed kicks were it not for the leprous stump stretched out before him which had created an eddy in the flow of people. His stubby fingers loosely gripped a battered pewter dish containing a coin or two and he looked up imploringly, but the young stranger could only offer a smile. William, the son of the mayor of a sizeable city, had little more wealth about his person than a ragged leper. He would have to find work soon to be able to eat, let alone to continue his journey.

Inside the gates the pungent odours reminded him that he had not been in a city of this size since Paris, and he shuddered. The swirling momentum of the crowd dragged him on, like flotsam on an incoming tide, deeper into the maze of winding streets which were already almost without daylight. He found himself in the butchers' quarter where legs, shoulders and heads of pigs and sheep hung on spikes outside the houses. A heavily bearded man with a bloodied leather apron pointed his grimy fingers up to freshly slaughtered stock: 'My friend, you look hungry!'

William forced a grin but did not respond and the man jeered once it was clear the boy with the golden hair would not buy. As he was swept on down the street, women in filthy aprons pushed baskets of silvery bass and bream, smelling of the sea, under his nose. He could understand the Occitane language of the south up to a point, but these crones cackled in an accent too harsh for him to catch, though their leering glances made their meaning plain enough. Children screamed and pointed at his hair and were wrenched away by their mothers. The people of Paris had been rude but at least they saw many strangers, and were too wrapped up in their own money-making to give them a second glance! But here he was outlandish beyond the ken of the people.

He was suddenly aware of a lad at his side, a few years younger than himself, casting him sidelong glances.

'Hello,' he said, 'my name is William – I'm a stranger here.' The lad grinned.

'I thought you might be!'

'I'm sorry I don't speak the Occitane tongue so well…'

'Well enough! But you speak it like a Frenchman. Are you from the north?' he asked, nodding at William's hair.

'Well, it depends what you mean, I'm from England.'

'Oh, I suppose I meant are you French. I don't really know where England is.'

'England is beyond the lands of the French king, and across the sea. But we speak the French language, as well as our older English tongue. Our kings came from Normandy. I've tried to pick up Occitane along the road; in fact I travelled for a while with a monk returning home to Marseille who was a good teacher. It's been a long journey...' William tailed off, but his new friend seemed to have heard enough for now.

'Well, I'm glad to meet you! I'm Gilles, by the way,' he said. They stopped walking for a moment and Gilles held William's eyes with his own and put a friendly hand on his shoulder. His face was well-tanned and he had an untidy mop of light brown hair.

They moved on together until they reached the crowded square in front of the foursquare cathedral, where the ground was strewn with rubbish and slippery with animal droppings and vegetable scraps from the market which was just ending. William asked Gilles if he knew where he might find lodgings for the night.

'Well, the city is very full, but my father lets travellers sleep in the hayloft sometimes for a few *sous*' – Gilles gave William another glance – 'or for a few hours' work if they don't have any money.'

William smiled. 'That sounds perfect, though I'd need to do the work!'

Gilles grinned and led the way across the market place and deep into a similar warren of narrow alleyways on the other side. At one point they came out onto a strip of rough land just inside the walls from where slit holes gave a clear view all the way to the sea. It was closer now and William could see one or two fishing-boats bobbing and white-horses whipped up by the stiff breeze blowing off the land. Gilles watched him and wondered, but did not ask, what he was staring at. The sea was just the sea.

A few more twists and turns – William doubted he would

ever find the place again by himself – and Gilles pushed open a heavy wooden door which led into a courtyard overshadowed by a lime tree. A woman with a rough red complexion, helped by a girl of eight or nine, was preparing the evening meal in a kitchen which opened directly onto the right-hand end of the courtyard. The girl was chopping vegetables to add to a blackened pot bubbling over an open fire.

'Mother, I've brought a visitor in need of lodging. I thought father might let him sleep in the hayloft.'

'Your father takes in all manner of waifs and strays!' the woman exclaimed, but then she turned a kindly eye on the newcomer. 'You are welcome, young man. You've journeyed far, I think?'

'Thank you, madame, I am grateful for the shelter of your home. Yes, I have travelled from the city of Rochester in the county of Kent, in England.'

'England – there was never a traveller from England before! What brings you…' But William was saved for now from the awkward explanations he mostly sought to avoid by the arrival of a man of some forty years with a full beard – though William saw at once the family resemblance to Gilles in the brown eyes and prominent nose.

'Ha! I saw you and Gilles together in the market-place. You looked as thick as thieves so I'm not surprised to find you under my roof!'

William introduced himself again and got only a grunt in response, but guessed from Gilles' grin that he should not be alarmed.

'Well, of course you can stay. But you must entertain us over our meal by telling us about your travels and what brings you all the way from England to our city!'

William smiled thinly and Gilles pulled him away to show him the rest of the house and his sleeping quarters. The kitchen was little more than a dark alcove off the courtyard, hung with gleaming copper pans, where Gilles' mother and the girl continued with their preparations. The main living area was at the rear, and was dominated by a great wooden table, olivewood William supposed, oiled over the decades to a rich brown and deeply indented with gashes from the meat-knives laid out ready for the meal. There was a well-carved wooden chair with curved arms at either end of the table for the mother and father of the household and a jumble of benches and stools for their son and daughter and any other guests. The fireplace at the left-hand end, open to the sky, was not made up and clearly only to be used in the depths of winter. The most striking piece of furniture was a massive wooden chest of some darker wood, also worn to a beautiful shiny patina by its great age, and firmly locked with a heavy metal clasp. The earthen floor was swept clean and the whole effect was of a home of some substance.

The left-hand end of the courtyard was taken up by a row of bed-chambers for the family. Gilles retrieved a blanket from one of these and with it under his arm led William up a rough wooden ladder to a hayloft above the stabling which lay behind the bed-chambers.

'This is where visitors sleep, I'm afraid.'

'It's fine, this is a fine house: your father must be a successful man.' William thought, but didn't say, that he had slept in much worse places in the last three months. He shuddered as the memory of the tavern in Rheims came back to him; he wouldn't be telling that story over dinner. But how much would he tell them? He felt a fondness for these people who had taken him in unquestioningly, and he didn't want to lose their respect. His travels had taught him that too much openness to outsiders could be unwise.

'Oh yes, father is well regarded in the city,' Gilles was saying, 'he owns one of the two bakeries which supply bread to the wealthier townsfolk. The poorer people bake their own, of course. He took the business over from grandfather but he's increased the trade and moved it to a better location near the market. When I was small this house was just two rooms and the old bakery, but father bought the adjoining land, which had been used for grazing goats, and built the courtyard, the extra rooms and the stabling. He even bought the goats and we make a little extra selling the milk in the market!'

William grinned, eased off his tattered boots and fell backwards into the straw, throwing up a cloud of dust.

'A bed fit for a king!'

'Well, don't go to sleep now – we're all looking forward to your traveller's tales! Dinner will be in an hour.'

***

The dinner exceeded William's expectations. There was a rich garlicky stew of pork and vegetables, mopped up with roughly hewn chunks of the soft bread to which he had become accustomed during his long journey south.

As the meal drew to an end, Gilles' father speared a last piece of goat's cheese with his knife and looked at William quizzically. William was a good story-teller, he thought, but he had noticed too that the boy had been careful to restrict his tales over dinner to daily life in Kent and the adventures of his journey, rather than the reasons for it. Well, that could wait; it would not be polite to press a guest too hard. In fact it was the youngest person present who spoke up, her eyes shining.

'One more story please, William! Did you say there is a sea between England and France that you had to cross? Is it as wide as our sea?'

He had been saving up the sea-crossing even before Liliane asked. Gilles' younger sister was a pretty, lively girl who showed no sign of shyness towards the stranger. William looked for permission to continue to his host, who assented with a nod.

'Thank you, sir! Well, Liliane, the sea I crossed between England and France is not as wide as the sea here, nor as blue. In fact for most of the year it is a grey sea, and it's often stormy, with strong currents and treacherous sandbanks.

'I left England from a place called Romney, three days' journey from my home in Rochester, just a church and a few houses sheltering behind dikes in the midst of a great marsh. The land is flat like the land here, but windswept and weather-beaten. It was an hour before sunrise and bitterly cold. Imagine two tiny figures struggling through mud which sucked and squelched and stank, lifting a dead weight on our boots with every step. Seagulls swooped and screeched overhead, frightening us off as invaders who might threaten them, beady-eyed and ready to peck at living flesh!'

He bunched his fingers in front of his mouth and made little pecking gestures at Liliane, who put her hands up to her face and screamed satisfyingly.

'These were ugly omens and we didn't wait around. Now we could see the boat loosely moored in the lea of the last mudbank before the open sea. A boat which was barely more than a rotting carcass, a broken shell of poorly caulked wood with a flapping sail. It was just waiting to crack and splinter in the rough seas beyond the backwaters! The boatman emerged from the gloom, glared at us angrily and shouted: 'Hurry up for sweet Jesus' sake, the tide won't wait!' We slithered in, covered in the foul mud, and huddled in the bottom of the boat amidst reels of rope and a few casks of ale which the boatman evidently intended to sell on the other side to increase his profit from the journey. As we eased out from the marshland into the open sea the first great wave struck us side-on with a sickening thud – the first of many!

'It took us eight hours to get across, constantly buffeted by the winds blowing up from the west. Many times I thought the boat would splinter and the sea would sweep over us and deliver us into the hands of God! I was throwing up the whole time, over the side as long as I had the strength, then when my guts were empty just curled up in the bottom of the boat and retching. My companion Edwin, when he was a young man, had sailed with the crusade to liberate Jerusalem from the infidel and he was not sick. But his older, wiry body suffered badly from the cold and damp and the constant battering.

'The boatman – a big, rugged man – ignored us completely once we were at sea. He was interested only in reaching land before nightfall and getting paid the rest of the money. He muttered once or twice about ending up in the Low Countries if the wind got any worse, but he knew his business and in the early afternoon Edwin sat me up to point out the thatched roofs of the settlements on the northern French coast, faintly visible behind long, low dunes. We struck land just east of Calais with several hours to spare. A good price that boatman took off us for our calvary too!'

The family sat back, mulling over William's story. Liliane was grasping her mother's skirts and asking whether seagulls really peck people. William felt a glow of satisfaction. His happiest childhood memories were of sitting round the embers of the fire in the moot house in Rochester on winters' evenings, listening to the travelling story-tellers who would arrive out of the blue and recount the epic poems and romantic stories of love and war and adventure. Best of all had been the yearly visit of a troupe of players who dramatised one or other of the epic poems, or sometimes a story of their own invention, on the well-kept greensward in front of the great stone keep.

By the time William left Rochester he had learnt to retell some of the stories accurately enough to entertain his friends, and had shown a gift for picking up other scraps of local history and lore and winding them into stories of his own. This facility, sometimes accompanied by a musical introduction on his home-made wooden flute, had sustained many a long evening and even earned him a little money in inns along the road on the long journey south. It had been his greatest comfort during those lonely weeks.

Gilles' father had been watching the visitor thoughtfully, until finally he broke the silence:

'You have told your stories well, William. It is late now but we must have more another evening. But you should know one thing: in this house we do not believe that our souls are delivered to God when we die.'

William pulled himself out of his reverie and recalled using the words. He knew from talk he had heard along the road that there were heretics in these border lands which were barely under the control of either France or Aragon, or even of the Church. But he had not knowingly met a flesh and blood heretic before and he found the words faintly alarming. They did not accord with the kind-hearted family who had taken him in, but he heard himself mumbling:

'Thank you, sir, I will remember what you have said.' He would ask Gilles to explain what his father had meant in the morning, but suddenly now he felt the waves of tiredness sweeping over him and after many nights sleeping in ditches the hayloft really was very inviting.

***

William slept better that night than he had for many weeks, but was woken early by Gilles, who to his surprise asked him if he could swim. When he said that he could Gilles told him to get up. He dressed quickly and Gilles led William out of the town gates as soon as they opened, then off the road and along narrow paths through the marshland until they emerged onto a curving bay backed by shoulder-high reeds. In front of them golden sand shelved gently into a wide channel with similar reed beds on the opposite side. William turned to his friend, laughing, already pulling off his clothes. The water was warm and lapped gently in the shallows, but as they waded out the ridged sand under their feet shelved more steeply and William pushed forward against the water, marvelling at the swarms of tiny, glittering fish, then glided into a gentle crawl. He flipped over onto his back, smiling and waving to Gilles who was some way behind. Now that he was clear of the shore he saw that the sea opened up to the left round the last bend of the waterway, flipped over again with the ease of a confident swimmer and struck out into the open sea. Gilles was slower off the mark but followed, gaining on him, and after a while caught up. There they stopped, panting and treading water, tiny specks pinned between the sea and the sky, free of all the cares of the world. William put his hands on the sides of Gilles' shoulders and they bobbed about on the gentle swell, supporting one another.

'You swim fast, William!'

'You have to in the sea where I come from, it's so damned cold – not like this! But I've always loved the water.'

'Me too. I learnt to swim at this spot, just taught myself really. It was as if I'd always known. Perhaps I was a fish in a previous life!'

William half frowned at this remark, then grinned. Gilles pointed out that you could just see the tower of the cathedral above the reeds. When they had got their breath back they pushed apart and swam back to the beach. It was harder work against the gentle current flowing out of the inlet.

Exhilarated by the physical effort and by the clean, clear water, the two boys ran up the beach and threw themselves down on the warm sand to dry off in the sun, gazing up into a perfect blue sky, each sunk in his own thoughts. It was Gilles who broke the silence.

'So what did bring you on this long journey, William?' He could hear William breathing deeply, and wondered for a moment if he had fallen asleep. William had been expecting the question. He relished telling his own story for the first time, though he was aware he must be careful about how much he shared until he had got to know his new friend better.

'Well, I mentioned my companion Edwin last night, the one I crossed the Channel with. He gave me the idea, really. I'd known him for as long as I can remember. He'd fought in the crusade to free Jerusalem from Saladin when he wasn't much older than we are now. He was full of stories about those days and how he'd have been happy to continue his life as a soldier, but he'd lost the use of his right arm in the crusade, shattered by an axe-blow. Anyway, he couldn't hope to fight again. He had no close family apart from his widowed mother and he never really settled back into life in Kent; instead he dreamed of returning to the Holy Land to finish his days there. Apparently there are communities of monks who take in lay members who can work and offer some protection from marauders.'

There was a silence which lasted so long that Gilles propped his head on his hand and looked at his friend, whose eyes were shut.

'That tells me a bit about him. What about you?'

'I'm not boring you?'

'No, not at all – go on!'

'Well, me then…if you're sure you want to know?'

William opened his eyes and looked round at Gilles who nodded encouragingly.

'I asked, didn't I? That's if you don't mind talking about it.'

'Well, I certainly didn't talk to anyone along the road about my reasons for leaving home, but my long journey gave me plenty of time to think it over, and…and I'd like to share it with you.' He paused and looked calmly at Gilles, who returned his gaze expectantly.

'Where should I begin? Well, my father is the mayor of Rochester, which is a city in the county of Kent, on the old Roman road between London and Canterbury. He has done well in life. Most of the positions of authority in England, including mayors and burgesses, are held by folk of Norman French descent, but he had worked his way up, in spite of his mostly Saxon blood – that's where my flaxen hair comes from! Anyway, my father started out as a trader, buying up supplies of wool, employing women from the town to spin it into cloth and then arranging transport to London and selling it for a profit in the cloth-markets there. That gave him a position in the local community, and over the years he worked his way onto the town council on the back of his success as a merchant. I'm his eldest son, so he always expected me to follow in his footsteps. He was grooming me both to take over the business one day and to follow him onto the town council. From my twelfth birthday I had to attend the meetings of the council – well, could they talk! A discussion of property rights or tithe payments might last for hours – and that's the future he was lining up for me! He even had my future wife in mind, a girl called Agnes, the daughter of the chief of a nearby town. Perhaps you thought it was only kings who married their children off for reasons of state? Oh no, my father was at it too!'

William paused for a moment to check that Gilles was still following him, and Gilles, head propped up on one arm, immediately urged him to continue.

'Don't get me wrong,' he continued, 'I loved and respected him for what he had achieved. But, for all sorts of reasons, I knew I didn't want a life like that, laid down for me. I dreamed of travelling out of Kent and seeing something of the world.'

There was another pause, which Gilles filled: 'It's funny but

I've never really thought of travelling anywhere. I like it here!'

'Maybe you're the lucky one, happy to stay put! Most people from my village seemed to feel the same way. But not me, and not Edwin. Apparently when he returned from the crusade he'd been greeted as a bit of a hero. I was very young then, but I learned about it from others as I was growing up. He moved back into his mother's cottage, picking up odd jobs around the town to pay his keep. But he never really settled back into local life, and without a family he was inevitably an outsider. He didn't have many friends, but somehow he and I saw eye to eye. We seemed to understand one another.'

'You were fellow-spirits?' Gilles suggested gently. William frowned.

'Yes, perhaps we were. Anyway, after his mother died a couple of years ago he told me about his plan to return to Palestine and I started to think that I should go too, that it would be a way out. I didn't say anything to him of course; he would certainly have said no, maybe even told my father! Then the plans started for the wedding to Agnes – it was to take place around now in fact. She was a sweet girl but I knew that marriage would trap me into a life I didn't want, or at least wasn't ready for. And …I knew I couldn't love her.'

He paused again and looked across at Gilles, hoping for a glimmer of recognition. But all Gilles said was:

'So what did you do?'

'Well, I made my plans in secret. Edwin had told me when he was leaving, but I was pretty sure he hadn't told anyone else. I reckoned his departure wouldn't be noticed for a day or so. His mother's cottage where he still lived was quite a way outside the village. So I packed a few belongings and ran away from my home – and my responsibilities! I knew Edwin planned to leave from Romney and I caught up with him as he was waiting for a boat to cross the Channel.'

'And what did he say when you turned up?' Now Gilles did turn to look at William, caught up in the story.

'He was angry at first, but what could he do? He didn't want to go back. He was a wanderer at heart and I like to think he saw something similar in me. The boat I told you about last night was leaving that evening, and the boatman was only too ready to squeeze in another passenger. That was only a little over six months ago, though it seems like a lifetime. A lot's happened in those six months. What I was doing felt right then, now I feel I've travelled far enough. Maybe because I already have a strange sense of belonging here…'

William looked across at his friend shyly as his words tailed off; it was so difficult talking about yourself! Gilles looked back at him, wanting to hear more but aware that his curiosity had already probed into dark corners. Anyway, it was time to get back and he stood up, brushing the dried sand off his body unselfconsciously.

'Come on, we should go!'

William turned and looked up. He didn't want to go yet but realised that the moment had been lost; Gilles had turned away and was buttoning his chemise. William stood up and pulled on his own clothes.

***

The way back seemed longer than when they had come, and William steered the conversation away from himself and onto the faith of his hosts, which he wanted to know more about. What had Gilles' father meant about not believing that men's souls are in the hands of God when they die, and wasn't it blasphemous to talk about having been a fish in a previous life? Gilles seemed as shy of talking about these things as William was about his past and the reasons for his journey, but when William promised not to speak of it to others he started to explain, hesitantly at first, but with increasing confidence.

'Well, we follow the Cathar faith, though usually we call ourselves *bons chrétiens* – good Christians, or just *credentes* – believers. That's not how the Church of Rome sees us though; they call us heretics, plain and simple! But, you see, we've gone back to the simple truths which the Roman Church has forgotten, and that's what they don't like. The priests of Rome talk about living humbly and urge us to confess every little sin, but they live like kings on the tithes the people have to pay them. Is it any different in England?'

'Well,' William said, 'the priests are certainly not poor like the common people.'

'There you are, then! So we *credentes* follow the faith of the wandering preachers, good men who genuinely live a life of poverty. They speak well, like you! They teach us that there are two worlds. There's this corrupt and fallen one we live in, and somewhere else there's the perfect world of the spirit. As father said last night we don't believe our souls are delivered to God when we die. The Cathar elders teach instead that we will eventually get to heaven, but only after we have lived many different lives in this world, becoming better people as we do. So you see I may have been a peasant or a serving-girl in previous lives!'

'Or a fish!'

'Well, not a fish, actually! But then there are some believers – known as the 'perfect' – who have freed themselves so far from all the temptations of this world, that when they die they won't return. They'll finally become part of the spiritual world, a world of pure goodness which we can't see – but it is there.'

Gilles' eyes shone as if he could actually see this other place. William asked nervously: 'But you believe in the Holy Trinity and the Lord Jesus?'

'We believe in Jesus and that he brought a message of truth from the spiritual world. But that message has been lost in the ritual and wealth of the Roman Church. All that finery hides the simple truths which we follow.'

William felt he was getting out of his depth again. He had always accepted the teaching of the Church about the Holy Trinity, the Day of Judgement, Heaven and Hell, though he couldn't say that he exactly understood most of it, and some of it just terrified him. So he was shocked by what he had just heard, but fascinated too. He knew that what Gilles was describing was some sort of heresy, but Gilles and his family didn't look or act like agents of the devil. How could they believe such strange things? And then again, when Gilles talked about this other world of pure spirit it sounded so simple, and so beautiful.

'Perhaps I could introduce you to my father's elder brother who is one of the perfect I was telling you about,' Gilles suddenly continued. 'He lives very simply, eats little and certainly no meat or other foods that come from animals, not even butter or milk. And of course, as a perfect he has taken a vow of chastity, though as he is over sixty years of age…' Even as he said this Gilles realised it sounded disrespectful and shrugged sheepishly, and William repressed his own grin. They walked on in silence for some way until William returned to the topic.

'So is your father one of these perfect?'

Gilles laughed. 'Oh, no! I think he's too attached to the things of the world! Didn't you see him tucking into the pork stew last night? No, we're just credentes. We try and live as best we can and we hope to come back a little closer to becoming perfect ourselves in a future life. In that way maybe in the end we can return to the spiritual world. To be honest, I don't think about it that much. I'm happy enough in this world for now!'

William laughed and put his arm round Gilles' shoulder as they walked back towards the city. He was stunned by all that

Gilles had said and he had more questions, but now was not the moment. The crowds on the approaches to the gate were as large as the day before, but this time the throng was of buyers and sellers from the outlying settlements coming into the city for the market. Once again William was absorbed by the spectacle and the thrilling sense of being drawn into the life of an utterly foreign land.

Rochester, 1202: The Seed is Sown

William had been following the activity going on around the castle all day. As soon as his schooling was over he had put out of his mind both the Latin which he rather enjoyed, and the arithmetic which he despised. As soon as he could sneak away from the duties which his mother usually found for him during the afternoons, he had run round to the castle to keep an eye on the preparations for the evening. He had offered to help the men of the troupe when there was carrying or lifting to be done, but they had only laughed and amiably but firmly told him to get out of the way; this was heavy work and not for a slip of a boy! Still, nothing could stop him from watching as first the stage was set up and then the curtain was hung which would keep it out of sight until the performance actually began.

He recognised the beautiful embroidered curtain which had maintained the suspense last year too, and he recalled the excited buzz which had gone through the audience when it had finally been pulled back to reveal a rugged scenery of rocky cliffs – unlike anything to be found in north Kent! – with one crenellated tower in the left foreground. His mind drifted back to the story of Tristan and Isolde which the troupe had played out that evening, when for the first time he had seen the possibility of a wider world, beyond the confines of Rochester and north Kent with its wooded hills and winding rivers. The castle and the cathedral, and the town huddled in the protection of both, were all he had known in his life so far, but the troubadours had conjured up the stormy seas and forbidding moorlands of distant Cornwall and Ireland, just as they had conjured up love and tragedy, passion and adventure. The twelve-year-old William had been transported from the mundane reality of life in Kent and even now he could recall every twist and turn of the tragedy.

Indeed, William had made something of a name for himself locally in the last year by recreating the performance in the corner of the bailey which surrounded the castle, with other older children taking the roles of King Mark of Cornwall and his intended Irish bride, the beautiful Isolde, whom Tristan brings back from Ireland for the King. Of course, William had taken the lead role as the heroic but tragic Tristan, who falls deeply in love with the beautiful Isolde himself, after they have both been tricked into drinking a love-potion during their return journey. He played the final tragedy, when Tristan is ruthlessly killed by the wronged King, for all it was worth. He had even introduced some new elements of his own into the story, including the slaying of a dragon during Tristan's Irish adventures.

It had gone down very well with the audience, and only his father had been unenthusiastic about William's efforts. He had sat stony-faced through the performance and afterwards the best he could say was: "You show some talent, my boy, but you should turn it to other ends. Perhaps I should send you to London to learn more about trade! The play-acting is not the right way in life for my son and heir." Then he had turned on his heel and walked away.

***

William took his appointed place in the front row in plenty of time, still replaying last year's performance in his mind and imagining what the evening might bring. The hand-painted banner which had been hung on the wall of the keep behind the stage promised: "A Tale of the East" and the players had refused to say any more. But it was enough to pique William's interest and to make him wonder whether the play could be connected with the experiences of his friend Edwin during the crusades, which fascinated him. Of course, Edwin's story since his return was not a happy one: he had come back from the east unable to do any real work because of his injury, and he had missed the chance to settle down and start a family. His only close relative was his old and sick mother whom he looked after. This inevitably made him something of an outsider in a community based on extensive family ties. Some of the more kindly townspeople took pity on Edwin and paid him now and again for odd jobs which he could manage despite his damaged arm, but William sensed that none of the grown-ups really trusted him. His own father was certainly hostile. But William and the other children loved him for his stories and for the way he treated them as equals. William in particular could listen for hours to his tales.

By the time the benches started to fill up around him William had drifted off into mysterious Palestine. He imagined himself in that land which Edwin had described to him: a land of searing heat, of endless barren hills and occasional oases of shade and cool water, and of warriors on horseback – or even riding camels, though William still wondered if Edwin had not invented those stinking, spitting, hump-backed beasts. He was brought back to the here and now as his mother sat down next to him and gave him a friendly hug, though he wished she wouldn't when everyone could see; he was twelve now, almost a man!

'Looking forward to the performance, my boy? Just don't upset your father by appearing too interested. You know it will displease him.'

'Yes, mother, but... but I love the players' stories so much. They let me dream and see other places! Isn't that a sort of learning too?'

She laughed. 'Well, yes, I suppose it is learning of a kind, but not one your father would approve of. You know your future is here!'

William pulled a face and retreated into his own thoughts. Beyond his mother's place was the finely carved wooden chair in which his father normally sat to lead the meetings of the village council, and beyond that the cathedra, the Bishop's own chair which had been brought out from the cathedral for the occasion. There were more modest chairs the length of the front row for other notables, and rows of benches behind for the common people. The landless farmers and the churls would stand wherever they could at the back and the sides. William knew he should be grateful for his honoured position, but still he looked longingly to the grass in front of the seating where his friends were gathering, chatting, giggling and sucking on the honey sweets which the bakers' boys were handing out free for the occasion. (William's father had explained to him that these were in fact funded by a donation given by the council, but William hadn't been listening.) He sat back in his chair, scuffing the bare earth with his heels and wondering if he could get away with slipping out of his seat once the performance began. He concluded that he couldn't; it would annoy his father too much and probably lead to some kind of punishment or extra instruction in the work of the council.

All the local notables were taking their places now – apart from his father, and the Bishop of course who would arrive at the last minute in his mitre and ceremonial vestments. But old Father James, who actually took most of the services in the cathedral on the Bishop's behalf, was there wearing his habitual black cassock and severe expression. Simon the baker was just arriving, red-faced and cheery and still with flour in his hair, and his brother Geoffrey, the blacksmith. Gudrun the butcher would shuffle in at the last minute, hot and flustered from his duties preparing for the feast which would follow the performance. Apart from

Father James they were accompanied by their wives, dressed in their most respectable chemises and long skirts. Simon ruffled William's hair and gave him a friendly slap on the shoulder as he passed, and Josephina his wife leant down and whispered: 'You should sit in front with your friends!' William pulled a face which Josephina interpreted correctly. She bent down again and he felt the hot breath in his ear as she whispered: 'Well, afterwards then!'

When she had gone William's mother turned back to him.

'Are you planning your own version again, perhaps?'

'Oh, yes, mother! I hope so, if father doesn't mind. Uncle Edwin has been talking with the troupe about his adventures in Palestine and gave me some clues about what they will be performing. He swore me to secrecy so I can't tell you, but it sounds wonderful!'

His mother laughed. 'I'm sure it will be! But don't tell your father you've been spending more time with Edwin. He isn't a real uncle, remember, and you know it's better if you don't see him too often. And, dear boy, you shouldn't say too much about putting on your own performance, for now at least. I'll put in a word for you, but your father might say you're getting too old for play-acting.'

'But the players are much older, mother!'

'You know that's not the point, William.'

'I know, mother, but …'

'Enough, my child! Ah, dearest, there you are. Take your place quickly before someone else corners you.'

Her husband did as she said, but turned to her with a tired smile.

'I have to listen to their problems. These aren't easy times and all over north Kent the planting is way behind. They're all worried that there won't be sufficient food stocks for next winter. I try to reassure them, but I fear they may be right.'

'Yes, well, these things are usually not so bad when the time comes,' she replied distantly. 'Now, try and enjoy the play!'

'As if I had time for plays – what's this one about anyway? More romantic stuff like last year?'

***

By the time the final curtain fell young William had slipped down to sit cross-legged on the ground for the third time, and his mother with a touch of her hand and an imploring look had finally dissuaded his father from hoisting him back up again.

He turned round and looked up at his parents, his eyes shining with excitement at the exotic world which had been conjured up before his eyes. But his father had already turned round and was deep in conversation with one of the burgesses about some matter or other, and his mother put a finger to her lips and nodded that he should run off somewhere with his friends while he had the chance. William grinned and was gone.

***

Later that evening William sat with Edwin on the edge of the Medway, the earth cut away below them by the great bend in the river on its journey northwards to the sea. The light was fading fast and the swooping heron would soon settle for the night. It all seemed so dull to William, compared to the wonders of the east which the players had conjured up just an hour or so before.

They talked first of the play, which this time had not been based on one of the traditional ballads. Instead it told a story written by the leader of the troupe, about a band of crusaders who become separated from their comrades, and are taken prisoner by a group of nomadic people of the desert. The nomads lead their prisoners up into a mountain stronghold overlooking the plain, where they lock them into a cave with an iron gate. One of the nomads speaks some French, having traded for a while with the Frankish kingdoms in Palestine, and explains that they mean their hostages no harm but intend to extract a ransom for their release.

Gradually the two sides become friendlier, until finally one of the guards gets too close to the barred gate and a crusader manages to get an arm round his neck and force him to hand over the keys. Once free of the cave, the crusaders slaughter the rest of their captors and return triumphantly to their own people where they are feted as heroes.

'I still can't really believe that you have actually seen those deserts and bare red mountains, and those fearsome infidel warriors!' William sighed.

'Yes,' Edwin replied, 'I have seen them, and I returned to tell the tale, which is more than many of my fellow crusaders did. But I didn't enjoy the play. Things are never as simple as they seem. Those nomadic people treated their prisoners fairly by their principles, and yet they were slaughtered. Of course, they were infidels, you will say, and that is true. But I don't think they deserved to die.

'You mustn't get the idea that it's easy to say what is good and what is bad, William. In Rochester, maybe, it seems simple. But the world is a bigger place and men are more ruthless than you can imagine, sitting here.' He swung his arm out to take in the river valley before them and added: 'Yes, I have seen the world, and my advice to you would be: stay here amongst your own people, marry that local girl your father has in mind, and have children of your own!'

'But I want to see the world for myself, when I am old enough!'

'Of course you do, William, of course you do,' Edwin murmured. 'Just as I did!'

Beziers, April 1209

Gilles' family quickly took William into their hearts. They seemed to take it for granted that he would be staying with them in the short term at least, which of course he was delighted to do. Gilles' father had not mentioned payment, so on the second evening William himself asked what work he could do to cover his food and lodging, adding that he had worked part-time for a carpenter in Rochester for a year before his departure. Gilles' father laughed and said that he could certainly find some woodworking tasks for him to do around the house: repairing the stairs to the hayloft and making small items of furniture. Over the next few days, he also put out feelers for more work from friends and neighbours, and quickly found interest. A lot of people were moving into the city from outlying settlements, which created a demand for new beds and chairs and even extensions to houses where there was any free space in the warren of narrow streets and tiny homes.

William woke in the mornings to the sound of the day beginning in the city all around him, and washed quickly from the water-barrel in the courtyard before breakfasting on fresh rolls, goats' cheese, and diluted local wine. He pleased Gilles' mother by offering to take on the task of collecting the bread. This came from the family's own bakery a few streets away, a place which he loved because of the warm and reassuring aroma which filled the oven-room behind the shop. His mornings were soon fully occupied helping out at a carpenter's workshop behind the cathedral, and on jobs for the same man in the bigger houses around the city. He even had a hand in the preparation of new choir stalls for the cathedral itself, though as a newcomer he was only trusted to work on the sawing and planing, not on the elaborate heads for the ends of the armrests and the stalls. These were carved by master-craftsmen whose work William watched with fascination when his own simple tasks were done.

The detail of the heads was left to the individual craftsmen, who took their inspiration from biblical stories, but adapted them in their own ways. William's colleagues welcomed him into their midst and, when they took a break, would explain the further levels of meaning in the heads. The plump-faced and jovial Noah was a tribute to a popular old gentleman who had been a fisherman all his life, noted for taking his boat out in all weathers. Although he was now too old to go out in the fishing barks, he still spent his days at the fishermen's quay, repairing ropes and sharing tales with the other greybeards. The weeping figures of Adam and Eve, carved full length on the end of one of the choir-stalls and covering their private parts with their scrawny hands, were a crueller reference to a local couple who had been taken in adultery and forced to leave the city in disgrace. William smiled at the idea that future generations would see only the biblical figures, and would have no inkling of the references to real people which the carpenters had carved into their work.

From the stories carved into the wood, but mostly from the friendly chatter in the baker's shop and amongst his colleagues William's knowledge of the city and its people grew rapidly, as did his fluency in the Occitane tongue. He began to lose the odd vocabulary which had made him sound like a Frenchman to southern ears, though the nickname François had stuck in the carpentry shop. When the two young men were both free in the afternoon Gilles showed his friend more of the city and introduced him to other friends who quickly accepted him into their circle. As William became drawn into the life of the city, he also picked up a growing concern about the possibility of conflict with outsiders because of the supposed heresy of the people. But for now this talk meant no more to him than a distant cloud in an otherwise sunlit sky.

In the first few days Gilles' father and mother had both made one or two attempts to find out more about the reasons for William's journey, but they had let the matter rest when they saw that their questions embarrassed him. Gilles had spoken to his mother one afternoon when his father was out, explaining that he thought there were painful memories which she should leave William to share when he was ready. He did not tell her that he already knew part of the story and understood that there was more, because he hoped that William would want to confide in himself first.

Gilles was aware too of a growing fondness for his new friend – a fellow-spirit indeed – who had arrived so unexpectedly from so far away. His arrival had stirred up feelings which he only half understood and which in the past he had kept locked away in a hidden corner of his mind. The two friends had not swum again since the day of William's arrival, partly for the simple reason that their work kept both of them busy for most of the day. But Gilles had also not suggested another visit to the sea because of where he suspected it might lead. Of course he had noticed the way William had glanced at his body as they lay on the sand, and he had made a point of getting dressed just as he felt William might do something more than look. But the disappointment in William's eyes that afternoon had stayed with him. He had never shared his own most secret feelings with anyone else, and the possibility that they would finally come to the surface was something he longed for and feared in equal measure.

***

It was William who suggested swimming again. One afternoon when the carpenter had no work for him he found Gilles munching an apple in the courtyard and cutting slices off for Liliane who was stuffing them eagerly into her mouth, already looking up to her brother for more.

'Do you have work to do this afternoon?' William asked.

'No, I don't think so. You?'

'No, neither do I. There's a push on to complete the carvings for Corpus Christi so most of the routine work has stopped. Perhaps we could go down to the shore again?'

'Yes, we could,' Gilles replied, 'if you want to?' He looked up questioningly.

'Well, I do, so that's settled! We should take something to lie on afterwards this time,' he said.

'Okay, you could bring one of the old blankets from the hayloft.'

'Fine!' William replied, and their eyes met briefly in a shared understanding.

Half an hour later they set off down the same track as before, chatting casually about the events of the morning. But this time as they approached the sea Gilles led the way a little further to the west. The narrow track led to a point where several inlets joined together to form a lagoon which was almost closed off from the sea by a low spit of land. At the back of the lagoon there was a narrow strip of sand backed by bamboo thickets.

'Nice place!' William said, noticing how well hidden it was.

'Yes,' Gilles replied, 'I've swum here sometimes and never seen any sign of anyone else.' Again their eyes met and Gilles felt the longing welling up in him.

They both felt a certain awkwardness in undressing this time, which they got over by doing so quickly and dashing into the calm water with boyish whoops. The sea shelved more gently here and they were only just out of their depth even in the middle of the lagoon. They swam short distances to and fro, trying to outpace one another, though William sometimes eased off a little to let Gilles win. Then they just basked and revelled in the warm water. At one point William lost sight of Gilles, until he felt something skimming his calves and caught a glimpse of a pale body rippling below him in the clear water. He raised his eyes to the cloudless sky and laughed for pure joy. On the next pass Gilles grabbed his ankles and up-ended him, and in a confusion of limbs they grappled and gasped for air and surfaced face to face. And then they were kissing.

When the embrace finally ended William put a finger on Gilles' lips to silence him, and led him out of the sea and up the beach. When they reached the blanket and the heap of discarded clothes he stood face to face with Gilles again, holding his glistening body by the shoulders and silencing him again with a look and a finger to the lips. Then, after another, briefer kiss, he let his hands and his mouth begin to explore further. He was sure now that Gilles wanted this as much as he did, but that he must take the lead. There was no need for words.

***

Afterwards they swam again languidly, then lay in silence side by side for a long time, fingers gently entwined. It was Gilles who finally spoke.

'I…I don't think that was your first time.'

William laughed, and although it didn't sound like a question he still gave the answer. 'You're right, it wasn't – but it was never so good! But shush now…' He kissed Gilles gently to silence him and then, curled against one another's bodies, they dozed and drifted through the warm late afternoon until it was time to make their way back to the city.

Rochester, 1205

Indeed, it wasn't the first time, but it had never been so good before.

It had begun with knowing nods and glances from Richard, the son of a tenant farmer who eked out a living on a half-acre between the river and the forest. Richard was a year or so older than William, and had barely spoken to him. He had thick black stubble and straggly hair, was muscular but not good-looking and had few friends. William had not exactly returned Richard's discreet signals, but he had not rejected them either. Eventually Richard had snatched a furtive conversation with him in the shadow of the east gate of the city, and made a rendezvous for the end of the next working day, at a spot on the edge of the woods.

Towards the end of the following afternoon William left the town by a little-used side gate. Richard was waiting for him when he arrived at the agreed spot, and wordlessly led the way deeper into the woods, to a small clearing of tussocky grass in the midst of bramble thickets. It was a fast, furious encounter, without preliminaries. Buttoning up afterwards, Richard's only words, with a twisted half-smile, were: 'Seemed like you were ready for that! See you here again next week?' William nodded dumbly, still trembling with the suddenness of it all, and the discovery that his secret longings were not his alone. It was exhilarating but it was terrifying too: 'If a man lies with a man *as with a woman, it is an abomination. He shall surely be put to death...'*

Only when Richard had slunk away did it occur to William that the older boy might have a schedule of similar encounters in the clearing. During the week he resolved not to go back, but when the appointed time came he was there. He took a fishing-rod and nets and caught a few fish in the stream on the way back to justify his absence to his family.

Beziers, May 1209

For the rest of their lives, William and Gilles would look back on the following weeks as a time of great happiness, and of blessed innocence before the calamity which was to come. William's carpentry skills improved rapidly and before long he was trusted to do some of the preparatory work on the carvings for the completion of the choir stalls, though not on the detail of the figures themselves; for that he had neither the requisite skill nor the local knowledge. On the surface Gilles' life carried on much as before. He worked in the bakery in the mornings and did odd jobs for his father in the afternoons, played bat and ball sports outside the city walls with the other boys some days and practiced archery with an old soldier who tutored whichever of the young men showed an interest and an aptitude. Again William picked up hints of some darker fear amongst the people, of a gathering storm. Nothing explicit was said, at least not in his hearing, but he noticed that when Gilles' father praised his son for developing his archery skills, his mother remained silent.

And whenever the two of them got a chance to slip away together, usually just for an hour at the end of the afternoon so that their absences would not be noticed, William and Gilles went down to the hidden lagoon. As Gilles' confidence and skill in love-making increased so did their secret happiness. The two of them seemed to have an unspoken agreement not to examine too closely what was happening between them, or where their forbidden pleasure might lead, not yet at least, though William felt in his heart that it could not last for long. Sometimes too, before he fell asleep, William wondered how what they were doing could be reconciled with the religious beliefs of Gilles and his family. He already knew only too well how it was regarded by the rigid religious tradition of his own upbringing in England. He had heard enough sermons on the wages of sin delivered from the lofty pulpit of Rochester Cathedral.

At the same time, William was becoming aware that religion was much more freely discussed in the Languedoc than it was in England, no doubt partly because there were different beliefs competing with one another rather than one unchallenged faith. The topic was often in the air around the family dinner-table, with talk of notable Cathar perfect, and of priests who were known to turn a blind eye to the heresy. But there were other priests who were viscerally opposed to the Cathar faith and liable to denounce those they suspected of being amongst the perfect or even simple *credentes*.

William soon understood that the family themselves were at some risk, and not only because one of their own was a perfect. Gilles' father and mother sometimes held late-night gatherings of a dozen or so believers around their dining table, where one or two of the perfect would share their wisdom and experience. Gilles went to these gatherings, but William was politely asked to go up to bed before they began, and although no reason was given he guessed it was because he might be putting himself at some risk by attending. From the hayloft he could hear only the faint murmuring of voices from below, interspersed with periods of silence.

On other nights, when there was no gathering, Gilles would join William in the hayloft for an hour or so after dinner.

They would lie companionably in the straw, gazing up at the cobwebbed rafters and glimpses of the night sky through the cracks, and exchanging tales of their childhoods and of the differences between life in Kent and in the Languedoc.

Gilles had never given much thought to what life would be like elsewhere. Beziers was on the *via Domitia*, the old Roman road which ran from Rome itself to Catalonia and beyond, and all manner of travellers passed through. There were the troubadours who performed in the square outside the cathedral for an evening or two, merchants bearing luxury goods to and from Hispania and Italy, pilgrims following the ancient routes which led to the holy shrines – westwards to the tomb of Saint Jacques at Compostela, eastwards to Le Puy en Velay, or even to Rome itself. Gilles knew all the names, but at heart he loved his own land and had little wish to travel far.

William had also been brought up with experience of other peoples, since his home lay on the main road – also Roman in origin – between London and the shortest sea-crossing to France. As the son of the mayor he had been introduced to merchants from France and the Low Countries, and even to the noble and clerical travellers who sometimes passed through. He remembered especially the papal delegation which had stopped for the night a few years previously, on its way to London to parley with the rebellious King John, and how they had come with a complete entourage of servants and cooks, and their own magnificent and colourful tents in which to sleep and dine. William had chatted with some of the papal servants who found their way into the taverns at the end of the day, and he had marvelled at their descriptions of Rome and their tales of intrigue. This experience had added to his desire, already primed by Edwin's tales of crusade, to see the wider world.

Rochester, 1208: The Impasse

William lay awake in the bed-chamber he shared with his brother Philip. The younger boy always fell asleep as soon as his head hit the pillow, and William could hear his breathing now, deep and calm. He wished he could still sleep so well himself. Instead he often lay awake into the small hours, turning over and over in his mind the same questions. On this particular night the questions felt all the more urgent, but the answers were still no clearer.

William understood only too well the expectations which his father had for him as his elder son, and which plenty of the other young men in Rochester would have given their eye-teeth for. The best that most of his peers could look forward to was life as a simple tradesman if they were lucky enough to be born to it or managed to obtain an apprenticeship. For the rest, their life would almost certainly be spent working on the land. He knew what that would mean: a back-breaking round of long days with little rest, and the constant fear of famine if God withheld his favour and allowed the harvest to fail or disease to take the animals. Some would technically be free men, but in practice they would have little choice but to remain on the land if they and their families were not to starve.

But William was lucky. He was the son of a line of bold and successful men who, over seven generations stretching back to the time of the Conquest, had built up a substantial landholding. This *had enabled them to retain increasing numbers of other men as tenants or serfs to do the hard work, allowing first his grandfather and then his father to provide a life of relative ease for their own family. William and Philip could look forward to profiting from the good fortune of their birth, but William as the elder son could look forward to the most. And yet, William lay awake at night, listening to Philip's peaceful breathing and wishing he had been born the son of a blacksmith or a tenant-farmer, or at least as a younger son.*

The questions had all came up in another difficult interview with his father that day, which had ended with his father storming out, snarling in his fury that he would return to the matter. Before his parents went to sleep that night William could hear their muffled voices from the adjoining bed-chamber. His father was evidently doing most of the talking, though William was only able to catch the odd word. At times he also heard his mother's voice, quieter and more emollient. No doubt she was asking her husband to allow his difficult son more time to recognise the honour and the responsibility which came with his fortunate birth. William loved his mother dearly and realised how much she spoke up for him, but then, how could she understand the depth of his resistance to the life which was laid out for him? In the end she was no less beholden to her husband than William was to his father, and William knew that the matter could not be put off indefinitely. He slept little that night.

* * *

When William came down for breakfast the next morning, dark rings round his eyes, his father had already gone out, but his mother was waiting for him. They greeted one another in the usual way, then sat in silence as William ate. Finally, his mother asked quietly:

'Your father spoke to you yesterday?'

'Yes, about my responsibilities.' There was another long silence, during which William chewed the last piece of bread slowly. 'Mother, you know how I feel. I understand how fortunate I am and all that it means. I sit through those council meetings, and try to follow the discussion, but my mind is elsewhere. I'm young, I've seen nothing, been nowhere, but I've talked with the merchants and pilgrims who pass through, I've heard their tales and seen the wider world through their eyes.'

'And you've talked with Edwin of his travels?'

William sighed. 'I know you and father don't approve of my friendship with Edwin. I know he's alone now and his lot is not a happy one, I know people don't trust him because he hasn't taken the normal course in life. But he followed his heart as a young man and he does not regret it, whatever other people may think.'

'Maybe not, but he didn't start out with your advantages,' his mother replied. 'And now he is alone, wifeless, childless and without prospects.' She did not pursue the point, knowing that William would not be shifted from his friendship with the solitary figure who lived alone in the woods. Instead she put an arm round William and said:

'You are young – of course you have dreams! Edwin has told you tales of the crusade. But he must also have told you that many of the men who went either did not come back, or did so injured in body or mind. Even if he didn't say it, you must know how dangerous and violent the world can be. In any case the time for crusading is over – thank God! – and you have a good future before you here in Rochester, even if you can't see it now. If you want to travel there will be opportunities to go to Picardy or the Low Countries with the merchants, as your father has done. Maybe even to Genoa and Venice which your father says are opening up for trade in new luxuries which soon everyone will want!

'You are eighteen, William; the time for dreaming is past.

When you are older you'll be grateful for the privileges you have by birth. You'll be respected and loved by the grateful townspeople in your care. I am sure of it.'

William held his mother's loving gaze for a long time, then embraced her. He could feel the tears welling up, fought them back and replied as best he could:

'I know you only want the best for me. And father does too of course.'

***

A couple of days later, William suggested to Philip that they should drink a glass of ale in one of the poorer taverns at the far end of the town after the evening meal, something they had taken to doing over the last year or so, and Philip readily agreed. The brothers got on well enough despite the difference in character and outlook. Philip was boisterous and had a wide circle of friends; and though he struggled with schoolwork he was already skilled in archery.

The two brothers sat down at a table in a quiet alcove, with full tankards of ale in front of them. Philip took a first appreciative draught and asked his older brother: 'So, father has had another of his talks with you?'

'Ah, you guessed what's been going on. Yes, another long lecture about my good fortune and my responsibilities, the second this week. Well, you know what I think about all that.'

'And you know what I think! I wouldn't mind being in your place – how hard can it be sitting around a table deciding how things should be run?'

Philip always made this comment sound like a joke, but William understood there was more than a grain of truth in it.

'You haven't sat through the discussions in the council,' William replied, as he always did. 'But there was a new angle to today's talk.'

Philip looked up enquiringly.

'Marriage! Father thinks it's time and has been exchanging letters with some wealthy miller in Maidstone about a betrothal between me and his daughter.'

Philip's eyes lit up. 'Ah, I thought that might be coming soon. But that's fine news – why d'you look so serious? Marriage – that might change your mind! What's the girl's name? What does she look like?'

'Her name's Agnes, and according to the letters I've seen she's "of comely appearance with fine golden hair and broad child-bearing hips". I think those were the exact words.'

'Ha, ha – sounds alright to me!'

'But marriage, Philip! I have other dreams, other ideas. If only there were a crusade I'd be off, and father could hardly stop me.'

'But there isn't, as everyone keeps telling you! That's all over, and a good thing too if you ask me. Make the most of the opportunities that come your way, that's what I would do!'

'It's all right for you, you're not under the same pressures to live up to father's expectations.'

'I suppose so, but frankly I wouldn't mind the chance! The girl sounds all right too!'

'Hmm, perhaps we should change places!'

The two young men laughed and the conversation moved on, though the idea, humorously meant, that the younger brother really could replace the older, lodged itself in William's mind. Perhaps there was a way in which everyone could get what they wanted.

***

When William reached the spot in the edge of the woods for his regular rendezvous with Richard, he wasn't there. This was unusual, as normally he arrived promptly and hurried to get back, *but William waited half-an-hour and still he didn't turn up. He returned home disappointed and a little concerned, catching a few fish on the way back to cover his absence. The same thing happened the following week, and after that he didn't go back to the woods, though he continued the fishing trips. There was no-one he could ask what might have happened without raising suspicions, and it would be several months before he heard the story of what had become of Richard, and by then he would have other plans. For now, the loss of these encounters, furtive and hurried though they had been, was a further blow.*

Beziers, May 1209

William sometimes pushed his conversations with Gilles in the hay-loft gently in the direction of the family's beliefs. As he now understood it, the followers of the Cathar faith believed that there were two entirely separate worlds. There was the physical world in which men and women lived out their lives, which had been created by and was ruled by the devil, the rex mundi. Then there was the spiritual world of pure goodness, the creation and domain of God, to which they hoped one day to return, if they succeeded in achieving the status of 'perfect' in this fallen world.

There was always a light in Gilles' eye when he talked of this spiritual world, and the beautiful idea of it continued to fascinate William in a way that the austere ritual and the fire and brimstone sermons delivered by the black-clad priests of his own religious background never could. When he tried to explain this to Gilles, his friend shrugged. The Roman church with its hierarchy and ritual, not to mention the power of kings and princes, were simply irrelevant to the *credentes*' way of thinking. Instead, the purpose of life was to achieve release – but only after many incarnations – from the temptations and the suffering of this world, into the world of pure spirit. This brought the subject back to the perfect, who were believed to be ready to achieve this when their current life ended.

William hoped that one of these conversations with Gilles

would lead on to what it meant for their personal lives and secret happiness, which in his own tradition was a mortal sin. However good and right their passion felt at the time, in the eerie darkness of the hayloft before he went to sleep, or in quieter moments during the day, he would recall the sermons of the bishop and priests in Rochester on the subject of Sodom and Gomorrah. One priest in particular had returned to this theme time and again. He was old and bearded and rather frightening, and on this subject, as on any other, he left no room for doubt. Unless he repented while there was still time, a man who laid down with a man would be damned to eternal torment in the flames of hell. It was a fearsome idea just to put aside.

William had told Gilles very little about his own previous experience with Richard, partly because he was not proud of it, partly because it seemed irrelevant now; those urgent, furtive encounters had borne no resemblance to the closeness and tenderness he now shared with Gilles. In any case, some time after the encounters in the woods had come to an abrupt halt William had heard the reason; Richard's father had married him off to a podgy girl from a village ten or twelve leagues away. William had assumed that the father had got wind of his son's activities in the woods and had imposed the only possible solution. Perhaps Richard had got off lightly; one heard of fathers killing their sons for less.

Gilles certainly intended their secret to remain just that, but he also showed no particular wish to talk about it with William. William assumed that the key must lie in the strange beliefs of his people. Perhaps Gilles didn't talk about it because he simply didn't see it as a problem in the way William did. When he thought this over he recalled Gilles' promise to introduce him to his uncle who was one of the perfect. The offer had not been repeated, although the gentleman had been mentioned respectfully around the dinner table on a number of occasions, at which point everyone murmured a brief blessing. William assumed that he attended the late night meetings, thought it had not been said and he had not caught sight of any of the visitors on those occasions. He even began to wonder if the uncle was already some kind a spiritual presence rather than a man of flesh and blood.

Gilles meanwhile was itching to know more about a quite different subject, and one evening as they lay on their backs in the straw he broached it.

'My father was asking again last night if I knew what has brought you so far from home.'

'Oh, what did you tell him?'

'Don't worry, I didn't betray your trust. But I still hope you're going to share some more of your story. You've told me a bit about Edwin and how his tales of the crusades encouraged you to leave home and set off half-way across Christendom. But, oh, I don't know, I just feel there must be more. And now that we are so close… I wondered if that's another part of your story. Then again, you've never told me what became of Edwin. I've been waiting for you to tell me, but I suppose I've got tired of waiting!'

It was a while before William spoke. But once he got started he couldn't stop, and the story just poured out.

'I've wanted to tell you, or perhaps I've been waiting for you to ask. But it's difficult; there are such painful memories, awful things. I mean, what happened to Edwin, it was so senseless. When you know more of his story you may understand better why I've ended up here!'

There was a long pause, during which Gilles waited patiently. Finally William began.

'Edwin was someone I could talk to, a fellow-spirit like you said. I suppose we were both outsiders in our different ways. He talked to me a lot about his life as a young man, when he'd travelled all the way across Christendom, not just half-way like me! That was with the crusade of course. I'm not sure he did it because he really believed it was right, or at least that wasn't the only reason. I think he did it mostly because it was a way of getting out of Kent, and seeing something of the world.'

Gilles interrupted: 'Oh, there are a few old crusaders here too, but amongst the devout Christians, not the *credentes*.'

'Well, you'll have heard some tales too. There's no doubt it was a violent and bloody business of course, but Edwin survived and came back with a wealth of stories. He also had just enough money to rent himself a plot of land, though he found tending it hard with his damaged arm. There was one thing he did regret, but we'll come to that.

'He must have been approaching thirty when he returned, with a useless arm and without wife and family. Some people felt sorry for him, some mistrusted him. But I saw it differently, because I knew him better. I could see the excitement in his eyes when he talked about how he had sailed across the Middle Sea, seen the islands of Greece, walked the alleyways and markets of Jerusalem. He'd crossed barren deserts and bare mountains, where you might suddenly come upon a paradise of flowing water and abundant green. Oh, the things he spoke of! The great fortresses of the crusaders which rose out of the burning sands; the bearded infidels who dressed in flowing head-dresses and wore robes like women, but who were merciless killers with their great curved swords. Some of them rode not on horses but on great hump-backed beasts which smelt fouler than you could imagine and had vicious tempers! Such tales he used to tell!'

William fell silent, lost in Edwin's stories of far-off lands. Finally Gilles had to ask again the question with which he had started.

'But what happened to him after you crossed to France? Please tell me.'

When William looked up again Gilles could see that he was

fighting back the tears. He put an arm round his shoulder to comfort him.

'I'm sorry, if it hurts too much...' But even as he said it he hoped guiltily that William would continue.

'No, no, I want to tell you, but it's still so hard, only three or four months ago.'

Gilles squeezed his shoulder again and kept silent. Finally William began.

'It was in Rheims that it happened. Have you heard of Rheims? It's a busy merchant city in the French domains, with a fine cathedral. Edwin and I were thinking of stopping there awhile to work and replenish our funds, before...before Edwin was killed.'

He stopped, steadying his breathing, and Gilles waited.

'We rested there two days and on the second evening we were in the tavern where we'd found lodgings. We shared a dormitory under the eaves with space for ten or twelve, though there were only two other travellers that night, merchants just arrived from Saxony. Their Saxon tongue was not so different from English, though God knows they had a rough way of speaking and we didn't warm to them. Edwin had a dagger always hidden in his cloak in case of trouble, and I noticed him checking on it once or twice during the evening.

'Still, there was little other company apart from the tavern-keeper, a surly individual who seemed to regard us as no better than Normans, whom the French despise. So we supped and drank the weak French beer with these two. I already had an uneasy feeling about them, and I think somehow they'd got the idea we had more money on us than we had. Perhaps if we had told them we needed work to pay for our next dinner things would not have turned out as they did. I wondered afterwards if they were in league with the innkeeper and he had added something stronger to our drinks.

'Anyway, by the end of the evening we'd all drunk quite a

bit, and I was feeling it badly. I remember stumbling upstairs to our billet with a pounding head, wrapping myself in the grubby blanket, then…nothing. At least, not until I was dragged from my sleep by a terrible scream. I thought it was a nightmare at first, but somehow I pulled myself awake and staggered to my feet, trying to understand what was happening in the pitch black. None of it made any sense. I could hear groaning where Edwin had been lying next to me, and reaching down felt him… felt the stickiness on his skin…heard him groan softly, then a dreadful clunk as he tried to sit up and his head fell back on the floor. There was frantic scrabbling and cursing as the two Saxons fled the scene, taking with them Edwin's money-pouch as it turned out. Much good it did them: it contained no more than enough coins to buy a loaf of bread.'

William stopped talking and Gilles put his hand round his friend's shoulder, comforting him silently, and waited for his sobbing to end. After a few minutes he was able to continue, his voice flat and emotionless.

'The tavern-keeper appeared with a lantern when he was sure the danger was over, and the horrible bloody gash across Edwin's arm and chest was revealed in the flickering light. The bastard just grunted and seemed more concerned about the stains on his blankets than the death of a man. Oh, there had been no need to attack him so viciously; we would have given them what little we had! I think Edwin must have been woken from his sleep by their attack and pulled out his dagger instinctively like the old soldier he was. They probably killed him in fear of their own lives!'

William fell silent and Gilles waited, the comforting arm still on his shoulder, until he was able to continue. When he did it was in a dull, flat voice.

'There was nothing to be done of course. Nothing could be done in the middle of the night and the bastards were long-gone by morning. I was left all alone, but I had one piece of luck: the local priest was a kindly man. When I told him that the dead man had fought against Saladin's army in the crusade, he provided a shroud for Edwin's body and paid a few local lads to help me bury him on the edge of the cemetery. I remember they were chatting and laughing about the local girls whilst they dug his grave.'

'It must have been terrible.'

'Yes, it was. I've not spoken of it to anyone since I left Rheims. But there's one more thing you should know. It's about Edwin, but now it's about me too, and it's what decided me to continue my journey alone, even after he had been killed.'

Gilles squeezed William's shoulder and waited for him to resume his story.

'Well, I told you that Edwin was returning to the Holy Land because he wanted to finish his life with the monks in the desert, and that's true, so far as it goes. But as we went along I discovered that he was returning for another reason too.'

Gilles said nothing, looking into William's eyes and willing him to continue.

'Edwin hadn't told me about it before we left Kent, but I suppose once we were travelling companions he thought I should know, or maybe he just felt freer to talk. So as we walked on the second day after the sea crossing, he told me more about his adventures on the crusade, much of which I hadn't heard before. In fact I don't think he'd told some of it to another soul since leaving Palestine. It's strange how you open your heart to someone when you're walking for hours on end; I shared quite a lot with people I met on the road as I journeyed on alone. Partly because stories help to fill the time I suppose, and partly too because you don't catch the other person's eye; maybe it's a bit like the confessional!'

'Oh, we don't go to confession!' Gilles said.

'No, of course,' William mumbled, not wanting to be distracted. 'Anyway, Edwin confessed to me one day as we walked across the wide plains of northern France. It was a strange story and I got him to repeat parts of it later until I knew it almost as if I had been there! I suppose you know about the great crusade he fought in, when King Richard the Lion Heart led the English army?'

Gilles nodded. He knew very little about the crusades or who this *Coeur de Lion* was, but he didn't think it would matter and he didn't want to interrupt William.

'The English crusaders travelled overland at first like me, but they made the last part of their journey by ship from Italy. There were some adventures along the way, and some fighting over an island called Cyprus after they were washed up there by a storm. But, well, that's not really the point. They finally reached the Holy Land at a place called Acre. Oh, how Edwin's eyes shone as he told me of his first sight of this fine city. The ship approached it across a suddenly calm sea. Its citadel rose above the horizon first, and as they came closer they could see the massive ochre-coloured walls which protected it. Then they started to pick out the tiny figures of the crusader forces from other lands who'd already arrived, and the outlines of siege engines set up to the north of the city, ready for the battle to come.'

William stopped, gathering his thoughts. Gilles, eager to hear more, waited and after a while his friend picked up where he had left off.

'The English were very excited to have reached their destination. They ate and drank their fill for the first time in months, and joined the preparations for the battle. King Richard himself oversaw the building of more siege engines to add to those already in place. Apparently he didn't really trust the French design which had been used so far! They also built defences around their own camp against Saladin's forces who were on the way to try and save the city from the crusaders. Edwin said that with the English arrival our side were sure they had an overwhelming force. There was a vast host already, with French and Hispanic armies, and smaller forces from all over Christendom, but with King Richard and the English too they couldn't fail to retake Acre, and then Jerusalem itself!'

Gilles looked up: 'Not so many men from these parts though, I don't suppose!'

William smiled briefly. 'Well, maybe not. Anyway, the siege engines and the deadly rocks that the English lobbed into the city soon broke the fighting spirit of the defenders. Envoys from the infidels found their way out and sought peace terms, and by the time Saladin heard about it, gathering his own armies to the south – well, it was already too late! Acre was liberated without any real fighting and the Christians took over the city.'

'Quite a piece of luck!' Gilles exclaimed.

'Maybe, but it didn't last. Of course, the soldiers were relieved and excited and the army rapidly headed on down the coast expecting to continue their success with the liberation of Jerusalem. It was a gruelling march, but they won a battle along the way without too much difficulty or losses – I can't remember what that one was called! Then they marched on to another place further down the coast called Jaffa, where the people threw open the gates to avoid a long siege like the one at Acre, which of course they knew all about. Now the soldiers were sure God was on their side and they expected that Jerusalem would soon be theirs.'

William paused for a moment, ran his hand through his hair and turned to Gilles:

'Are you tired? Shall I stop there?'

'No! I want to know what happened!'

'Fine, I'll go on then. So, as Edwin told it, the kings and their lords started to argue about what to do next. Some were eager to make the push inland, but others doubted whether they had the forces to fight on now that the infidel had mustered so many reinforcements. The arguments dragged on, and the soldiers were left hanging around in an encampment outside Jaffa. That seems to be what soldiers do most of the time!'

'Better than fighting, I suppose!' Gilles suggested, and William grinned.

'Well, maybe! They played bat and ball games when it got cool enough in the evening, drank what little ale remained in their supplies and then drifted into the city looking for loose women. They soon discovered that the infidels kept their women well-hidden: they barely appeared in the street, and when they did they were dressed from head to foot in black, like walking tents Edwin said! But there were enough Frankish women ready to oblige the soldiers, who hadn't got close to a woman for months.

'Edwin was a devout man, but he was still a man! So he and a friend of his named Oliver went into the city and soon found their way to the Christian quarter. They certainly found some life there! There was wine on sale in unmarked taverns, and there were women who called out to the soldiers from the doorways once they found their way to the right district.

'Edwin and Oliver followed one of these women into a house where she introduced them to others. They drank some wine and made their choices. When they emerged from the house late that night Oliver slapped Edwin on the shoulder and said they'd better get back to the camp if they didn't want to get into trouble for defying the curfew, and Edwin reluctantly followed him.

'But the next morning Oliver could see that Edwin was distracted. He asked him what was wrong: hadn't he had a good time? That's when Edwin told him he'd been awake most of the night. He'd been thinking it over and he had to see the girl, Emilia, again. I got the impression that Oliver was shocked and tried to stop him, but Edwin was determined and slipped away almost at once with only a small pack of belongings. He found the girl again easily enough, rented a room for them both and they lived there like man and wife for the next three weeks. I could see in Edwin's eyes how happy those three short weeks with Emilia had been, and he assured me that she'd been as happy as he was. He didn't say it but it was clear to me that he'd fallen in love with the girl, like Tristan with Isolde or Abelard with Eloise! He bought her little presents from the market, trinkets and sweetmeats, and gave her money besides so that she could stay with him all the time. Because of the heat, at night they went up to sleep on the flat roof of the house, under the desert stars.'

'It sounds like a dream, or a fable!' Gilles murmured.

'Oh, it was real, all right, and maybe that's why their happiness couldn't last! The light went out of Edwin's eyes and his voice was flat as he told me what happened next. Apparently so many of the crusaders had found their way into town by the end of the three weeks, that a party of Hispanic mercenaries was sent in with the task of rounding up the "deserters" and getting them back to the encampment. The advance inland towards Jerusalem was starting, and they needed all the men they could get. The mercenaries were brutal men and they stormed all the likely looking houses, grabbing any crusaders they found at the point of a sword and gathering them in the town square. Then they marched them out of the town under close escort before they could slip away again. It was awful; the only time I saw Edwin sobbing openly was as he told me about his last minutes with Emilia.'

Gilles put an arm round William's shoulder again, silently willing him to continue, which after a few minutes he did.

'They'd realised what was happening from shouted warnings and screams. Emilia was trying to hide Edwin in a clothes chest in one of the bedrooms when a couple of the Spaniards broke in, merciless and half-drunk, and ripped him from her. One of the brutes came right up to the terrified girl, and Edwin only saved her by grabbing him from behind and tightening his arm round the man's thick neck. The Spaniard swung round in a rage and hit Edwin across the chest and left arm with the back of the axe he was carrying. The mercenaries had been told to bring the men back in a condition to fight, or he'd probably have used the blade and killed Edwin on the spot! Instead he grabbed him and dragged him out of the house and down the street. Edwin was stunned from the axe-blow. He tried to fight back but it was hopeless. His last view of Emilia was of her being pushed to the ground by another of the escort as she tried to run down the street after him...'

William fell silent at this point, as Edwin had when he had told the same story all those months ago. Gilles didn't speak for a while, but now that he was released from the tale he had a question.

'But didn't Edwin go back to try and find the girl, if he loved her so much? Surely when the fighting was over he could have got away again?'

'That's what I asked too,' said William quietly, 'and a lot of the men rounded up that day did escape, or were regarded as hopeless cases and were just abandoned to melt back into the city or make their own way home. Edwin was much weakened but his sword-arm was uninjured and he was still considered a good fighter. So he was put into a contingent with other "deserters" who were kept under guard as the crusader army advanced inland towards Jerusalem. But by the time they got there the Kings and their Lords were convinced they didn't have sufficient resources or siege engines to make an attack on the Holy City itself. Their spies told them it was strongly fortified by an infidel army which was growing in size every day as new recruits streamed in, and they feared a counter-attack.

'Edwin remained a loyal soldier of course, and would have fought if necessary, but his injury was not healing properly and he went down with a fever. He had very little recollection of the journey back to Acre or of boarding the ship, and by the time he recovered any real awareness he was back at sea on a ship bound for Marseille. He had lost contact with Oliver and never knew what became of him. On the ship he was tended by other returning soldiers, who seem to have feared for his life. Edwin didn't have the strength to disembark at the ports along the way, but when the ship finally reached Marseille he came ashore and rested up for a month to regain his strength. I think he was surprised to be still alive. By then most of the other English crusaders had started to make the journey north by one route or another and he felt very alone.

'Then he ran in with a couple of English traders who had contracted passage on a barge to make the long journey back north on the great river which flows into the sea west of Marseille. There were no more crusaders heading east and there seemed little chance of returning to the Holy Land now, so when these traders invited him to join them he reluctantly agreed. When Edwin told me this part of the story he looked more sombre than at any other. I understood then that he regretted this decision more than anything else. He had not stayed true to his love! Now, twenty years later, he was making the journey east again, while he still had the strength, in the hope of finding Emilia again before it was too late. Of course, he knew that the chances of her still being alive, let along having waited for him, were very slim. But he had to try, and if he failed he would retire to one of those monasteries I mentioned to live out his days in the land where he had been happiest.'

There was a long pause before either of them spoke. Finally Gilles propped himself up on one elbow and turned to look at his friend.

'It's a moving story, and a terrible one. But I can't see why it would make you want to continue the long journey you're now on – least of all alone.'

'Well, maybe one reason is that I'm a traveller at heart and you're not! But there's one more thing I haven't yet told you; then I hope you'll understand better. The evening of the day when Edwin told me his story it started to rain and we were lucky enough to be offered quarters in a farmer's barn for the night. As we were about to turn in Edwin said he wanted to ask me a favour. I said of course, I would do whatever he wanted, but he shushed me and told me to wait until I knew what it was. Then he brought out of his pack a tiny pewter casket I had never seen before. He opened it up to reveal a curl of auburn hair. Edwin and Emilia had exchanged locks of their hair as tokens of their love, and he had carried hers with him all through his arduous journey back to England. But the longer he had stayed in England the more he felt that his life there was meaningless. That's why he'd finally decided to return to Palestine before it was too late.'

William paused, though Gilles sensed there was more and knew better than to interrupt. Sure enough his friend's voice started again, but more softly.

'In the cold barn, with the rain coming down outside, Edwin said he already felt like an old man. He was feeling the strain of the journey in his tired joints and in his wounded arm, and indeed I could see that his injury gave him much pain.

'The favour he asked me was this: if he died on the journey, I should take charge of the casket with the lock of Emilia's hair to keep her memory alive. That night I was fired up with enthusiasm for adventure and I said at once that I too hoped to travel as far as the Holy Land and that if I should get there… But he stopped me with a raised hand, and he warned me, as he often had, that the world was big and full of dangers. He said he'd be content if I just agreed to look after the casket and keep the memory of his and Emilia's love alive. I blurted out at once, with tears in my eyes, that I was sure he would fulfil his journey. But I swore to him too that if the worst should happen, I would of course do what he asked. Neither of us imagined then how close the dangers of the world really were! Just a few weeks later he would be dead and I would be the guardian of his precious legacy.'

As he said this, William withdrew the casket he had just described from an inner pocket of his jacket, and opened it for Gilles, revealing a gleaming twist of auburn hair in the candlelight, then closed it again and put it away carefully. This time the silence lasted much longer, and it was Gilles who broke it.

'So you think of journeying all the way to Palestine to fulfil your promise?' He could not hide the doubt in his voice.

'Yes,' William replied, though his own voice trembled too. 'After Edwin's death I was afraid to continue alone, but I didn't feel I could return to Rochester. That would have meant total defeat, and a shameful return to the life my father had planned for me – if he would have had me back. I might even have had to marry Agnes after all! So I continued, sadly at first but with more confidence as I walked, day after day, south towards the sun. There was my promise to Edwin, and there was still my dream of reaching the Holy Land, as he did. It has become my quest.'

Gilles smiled. 'Hmm, the Holy Land; my uncle would tell you that nothing of God exists in this world, not even in Jerusalem! He says we can only find God in our hearts, not in this fallen world. And you're right, I've never really thought of living anywhere but here.'

But both of them were too tired for further talk, and after a fond hug and thanking him for sharing Edwin's story, Gilles crept down the ladder to his own bed. William drifted into sleep where he lay, still turning over in his mind the conundrum of his journey, and the new consideration which had so far remained unspoken: his love for Gilles.

***

During the next few weeks William and Gilles were both kept busy by their respective work and they had fewer opportunities to spend time at the lagoon, though on each occasion when they did snatch an hour or two there their happiness only grew. It was the one subject they didn't talk about. William kept silent because he feared to break the spell of their love, as the spell of love had been broken for Edwin. As for Gilles, he knew that those who wished to attain the status of the Cathar perfect must renounce the pleasures of the flesh, but for the *credentes* these pleasures were simply another sign of the fallen world they lived in. At the same time, his simple faith had already taught him to accept the unexpected joys along with the inevitable sorrows of earthly life.

The possibility of such sorrows was certainly growing. Even William had picked up snatches of the furtive conversations which went on not just among William's father and his friends, but also in the carpentry workshop, the bakery and on street corners. The Pope in Rome had proclaimed a crusade against the so-called heretics of the Languedoc, and the King of France – and the Kings of other lands – were calling on their Lords and Barons to raise armies to respond to the call.

William had always thought of crusade as meaning Christians fighting infidel warriors of the east, and he was shocked at the idea that the Church to which his own people belonged was planning to attack these fine and decent folk among whom he now lived. Gilles seemed oddly unconcerned, and again William attributed this to his calm and confident beliefs. Or perhaps he was young enough not to take the danger too seriously as yet.

But the small cloud on the horizon was quickly growing larger and harder to ignore. One evening after dinner, Gilles' father looked round the dinner-table and announced that there would be a gathering of a small group of perfect and *credentes* in the house that night, to discuss the situation. William was surprised that this had been said in his presence, but the head of the family now turned to him in particular and said:

'William, I think you should join us. I know you don't share our beliefs, but you're living under our roof and your safety is my responsibility. I have that duty to your father in far-away England. In any case, we will talk mostly about practical arrangements for the dangers we face rather than matters of faith. But I leave the decision to you. It may be that you find our beliefs strange.'

William had not been expecting such an invitation, but as all eyes turned to him he had no doubts about his answer.

'Sir, I am very grateful to you for welcoming me under your roof, and for allowing me to stay here for so long. I am very happy here. I find what Gilles has told me of your faith, well, I find it surprising, but very beautiful too. I would be honoured to stay for the gathering if it is your wish.'

'A fine speech, William; you will be welcome amongst us. Now, let us prepare the room and some refreshments for our guests.'

William would not remember a great deal of the talk that evening, which went on late into the night and covered all kind of practical details for protecting the perfect, bringing people into the city from outlying villages and preparing safe places of refuge, as far as possible, for the women and children. He would remember instead the flickering candle-light, the calm, serious faces gathered around the ancient table, and the respectful nature of the debate, considering the seriousness of the situation. He would remember in particular the face of Gilles' uncle Eustace. He appeared perhaps ten years older than his brother, with calm blue eyes – a rare colour in this part of the world – and a stubbly grey beard. He wore a simple brown robe made of rough cloth and bound at the waist with a thick rope.

William was presented to the old man as a traveller from England, and he felt a curious feeling of calm as the old man looked him in the eye, appraising him, and then said simply: 'I hope you find what you are seeking.' William stumbled over his reply, mumbling something about being very happy to have been given shelter in his brother's house, but the old man nodded approvingly and grasped his hand with surprising firmness.

The part of the evening's proceedings which William followed most closely was the discussion of who should and who should not be required to fight. The perfect were excused automatically; most were too old to be useful with the sword, and in any case their role would be to support and comfort the wounded and to perform the rite of *consolamentum* for believers as they faced their death. William understood by now that this was a kind of religious observance which would increase the believers' chances of returning in a more favourable form in their next life.

Otherwise all healthy men from fifteen to forty were expected to take part in the defence of the city, and if necessary to engage in fighting outside the walls. Men over forty would be free to volunteer. William caught Gilles' eye: this would mean both of them would be involved, but Gilles shook his head and nodded towards his father who was already leaning forward to intervene.

'Gentlemen, I do not think that our guest William should be included in this call-up. I have invited him into my house and I owe a father's duty to his father in England to protect him from harm. In any case, this is not his fight, indeed some of his countrymen may be fighting with the crusade.'

There were nods and murmurs of assent from around the table, which fell silent when William himself tentatively raised his hand to speak. Gilles' father attempted to intervene, but the oldest man present who seemed to have a role in leading the debate raised his own hand and said quietly:

'Gerald, we understand your concern for the boy's safety, but he should at least have a right to speak like anyone else here.'

Gilles' father – it was the first time William had heard him called by his first name – did not look best pleased but he sat back and signalled to William to go ahead.

'Sir, I beg your pardon for questioning your decision in this matter, but in the few weeks that I've enjoyed your hospitality I've come to love the kind and generous people of Beziers. You have shown me more kindness than any other I have encountered on my journey, and I can only think it comes from the beliefs of your people. I am twenty years old, my father saw to it that I was trained in archery and I beg your permission to fight to defend the city alongside Gilles and the other young men.'

'Another fine speech, William, but I still forbid it,' Gerald declared bluntly before William could continue, but he was obliged to back down by his brother, who calmly raised his own hand and said quietly:

'Gerald, let's leave this for now and discuss it as a family later.'

This deferral was quickly confirmed by the leader of the debate, and Gilles gave William a conspiratorial grin as the discussion moved on to other matters. By the time the meeting concluded late in the night William could hardly keep his eyes open. He was still a young man, and he marvelled at the stamina of the elderly perfect who would now continue the proceedings with a closed session of contemplation and prayer for the safe deliverance of their own followers and their fellow citizens, for it seemed that most of the Christian population of Beziers would remain and defend the city alongside their *credentes* neighbours.

***

William had a strange sense of time speeding up in the weeks which followed. Already on the day after the meeting, Gilles' father had asked both boys to stay behind after the evening meal. The rest of the family, obviously pre-warned, had slipped away.

Gerald was silent for a while after they were left alone. Then he looked up with the serious expression he now wore all the time and cleared his throat.

'We left unfinished certain business from yesterday's meeting: the question of William's role in the coming struggle. The French armies and other forces are gathering and making their way towards our tranquil corner of the world, where we have so far been relatively free to follow our own religious beliefs. We've kept our heads down and avoided too much of the persecution that the church has meted out to others, as have our Jewish brothers and sisters, many of whom live and practice their faith in relative peace in these lands. But now it seems inevitable that a reckoning is coming, and it will not be peaceful.

'William, I and my family have come to love you dearly during the short time you have been with us, and in particular you have become a good and wise friend to my own son.'

Here he smiled, for the first time, at both the expectant faces, before looking away again to gather his thoughts. If he noticed the awkwardness that both young men felt at his words he didn't show it.

'At the meeting last night, William, we talked about your part in the coming struggle. As you know, I was opposed to your fighting, and you know why. I will not repeat my reasons. My brother Eustace, who is a far better man than me, wisely closed down the discussion yesterday, but before he left this morning he and I had a further conversation about it.'

William and Gilles remained silent, awaiting the substance, though William was again marvelling at Eustace's stamina. He had evidently been up and about in time for a discussion and departure before he and Gilles were even awake! After what seemed an age Gerald looked directly at William and continued.

'William, Eustace has persuaded me - against my own better judgement - that I should not exclude you from the call-up, though the final decision as to whether to fight remains with you. Eustace is a fine judge of men and he told me that he sees in you an inner strength, and a desire to take the right course in life. He does not think we have the right to deny it. He is my older brother, he is one of the perfect, and I must follow his counsel in these matters.'

There was a long silence, and then William said:

'Thank you sir! I shall be - '

But the older man cut him off with a raised hand. 'Do not speak now, William. As I said, the decision remains with you, but please take your time. You are young. You have your whole life before you: love, marriage, children. Discuss it with Gilles - perhaps he has more wisdom than I give him credit for! Then, and only then, give me your answer. There will be no shame in refusing and I will do my best to get you out of the city safely.'

William bowed his head. 'Thank you again, sir. I shall follow your advice.'

And there the discussion ended.

***

The rumours of the approaching danger grew stronger during the coming weeks, and with the rumours William's uneasy sense that the time of his happiness could not last, just as Edwin's had not. He and Gilles were both busier than ever, as preparations for a siege of the city continued apace in the carpentry workshops, and Gilles was drawn further into his father's role in preparing for the protection of the city and the people.

But William felt no less strongly that he was also presented with a great challenge, perhaps the greatest he would ever face. Occasionally Edwin's warnings about the dangers of this life crossed his mind, but he put them aside. He was in no doubt that he should join the struggle to protect this land, this way of life, and this family who had taken him in and treated him as their own. For the first time, far from home, he had a cause to believe in. Gilles would fight, that went without saying, and William would be there at his side. The two of them talked it over, in the hayloft before sleep and once or twice when they snatched an hour or so at the lagoon, but William was in no doubt what he wanted to do and Gilles was equally fired up with heroic dreams. They were too young to take seriously the possibility of their own deaths, each instead secretly imagining saving the other's life in the heat of battle. Gilles had heard the wandering minstrels of the Languedoc recite the *Chanson de Roland* on warm summer evenings under the market hall, and he cast himself in the role of the trusty Olivier alongside the heroic and headstrong Roland.

The two young men's first experience of battle would come sooner than either of them expected, and it would be nothing like its depiction in the epic poems.

***

William and Gilles were making their way back into the city late one afternoon a few days later when they were hailed by a scrawny, unshaven man of perhaps thirty wearing a grubby, red tunic and leading a couple of ragged goats.

'Oh – Robert!' Gilles said, warily. 'We haven't seen you for a while. What brings you to the city? Don't you have a lot of work in the pastures at this time of the year?'

'Hah – there's always a lot of work for shepherds – you townsfolk don't know how lucky you are! But with what we hear it seemed better to come and enjoy your father's hospitality for a few days.'

'Well, you'll have to talk to father about that, after last time. But what news have you heard?'

Robert ignored the slight and was scornful. 'You haven't heard? Why d'you think so many people are coming into the city? Everyone in the hill villages knows it's begun. A whole army of crusaders coming this way – damn them! People say as they're less than a day's march away. Ten thousand fighting men, and more joining them all the time. Knights on horseback and thousands of hangers-on who'll fight for whoever pays 'em, and steal from honest folk along the way! People even say that bastard Count of Toulouse has joined them to save his own damned city. His sort always look out for themselves first!'

Gilles mumbled under his breath: 'Bit like you, then!' but all he said out loud was: 'So we may see you later.' Then he quickly dragged William away through a convenient gap in the crowd.

Once they were out of earshot William turned to Gilles: 'An unwelcome friend?'

'Worse than that – an unwelcome relative! Robert is my mother's half-brother from grandfather's second marriage. He inherited a few fields in the Minervois foothills north of here but the only crop is weeds most of the time. He uses the land for grazing a dozen or so sheep which he bred from a pair he stole from father originally, though he pretended not to notice; I think father thought it was worth it to get him off our backs. I hope Robert doesn't turn up later. I don't like the way he looks at Liliane for one thing, and if he sleeps in the hayloft you won't like it either: he snores and farts like a pig!'

William laughed. 'Well, I'm sure it can't be worse than what I put up with in some of the places I slept along the road! But do you think he's right about how close the crusaders have come? Wouldn't we have known by now?'

'He may be right. The shepherds move around with their flocks and are often well-informed. And haven't you noticed how worried – and busy – my father's been in recent days? I suspect he knows more than he's letting on but doesn't want to cause alarm too soon. I wouldn't trust Robert's word on anything normally, but I expect there's some truth in this. It would be typical of him to turn up when he needs us. He may be right about the Count of Toulouse, too. I overheard father and some of his friends talking after dinner a few days ago when I was clearing away. In theory Beziers is under the Count's protection but they reckoned he might well decide to fall back on Toulouse if he doesn't think he can protect everything. Let's get home and hear what father thinks about it.'

But they didn't get that far. The throng of people turned into a solid mass around the market square and the reason spread rapidly through the crowd: Count Roger Trencavel of Carcassonne was in town and was going to address the people from the steps of the cathedral an hour before sunset. Gilles quickly explained that Trencavel was the vassal of the Count of Toulouse and the overlord of Beziers. That made him the people's main hope for protection in the coming crisis – if he didn't betray them too.

Gilles grabbed William by the arm and shot off down the side of a bakery into alleyways William hadn't seen before. They scrambled over a crumbling wall and through a back-yard where clucking chickens scattered in all directions. When they'd scaled the wall on the other side William saw the point. He found himself perched on a ledge the height of a man above ground level with a perfect side view of the cathedral steps. A sea of people stretched out before them: townsfolk, peasantry and here and there the glint of arms. At the centre of it all a dozen men of the town militia stood facing outwards. They were armed with halberds whose sharpened blades glinted in the late sun, staring forwards and holding open a space for the Count to address the crowd.

'No-one in Beziers really trusts Trencavel of course,' Gilles muttered, 'he's Count of Carcassonne first and foremost and sees us as a source of revenue and fighting men. His father slaughtered dozens of townspeople in some sort of feud forty years ago which hasn't been forgotten either. But he might feel he needs us now so I reckon he'll make a rousing speech with a lot of fine words about his obligation to protect us and our feudal duty to him!'

William marvelled at how much Gilles seemed to know about political matters, and he guessed a lot of this knowledge came from his father. William's own earliest memory was of seeing King Richard pass through Rochester on his return from captivity in Austria after the crusade. He liked to tell the tale of the returning king, resplendent in a scarlet tunic embroidered in gold with the holy cross and riding a white stallion which pawed the air when the king stopped to address the crowd. No doubt this had all been designed to impress the people who had forgotten him and sided with his brother John when he had attempted to usurp the throne in Richard's absence. William's father had shared the general view that 'good King Richard' had been a better king than John who succeeded him, but most of the time the outside world had impinged little on daily life in Kent. But here in Beziers where there were great events in the offing everyone seemed to have a view on them. William put an arm round Gilles to steady them both on the ledge and waited expectantly.

They didn't have long to wait. The Count's party approached

from the direction of the Porte de Carcassonne, forcing the packed and turbulent crowd apart to let them through. Trencavel swaggered forward in a long crimson cloak trimmed around the collar with white fur, left his henchmen behind with an imperious sweep of his arms and stepped up and onto the impromptu podium alone. William realised with surprise that the Count of Carcassonne could be no more than mid-twenties, only five or six years older than himself, but he puffed up his chest and lengthened his step to create an air of authority. The crowd fell silent, but there was no applause or other sign of welcome. The people of Beziers were beholden to no-one and even Trencavel – especially Trencavel – would have to make his case.

'My Lords, members of the Council, good people of Beziers,' he began. 'Your city is in great danger. As you must know by now, an army under the orders of the Pope and the French king is only a few hours' march away. It's a large army but it is not well disciplined or well led.' Trencavel paused for a moment and looked around the crowded square, judging the mood of the people. For now there was no response. 'I come to you directly from talks with the French barons and with Arnaud Amaury, envoy of the Pope' – a murmur ran through the crowd – 'and one thing is certain. They are determined upon besieging the city, unless..' – and here he paused again – 'unless the 222 men on this list are delivered up to them.'

The crowd leaned forward in unison, like an animal straining at a leash, to try and get a closer look at the parchment which Trencavel now unwound with a flourish, though most of them could not have read the writing even if they were close enough to pick out the spidery letters. But the great red seal which hung from the scroll like a huge drop of blood waiting to fall impressed everyone.

'The names on this list are some of the finest and the best

amongst you,' Trencavel was saying, 'the perfect of this city. The list includes all the *credentes* who are closest to release from the pain of life.'

The communal intake of breath was almost audible, and there were a few shouts of 'No!' or 'Never!'

'Can we accede to this horrible demand?' – the shouts were more general now – 'No, good people of Beziers, we cannot! I know that you and I have not always seen eye to eye' – he lowered his own eyes in a gesture of apparent humility – 'but in this hour of our need we must put those differences behind us and act as one to save our city and our people! Christians and *credentes* side by side!' He had to raise his voice now to be heard over the shouts of support. 'I can hear that you are as ready to fight this abomination as I am! I know now that I was right to have foreseen your courage. I have already told Amaury, that devil incarnate, that I am confident in my people, that we would never give in to his demands, that we would defend our city to the last man, woman and child.' He paused and scanned the crowd. 'Have I judged you aright?'

The cheers and shouts became one cry of defiance, in which the individual shouts could no longer be distinguished. Trencavel thrust out his jaw and held up both hands, fists clenched, in a gesture of solidarity and strength, to receive the acclamation of his people.

Having fired up the crowd, Trencavel now quieted them again and turned to more practical matters. He himself would ride with all speed to Carcassonne to raise an army from his vassals there and in the surrounding lands, returning within two days at most to defend Beziers. He would take the Jewish population of the city with him. He knew the people looked favourably on the Jews, who were a mainstay of the city's trade, but they would be among the first to be slaughtered if the invaders were to break in. He would leave the defence of the city in the safe hands of the town council until he returned. He had already established that there was sufficient food to last at least a week and, most importantly, there was access to drinking water. That, combined with the massive walls, made the city almost impregnable once the great gates were shut. They were shut every night in any event, but would not be reopened from now on until the danger was past, except to let the Count and his party leave at sunrise on the following morning.

Gilles turned to William: 'Heard enough? Let's go!' They scrambled back down from the ledge and returned by the route they had come. When they came to the patch of open ground inside the walls Gilles led the way up a narrow flight of steps cut into the stone and disappeared at the top. William followed and found him sitting in a wide embrasure with his feet dangling over a hundred foot drop and a view all the way to the coast, which stretched away to the south until it merged into the sea and a hazy sky. Graceful heron swooped lazily on the warm air. He sat down cautiously. It was the kind of spot he normally avoided and it made him feel queasy, but he wasn't going to show it.

'Your Count Trencavel talked pretty openly about the heresy.'

Gilles frowned. 'It isn't heresy, remember, William – it's the truth! I don't suppose Trencavel really believes one thing or the other, but he's always tolerated us, and he's right that we and the Christians live as good neighbours. Of course, he said what he had to say to win over the people. But he was right, too, when he said that the city is defensible for a few weeks against the most determined attackers. Just look at the height of these walls!' He pointed down but William could only nod faintly. 'I just hope he comes back, and doesn't decide to sacrifice us to give himself time to build up the defences of Carcassonne.'

They sat in silence for a while, thoughts drifting, until Gilles said:

'Are you sure about your decision to fight? Suddenly the

danger seems very close and very real. Perhaps you should get out tonight before it's too late, or join Trencavel's party at dawn. Carcassonne is a fine city, or you might be able to get away as far as Toulouse.'

William turned to his friend. 'I can't believe you're saying this. We've already talked this through and you agreed that I should stay and fight, if it comes to that. I'm not changing my mind because the battle looks to be close. As the Count said, the city is well placed to withstand a siege, and you just said you agree!'

'But as I've also said, Trencavel might betray us, and then we'll be in trouble.'

'Well, if he does you'll need all the men you can muster to fight. I've trained with the long-sword, you know, as well as in archery. And I don't want to go back on the road, to be alone again.'

Gilles sighed and was quiet for a moment, gazing out over the plain and the sea. Then he said, quietly: 'I know what you mean. But this seems so real all of a sudden. This is my people's battle, not yours. We are the ones they're fighting, not you!' He paused, then, still looking straight ahead, added: 'William, you mean so much to me, I don't want you to die.'

William put his arm round him: 'I feel the same about you, Gilles. That's why I'm not going to leave.' They sat in silence for several minutes, stunned by the conflicting emotions, until finally William said: 'Whatever happens, we should face it together.'

He turned to embrace Gilles, then jerked back as he remembered where he was. Gilles steadied him, laughing, and felt William's heart pounding.

'You have the fear of heights, William? That might be a problem when it comes to fighting on the battlements!'

***

Only just out of view from the point where Gilles and William sat, the main body of the French crusader army was making its way towards them across the sunlit plain. They had not travelled by the direct, upland route which William had followed a few months earlier. Instead they had marched southwards through the Rhone valley, adding to their numbers all the way, before crossing the great river at Avignon. The crusaders had been welcomed to the city with an open-air mass to bless their venture, which had to be held outside the walls to accommodate their great numbers; when it was on the road the host was said to stretch for more than a league. The next day they set off again, turning now to the south-west, and were guided through the treacherous marshes of the Rhone delta by Count Raymond of Toulouse himself. After years of turning a blind eye to the heresy in his lands, the Count had indeed changed sides when he appreciated the seriousness of the threat.

Beyond the marshes the crusaders had caught their first sight of the Middle Sea, and joined the great artery laid out along the coast by the Romans more than a thousand years before. This was, now as then, a major route for both trade and warfare, but despite its importance the road was not well-maintained. Working parties had been sent on ahead of the main army to repair bridges and fill in the deepest potholes, but even so the irregular and slippery stones had delayed progress and led to accidents and injuries.

The men of France cursed the dilatory southerners, though in their eyes the failure to repair the roads was the least of their shortcomings. At open air masses held all along the long march to the south, the accompanying priests had drummed into the soldiers' heads stories of the debauchery and devil-worship of the men they were to fight. The soldiers who would shortly besiege Beziers would do so in the certain knowledge that their enemy were men and women who espoused a foul heresy. The righteous crusaders would earn God's favour by wiping out that foulness without mercy! The priests encouraged the singing of hymns as the great host marched, both to keep up the men's spirits and to remind them of the holy endeavour on which they were engaged. But most of the men's minds were concerned with more practical matters. Their immediate objective was to keep on the move so as to ensure the best chance of a share of whatever food was going and somewhere comfortable to sleep at the end of the day's march. And for the men of the crusade, a city damned by its heresy was also a city ripe for slaughter and for plunder.

The great host had become very strung-out along the difficult road, and most were still unaware how close they now were to their destination, but by the end of the day the leading group could be in no doubt. Late in the afternoon a shout went up as the first men spotted the outline of the distant cathedral and the towers and walls of Beziers rising beyond the bamboo thickets which bordered the road, perhaps three leagues distant, or a couple more hours' march. The silhouette of the city was lit up by the setting sun, just as it had been when William first saw it, approaching from the hills to the north. The men of the crusade did not, of course, see the shining city which William, full of hope, had seen, but they shared the relief and excitement he had felt that a long-awaited destination was in sight.

It was late in the day when the first outriders of the crusader army approached the city, so they set up camp on the level plain to the east. From there a bridge led across the river Orb and up to the walls and the gates of the city itself. The command came round that no-one was to cross the bridge or do anything to incite the defenders until the crusader force was fully assembled. The army would begin its work at first light the following morning. They would set up the camp properly, ensure that all means of contact between the heretics and the outside world were closed off, and then they would make their preparations to besiege and storm the city.

***

During the meal that evening Gilles' father forbade discussion of the political situation, though this was of course the only subject anyone was interested in and the result was a brooding silence. But when the bones that couldn't be gnawed any more had been thrown across the courtyard for the dogs, and the family had pushed back their chairs and passed round the wine flagon, he turned to Trencavel's speech and the impending danger. There was little to be said about the family's own response to the situation: their home and all their immediate relatives were in the city and they would stay. Gerald checked the state of the family's food supplies with his wife. Liliane nestled up to her mother and William heard her whisper:

'It'll be all right, won't it mama?'

'Shush, my dear, your father will look after us,' but there was a catch in the mother's voice too and she led her daughter off to bed.

Gerald shifted uncomfortably in his seat at the head of the table and said that there were one or two other matters which needed to be cleared up.

'William, there's one change of plan, and it concerns you. You said clearly that you wanted to stay in the city come what may and I agreed, albeit against my better judgement. I don't like to go back on my word, but the matter has been taken out of my hands. The city elders agreed at the meeting this afternoon that all outsiders to the region should leave the city. This isn't just for their own safety, it's because of the realities of a siege. The city is well-protected and could hold off an attack for a long time, but our weak point would be the food supplies. The council has decided that anyone who doesn't normally live in the county of Beziers should leave for Carcassonne in the morning with Trencavel's party, preserving the stocks we have for our own people. This is the decision of the council and I can't be seen to make an exception for someone living under my roof. I'm sorry, William.'

William was stunned. He glanced at Gilles before replying but knew how he must answer. 'Sir, I understand this isn't your decision, and I must accept it. You and your family…'

Before he could say any more Gerald cut him off: 'Well said, William, as ever. Now, there are other practical matters we must…'

But before he could say what those matters were, the doors into the courtyard from the street were pushed open and Robert's ragged figure lurched in. As he approached the table he swayed slightly and his breath smelt of cheap liquor. The goats had followed him in from the street and could be seen nibbling the grass round the base of the lime tree.

'Cousin Gerald, good to see you, and Therese, charming as ever!'

Neither host nor hostess looked particularly pleased to see their guest, but they responded politely. Robert didn't address anyone else, but sat himself down on the bench seat in Liliane's place and reached across the table for the wine flagon. He poured himself a full glass, slopping some on the table.

'Well, here's a pretty pass! I wouldn't impose but it seems too risky to stay outside the city. You never know how long a siege might last of course – good thing I brought some supplies of fresh meat!'

'We never know how long your visits may last either,' Gerald replied coldly. 'I seem to remember you stayed most of the winter last time, and your animals too which you took away with you in the end.'

Robert banged the glass down on the table and glared at his cousin. 'So you'd throw your wife's blood relation onto the street at a time like this, would you? That wouldn't look very good, would it? You've done very well for yourself here, but you would deny shelter to me?'

'I didn't say that, you will receive the hospitality due to a relation,' Gerald replied calmly enough though his eyes blazed. 'I just meant don't push your luck too far, Robert. You can have Gilles' room for as long as there's a likelihood of trouble, but you'll pay us rent for it in cash or in kind. Gilles, don't argue, you can sleep in the hay-loft with William. There's plenty of room for the two of you up there.' He glared round the company. Neither cousin nor wife seemed very happy with this arrangement but everyone sensed Gerald's irritation, heightened perhaps by anxiety, and no-one challenged it. Robert snorted and changed tack.

'And who is the young man with the golden locks?' Robert sneered. 'We weren't introduced earlier.'

Before William could speak Gerald snapped back: 'He's a traveller from England whom I have chosen to give shelter to.'

William smiled to himself, pleased both by Gerald's staunch defence of his presence in the house and because his imminent departure was not mentioned. He introduced himself politely to Robert, who grunted a reply.

Gerald glared round the table and said: 'I think after all we should turn in for the night. There are matters to be discussed but I think after all they can wait until morning when we are fresh. There'll be work for all of us then, and we will need to be up early,' and here he looked pointedly at William. 'I suggest that we all rise an hour before dawn. We will meet here and say our farewells to our young guest. Then we will make what preparations we can, in particular identifying what weapons we have here in the house, cleaning and mending them if necessary and allocating them. We should hide valuables as securely as possible and make plans for getting my dear wife and daughter to safety if there seems to be any immediate threat.' He stopped and clasped Therese's hand in both of his. Then he continued: 'I think that's enough for now, apart from a short prayer for the safety of our people and our city.' With that everyone lowered their eyes and murmured the evening prayer which William had heard before, though he could never catch all the words which were clearly so familiar to the *credentes*. When it was over Gerald wished everyone goodnight, then stood up rather formally and led his wife from the room. William sensed that Gerald was holding back his own emotions and perhaps could not bear to say any more at this time. Those who remained looked round at one another blankly. Gilles offered to show Robert to his quarters and find him a blanket, and got another grunt by way of acceptance.

***

William had already bedded down by the time Gilles climbed the ladder, but he was not asleep. In the moonlight which broke through gaps in the roof he could see his friend as he laid a blanket over the straw and took off his tunic. Gilles lay down and moved in close for warmth. William waited a while before he spoke.

'Do you really think I should leave in the morning?' he asked, quietly. 'I've only been here a couple of months, but I feel so much at home here already, and you know I don't want to leave you; we've had so little time together.'

'Well, you must leave. You heard what the council of elders have ordered.' Then he softened his tone, put his arm round William and held him tight. 'Of course I don't want you to go. But I don't want you to stay here and face who knows what dangers either. Like I said, you can wait this out in Toulouse – you begin to sound like a local even if you'll never look like one! – and come back when it's all over. Now let's stop this before someone hears us. You wouldn't be so popular with my father then!'

Gilles turned away and after just a few minutes his breathing came deeper and longer. William sighed, turned over and tried to sleep too. He normally slept as long and soundly as any young man, but he doubted that he would get much sleep that night.

***

In fact William slept fitfully for a few hours, drifting in and out of strange dreams which he could not grasp afterwards though he sensed they had involved dark and frightening figures of men on horseback. He was awake and listening for the sounds of the household rising in the dark hour before dawn, as Gerald had ordered. He got up and slipped on his tunic and cloak quietly, but Gilles was sleeping deeply and didn't stir. He rested his hand for a moment on his friend's shoulder, then crept across the cold loft towards the faint gleam that seeped up from the torches in the courtyard below.

There was less activity in the courtyard than he had expected: Gilles' mother was tending the fire with Liliane but there was no sign of either Gerald or Robert.

'Good morning, William! I hope the sleeping arrangements were not too cramped?'

'They were fine,' he replied, taken aback and hoping he was not blushing. 'But I suppose the Count's party will be gathering soon?'

Therese looked up for the first time and shook her head with a tired half-smile: 'Well, I'm not sure, but I think they may already have left. Some of the other men were here an hour ago and took my husband off to some sort of emergency council. The women don't get told much of course, but from what I overheard it sounded as if Count Trencavel and his men left with most of the Jewish families soon after midnight – maybe to be sure they got away in time, maybe to avoid too many hangers-on. Either way I suspect you'll get your wish – and may God protect you – but my advice to you would be not to look too pleased about it when my husband returns!'

'Er…no, I understand.' William suppressed his immediate feelings and tried to gather his thoughts.

'And here they are. Gerald, what news?'

Gerald had stormed into the courtyard, with Robert trailing behind. 'News? Too much news! Bring wine first though, and bread and oil. Then we'll tell you.'

Robert leered unpleasantly at William. 'Ah, here's our young friend who wanted to show his English courage in whatever horrors are to befall us. Well, it looks like he's going to get his chance!'

'Do not speak in such a way!' Gerald snapped. 'In any case, we may still get William out of here before the French arrive, though the Council have already ordered the gates closed and no more departures. The enemy army are camped across the river in large numbers and more are streaming in all the time. It's begun!'

Therese brought a flagon and laid a hand on Gerald's shoulder.

'Ah, that's better – thank you. We'll need another flagon, I think. Well, Gilles, good of you to get up!'

'I'm sorry father, I…'

Gilles shuffled across the courtyard, his eyes still heavy with sleep.

'He looks as if he needs another eight hours! D'you think those boys smuggled a couple of wenches up there last night?'

'Robert, we know you have foul thoughts, but please don't speak them out loud in my house. Remember our faith at this time!'

Robert looked as if he was about to say something else, but thought better of it. Gilles was playing it safe and looking resolutely at the ground. William had reluctantly concluded in the dark hours of his sleepless night that he must leave early as had been planned, and was struggling to catch up with the speed of events. He felt a mixture of excitement and fear now that fate had taken the decision out of his hands.

'So it is true, sir, that Count Trencavel has already left?'

Gerald glared at him. 'Yes, William, it is. We may still be able to get you out, maybe even the remainder of the Jewish population whom Trencavel saw fit to leave behind, but I fear it is already too late. I've just come from a meeting of the city council, and the last few refugees who made it in from the countryside during the night have reported that the crusaders have been burning farms and taking the livestock as they approached across the plain yesterday. The council have sent out spies to try and get a clearer idea of how well-armed the enemy are, and how many more are still on the road. It sounds bad, but we should know more within an hour or two. In the meantime the gates are to remain sealed except to allow clearly identified local people and the spies back in.

'There is much to do: ensuring everything of value is well hidden, finding whatever weapons we have and passing on those we cannot use ourselves to the general levy. I have two swords – Robert can use the second one – and we can sharpen up the pitchforks in the stable for the boys. If it comes to a fight the women and children are to barricade themselves in the church of Saint Mary Magdalene. All able-bodied men will fight including Gilles and, if he's still here, William. I'm sorry, boy, but it may come to that.'

'I am not afraid, sir.'

Gerald turned a kindlier eye on him now: 'I never thought you were, William. I hope it doesn't happen, but you seem to have a strong spirit, and if my son is fighting…' He stopped speaking and put his arm round his wife, whose eyes were filling with tears, and his own mortal fear was clear enough. After this brief show of emotion he composed himself and, resuming his role as head of the family, made a short speech. Even Robert knew better than to interrupt.

'I can't hide from you all that we face great danger, but I have every confidence in our people. The men of the city are arming themselves and preparing the city to resist attack. We have built up good supplies of grain, dried meat and preserves, and luckily we have an excellent source of fresh water here in the city. In addition there is a reasonable supply of livestock within the walls, even in our own house, thanks to cousin Robert!'

Robert, who had been leaning against the door-post of his room throughout, gave a twisted smile, as if he rather thought the goats were his to dispose of as he saw fit, but he said nothing.

'Well, in short we have at least two months' supply of all we need within the city walls, more if we cut the rations. The leaders of the damnable crusade won't find it easy to keep their force together and provide sufficient food for much longer than that. Most of the fighting men will only be subject to feudal ties for forty days and are likely to start to disperse and go off looting elsewhere if we can hold them off that long.

'Finally, there is at least one piece of excellent news which I can share with you from this morning's meeting. Of course, we've always lived on good and neighbourly terms with our fellow citizens who follow the Roman church, but I've been worried about how they would react in the face of a crusade aimed at our supposed heresy. Well, I can tell you they will stand by us. Apparently spies from the crusader force have entered the city in secret in the past few days and offered all "true Christians of Rome" free passage out of the city in advance of any attack. Councillor Bonafet wanted the whole council to know that only a small minority seem to have accepted these offers and crept away before the gates were locked. The rest of our Christian neighbours are remaining to defend the city shoulder to shoulder with the *credentes*. We will stand together against the invaders.'

Gerald paused for a moment before continuing, and there was a general expression of relief at this positive news.

'But as I have said, we face great danger. My dear family, you must act as the perfect have taught us in this hour of need. Remember your faith and believe there is a better place beyond this earthly life which we should always keep in sight. Then God will protect you. Perhaps William can also find comfort in those words, even if he is not of our faith! Now let us all pray together for a few moments.'

William looked down, hearing again the tremor in Gerald's voice which had not been there before and which brought home to him more than anything the dangers that lay ahead. And yet at the same time he felt more alive than ever before, and an overwhelming wave of gratitude and love for this second father and for this family who had taken him in unquestioningly. Around him he heard the hurried murmuring of prayers, and he himself offered up the familiar and comforting words of the Lord's Prayer in his own tongue.

***

It was not long before Gilles' father was called away to another meeting of the council, leaving orders that the women and children should go straight to the church of St Mary Magdalene and lock themselves in at the first sign of incursion into the city, though that was not thought to be an imminent danger. All men of fighting age should in the meantime arm themselves as best they could. Gerald had glared at his wife's cousin as he said this. Gilles took William down into the cellar of the house where they found a pile of rusty pikes, and each selected one of the less corroded ones. For all William's swagger about his use of the long-sword, his experience was limited to trial combats on feast-days in distant Rochester where the likelihood of using arms in anger had been reassuringly remote. He was faintly relieved that he would not be expected to demonstrate his swordsmanship with a weapon of such weight.

When they re-emerged into the daylight, armed with the pikes which they had polished up as best they could and each with a short knife tucked into his belt, Gilles' father had returned and was engaged at the table in earnest discussion with several other grim-faced men. He broke off only long enough to tell William and Gilles that they should gather in the market square with all the other men of fighting age. The enemy would no doubt quickly start the construction of siege-engines, but those would take some time to complete. The crusaders might be harried from the walls if they approached too close, but arrows and other ammunition should not be wasted so long as the walls were not breached.

He had looked both boys in the eye and, his own eyes shimmering, spoken the most encouraging words he could summon: 'Gilles, my son, whatever you do, be worthy of our faith and of our family, and God will protect you. William, you know I didn't want you to be caught in our city at this time, but now there is no choice. I am sure you will act bravely and be deserving of God's protection.'

He embraced first his son, then the young visitor whom circumstance had so quickly drawn into the family, and he no longer attempted to hide the tears in his eyes as he did so. William felt the man's hot breath as he murmured into his ear: 'Look after my son: he is a good boy, but impulsive!'

'I will, sir, I will!' William murmured back, also close to tears, touched by the trust Gilles' father was placing in him and determined to live up to it. Then the older man returned to the discussion at the table, and the two young men left the house sunk in their own thoughts.

***

The urgent talk and serious planning inside the house, which like all the larger houses in the city faced inward to the courtyard, gave no clue as to the mayhem outside. The narrow streets were congested with shop-holders barricading their premises against possible looting and residents of the outer suburbs moving as many of their possessions as they had managed to load onto carts up into the citadel. There were also people from out of town who had made their way into the city the night before and were now desperately seeking lodging or, at least, somewhere to pile up their belongings and create some kind of resting-place for their children and elderly. A steady flow of women and children whose expressions ranged from the bemused to the terrified were making their way up through the throng towards the church of the Magdalene, which was already serving as a place of refuge, not least because today, 22 July, was the Holy Mother's feast-day. Isolated groups of men bearing makeshift arms, many of which were in no better condition than William and Gilles' own, were heading in the other direction. The crowd edged back to let the men pass, eyeing them anxiously or giving encouragement. This rag-tag force would be the people's only hope if the walls were breached.

William gazed at the spectacle with fascination. He had travelled far from home and seen many things, but for the first time he felt a world of unimagined drama and danger swirling around him, which filled him with excitement and fear in equal measure. He had left home to escape the certain pattern of his life in Kent, to see foreign lands and – maybe – to find his own place in the world. He marvelled at the spectacle of the events unfolding around him and relished the chance to test himself in the coming battle, though if he had known in any detail what lay just ahead he might have felt differently. For now he was brought face to face with the brutal reality by the wailing of an ancient woman with clouded, unseeing eyes, precariously balanced on the back of a passing donkey. A more religious soul might have taken it as a sign. William saw it simply as the first stage of the suffering which the siege would bring, and which could only get much worse if it endured for long, despite Gerald's encouraging words.

Now Gilles was tugging at his sleeve and, as before, ducking down alleys William wouldn't even have noticed, crossing the patches of kitchen-garden perched just inside the city walls and emerging onto the same ledge with the precipitous drop overlooking the coastal plain. Once again William blanched and tried not to look down. But here too, everything had changed since the previous afternoon.

The heron had been frightened off and the landscape was now overrun with the chaotic, colourful sprawl of the crusader army, encamped on the solid ground on the far bank of the river which flowed past the city, the one unchanged feature in view. Red and yellow pennants fluttered in the light breeze; the snorting and whinnying of tethered horses drifted up to the two friends; and smoke curled up from hastily constructed field-kitchens – apparently the besiegers would not go hungry in the short term even if the people of Beziers did. Further out across the level plain William could see the constant flow of new arrivals streaming in and joining the encampment.

'There are an awful lot of them!'
'That doesn't make the walls any lower!'

William grinned, but he didn't share Gilles' confidence. He had been thinking hard about the situation. The city had been deserted by Trencavel, who might not come back when he learnt the size of the host which was now assembling around it, if indeed he had ever intended to. There were certainly a good number of fighting men in the city, though William had not seen many who carried real weapons. There were already signs that the crusaders were assembling siege engines near the southern escarpment. These were great contraptions of wood, pulleys and counterweights which, as he knew from the stories Edwin had told him of the crusade, could be used to hurl rocks, burning rags and – in the later stages – even diseased carcasses into a city under siege. Any attack would take time, but time, he thought, was on the side of the besieging force, which had the supply lines the city did not. The excitement he had felt when they first came out on the street had drained away, to be replaced by an increasing sense of dread about what lay ahead and by simple fear for himself and for Gilles. He remembered Edwin's words about the battles he had fought in: 'I have never felt more alive than I did then, nor more aware of the reality of death'.

**

In the grandest of the tents, which William and Gilles could have picked out from their vantage point if they had known where to look, Arnaud Amaury, abbot of the Cistercian Order and ultimate spiritual leader of the crusade, sat in all his splendour, munching grapes one after another. He was a man for whom there were no half measures, a man of war no less fanatically than he was a man of God, and he had waited a long time for this day. He was pleased that the rhetoric and the parleying were over. Now he would act, with the direct authority of His Holiness, to wipe out the foul heresy with the sword of Christ.

His gimlet eyes beneath hooded brows swept the expectant circle of religious and temporal leaders. The Bishops of Autun, Clermont and Nevers returned his gaze with the calm inscrutability born of a lifetime of religious practice and devotion. They exuded sanctity, the mystery of God and their own closeness to the Almighty. Arnaud Amaury had no time for all that; what preoccupied him now was not the abstractions of the faith but practical, military intelligence. His gaze alighted on the Duke of Burgundy, the most experienced military leader of the assembled force, and the senior representative of the King of France, who himself had declined to lead the host on the grounds that he was preoccupied with his English enemy. The Duke was a man in his middle years, massively built, swarthy, heavily bearded and with part of his left ear missing.

'Well, my Lord Duke, how would you assess the military position?'

The Duke opened his mouth to reply but before he could do so Amaury launched into his own analysis.

'From what I as a humble man of God can see, the city is well defended and has massive walls. The people have known for some time that we were coming, and although we have given the heretics the chance to recant the heresy and save their souls very few have chosen to do so. It seems that the majority of their Christian fellow-citizens have also chosen to stay in the city and fight. So be it – they too will pay the ultimate price for their betrayal of the faith!

'We must presume that they have made their preparations, must we not, my Lord? Stocked up their food supplies, filled the cisterns with drinking water and so forth. We have the far greater force, but it is something of a motley army, and most of the best fighting men are only subject to forty days' feudal service. I wonder how long the force will hold together, especially if you cannot raise sufficient food supplies from the surrounding lands to fill the men's stomachs. From what I saw of the country we passed through there are as many fields of vines as there are of barley and other cereals. The fruit of the vine is hardly likely to sustain the fighting strength of the men – rather the opposite, I would have thought!'

With this he took a generous swig from the silver goblet on the side-table, seeming not to notice the irony, and gestured to the Duke to respond. The Duke glared round at the company to ensure he had everyone's attention before doing so.

'You have of course assessed the situation expertly, my Lord Abbot. We have some fine fighting men, mostly those brought by the assembled lords of France, but they are only the core of a wider and less reliable army. You're right that they would be difficult to hold together in the event of a long siege.'

He paused for some time, looking down and nodding thoughtfully to signify that he was applying his long military experience to the problem.

'The key therefore is to move fast. I have already set up working parties who even now are constructing the siege engines which will be needed to break the morale and resistance of the defenders – I mean of course of the *heretics,* my lord – and in due course to breach the walls. I've sent out a small group of men to work their way around the city, keeping under cover, to assess the weak points in the defences. Every city has its weak points; the art lies in identifying them correctly!

'I intend that we should be ready within three days, four at most, to launch a full assault on the city. We should do this just before daybreak, when we have the greatest element of surprise on our side, and the heretics will be at their least prepared. We will keep the smaller siege engines hidden as far as possible, and arrange some pretence of carousing in the camp late into the previous night, to trick the infidels into believing that we are not planning an imminent attack.'

The Duke sat back and looked round challengingly, and the assembled lords and bishops nodded mutely, waiting for Arnaud Amaury's response. The abbot nodded slowly, looked up and waited before replying.

'Very well, my Lord Duke. Move fast, yes! We must destroy all the enemies of Christ in the city – utterly destroy them – the heretics and their Christian sympathisers alike. That will send a message to the rest of the Languedoc about what is coming to them if they do not recant. A bloody massacre to put the fear of God into the rest of them. Good, good! The third day it is then. We are all agreed? Then go to it in the name of the Lord...'

***

Outside the tent the Bishop of Autun put a gentle hand on the Duke's arm, noticing as he did so its phenomenal girth and the iron hardness of the muscle.

'A word, my Lord Duke?'

'What is it, my Lord Bishop?' the Duke replied, folding his rippling arms to face him.

'Only this, my Lord. I have had my servants take soundings of the morale of the forces assembled here, and the impression they have given is of little enthusiasm for the hard grind of a siege. There are plenty of men ready for looting and pillage, indeed there has been enough of that already in the undefended villages along the road. But most of these so-called fighting men will fade away like dew in the morning sun in the face of real privation, or simply the boredom of a siege when there is nothing in it for them, will they not?'

'I know that as well as you, my Lord Bishop. Did I not tell your Lord and master that speed was of the essence? Maintain morale and wind the men up for a short siege and a quick result. That is my strategy! Don't forget, too, that there will be plenty of rewards for the men in the defeated city, though you gentlemen of the cloth may prefer to turn a blind eye! That should keep them interested for a while.'

'Of course, my Lord Duke, the army is doing God's work here and must have its reward.' But the Bishop averted his eyes as he said this.

'Exactly, my Lord Bishop, exactly… Now, if you will allow me I must return to my preparations.' With that the Duke grasped the bishop's shoulder companionably, then turned away and was gone. The bishop was left rubbing his shoulder, wondering if it was dislocated or just bruised.

***

The Bishop of Autun's spies had, if anything, understated the enthusiasm for looting and the lack of religious zeal amongst the assembled force. They had not wished to offend the sensibilities of their master whom they regarded as a devout but unworldly man of God. As they had made their way from camp-fire to camp-fire, the talk they overheard had mostly been of the rich plunder to be had in these fertile southern lands, the easy availability of wine and the sultry charms of the women. The foot-soldiers had no real contact with the people, whose speech they could barely understand, though they cheerfully condemned the "filthy heretics" and swapped lurid stories of their sexual depravity. Some of these slanderous tales involved camels and had presumably been around since the crusade to Palestine fifteen years before.

But most of all the men of the crusade looked up at the city which towered over them and talked of the rich plunder and defenceless women they would find behind its walls. They gave little thought to the difficulty and the danger involved in breaking into such a formidable fortress, and they would be ready to follow any leader – such as the Duke of Burgundy – who rallied them with cheering talk of a surprise attack and a quick result.

It so happened that the Bishop's spies did not pass through the area of the encampment nearest to the bridge which led across the river to the eastern walls of the city. There they might have come across a pock-marked man with a sneering expression, known to his friends as Elmo of Gaeta. He always had a circle around him, ready to listen to his tales, even if no-one who had had dealings with him took anything he said too seriously. His *pièce de resistance* was, of course, his account of the murder of Pierre de Castlenau which, as he grandly announced to anyone who would listen, he himself had witnessed. In Elmo's version of events, he himself was an heroic figure who had struggled desperately to protect his master by fending off the fatal sword blows of the gargantuan horseman. He wept as he told how the monster had nonetheless succeeded in fatally stabbing Pierre in the back and escaping into the dense mists and treacherous marshlands of the Rhone delta. In some versions Elmo had even held the dying Pierre in his arms to comfort him and, in the absence of a priest, to hear his confession.

What he failed to mention was that after the murder, the remainder of the papal envoy's party had left him behind when they took ship to return to Italy. They had had enough of his laziness and petty dishonesty. Left to fend for himself as best he could, Elmo had settled and taken odd jobs in the thriving underworld of Marseille. Then, when a recruiting party had passed through the city a few years later, he had tagged along and so found himself part of the crusade which Pierre's murder had unleashed.

Early in the morning, three days later, Elmo was not concerned with tales of past exploits, he was concerned with the present. He and a band of his cronies had set up camp as near as possible to the bridge which crossed the river and led into the city. They reasoned that this gave them the best chance of keeping out of the exhausting and dangerous business of besieging the walls. It also gave them some hope of breaking into the city through the main gates soon after it fell, and so being first in line for whatever rewards were to be had.

As fate would have it, the selfish little scheme of this band of chancers was about to alter the course of history.

***

Up on the battlements, Gilles touched William's shoulder and pointed down to where the main road into the city crossed the river on a low wooden bridge. He explained proudly that it had been built on the foundations of the stone crossing constructed by the Romans. Around the bridge the two friends could see a small group of camp-followers fooling around, pushing one another into the water and shouting taunts up at the city walls. Gilles said that these would be some of the *ribauds*, landless men who strung along with armies on the march and who might join the fray when the fighting began, but were not under any real discipline.

William and Gilles could not catch the words from their high vantage point, but some of the young men of the city, gathered on the walls just above the gate, evidently could and were giving as good as they got. As the two young friends watched, helpless observers, the idle disorder rapidly changed into something much more sinister. A ragged party now emerged from the gate, brandishing pikes and whooping, and began a disorderly charge down the slope towards the bridge, a distance of three or four hundred paces. The *ribauds* in their turn, catching on to what was happening, let out cries of excitement, gathered up their weapons and scrambled out of the river and across the bridge.

William could hear the fear in Gilles' voice as he muttered: 'Those idiots have opened the gate...' Wiser heads on the walls further down were already screaming at the ragged mob to get back inside and bar the gates, but the opportunity was equally clear to the band of *ribauds* coming up the hill towards the gate from outside, yelping for reinforcements. William touched Gilles' shoulder and pointed out across the plain. Gilles understood at once; men on the far side of the river who had spotted what was happening were shouldering their weapons and crossing the bridge. Further out into the crusader force there was a glint of arms as men hurried to shoulder their weapons and form into fighting groups. Soon they too would move towards the city. The sleeping giant had been woken and was rousing itself to strike.

'Those idiots,' Gilles muttered, 'all could be lost before it's begun!'

'We should get down there, get the damned gate shut again!'

Gilles grinned for a moment: 'William, you're swearing like a son of the Languedoc!' but his brief smile faded again fast. 'You're right, of course. If the gate is lost now ...oh, God...' William glimpsed the two ragged bands starting to engage in hand to hand combat on the bridge over the river, then he and Gilles jumped down into the vegetable patches and ran as fast as they could along the inside of the walls towards the gate. From here they could have no idea of what was going on outside, or whether others inside had already seen the danger, swung the heavy doors to and rammed home the great wooden bolts. Or perhaps they would not want to do that until the rabble was back inside, despite the catastrophe that could follow if they left it too late? Maybe from lower down they hadn't yet realised that the main army was already on the move?

Gilles seemed to know this corner of the city less well, or had perhaps just lost his bearings in his panic, and they found themselves in dead-ends once or twice. But suddenly they turned a corner and came out onto the main street from the gate to the centre, at the point where William had met Gilles on his arrival in the city. How long ago that seemed! Down here the danger was not visible, but there was a real sense of panic as word spread like wildfire that the gate was already breached. Preparations against a long siege were abandoned as men, and even some of the bolder women, grabbed whatever arms came to hand and headed down towards the gate. Gilles turned to William with an expression which he had not seen in his friend's eyes before, a blazing excitement which no doubt betrayed the impulsiveness his father had warned William against, overcoming his natural caution and his fear.

'Maybe they're not inside yet – there's still a chance!'

William was less sure, or maybe just less courageous, but in the heat of the moment there was no time to think. He nodded grimly and together they pushed through the melée. The men heading towards the gate shoved aside the women and children, many of them carrying screaming babies, who were coming the other way, still hoping to find safety in the upper town. The thought flashed across William's mind that there would be no safety anywhere within the walls if the crusaders broke through. More women now evidently thought the same and were going downhill armed with kitchen knives or pokers to add whatever they could to defending the city. One had her baby wrapped in a cloth cradle on her back, still sleeping in the midst of the chaos.

As they rounded the last bend in the street before the gate, the scene William had feared was before them. Inside the gate, a ragged scrap was already in progress between the foolhardy rabble who had run wildly down the hill less than a quarter of an hour earlier, and the *ribauds* who had taken advantage of their stupidity to bring the fight into the city. The attackers had the better weapons, long pikes and even swords, and several of the defenders lay dead or wounded underfoot. William steadied himself; he didn't feel in the least prepared for this. It was impossible for him to judge how the fighting would turn out, but he could also see that what mattered was that it was allowing time for the main crusader force to reach the gate and enter the city. If that happened there would be bloody slaughter at least, and most likely the city would be lost.

A few of the *ribauds* were hanging around the gate, presumably to guard it, but the main fighting was taking place a hundred paces inside the walls. Gilles gave William a glance and a nod, and William understood him at once. If they could only get round to the half-open gates and shut them, they might just save the day. William nodded, and they began to ease their way unobtrusively past the fighting. They collected a small group of other townsmen, most of them known to Gilles, as they went. William noticed a similar group edging along the opposite wall. There was still a chance!

As they approached the gates the *ribaud* guard spotted what was happening, raised their weapons and shouted for reinforcements, though in the confusion no-one responded immediately. In fact for a moment nothing happened at all, then William saw Gilles rush past him, brandishing his pike wildly around his head. As he reached the first of the *ribauds*, a rough-looking man of maybe thirty years, he brought the pike down with a sickening crack onto the side of the man's head. His victim stood for a second, staring into space as blood poured from the wound on his temple, then he crumpled heavily to the ground. There was a brief silence before his fellows roared in anger and turned towards Gilles, who himself seemed transfixed by the gory body at his feet. William lunged forward and fended off the nearest of the attackers, giving Gilles time to come to himself and take a swing at another man, though to less effect this time. The two young men were now surrounded by the braying throng, and the thought flashed through William's mind that perhaps this was where his adventure would end, hacked to pieces in a foreign city. Gilles raised his weapon again, keeping the mob at bay for a few seconds more, but neither side moved. The attackers were mostly boys, no more battle-hardened than the locals, and equally stunned by the sudden death. They eyed one another with fear and uncertainty, vaguely aware that the fight was continuing further inside the gate.

Then, with unimagined suddenness, the catastrophe struck. The great wooden doors flew wide open and slammed against the inner walls of the gate-towers with a thunderous crash, swiftly followed by the piercing scream of a *ribaud* who had been crushed between the gate and the wall. A shaft of morning sun lit up the remnants of the brawlers, bloodied and filthy and running with sweat, and through the gate there streamed a dozen rows of four horsemen riding abreast, their armour gleaming, their horses rearing and snorting and trampling underfoot whatever and whoever was in their path. Townsmen and *ribauds* alike scrambled for cover before the terrifying machine which had burst upon them, filling the narrow street and utterly beyond challenge.

William, immobile, was suddenly aware of Gilles tugging at his arm.

'Don't just stand there, you dozy English clod, let's get out of here!'

His arm was almost pulled out of its joint as Gilles dragged him over the low wall behind them and back the way they had come, unnoticed in the chaos that followed the irruption of the horsemen into the city. They could hear others on their tail, but didn't turn to see if they were townsmen or *ribauds*. Hurling themselves over walls, stumbling through potato patches, skittering down alleys, they just ran. William ran with one image burnt onto his brain: the head of one of the townsmen bouncing away into the dust, scythed clean off with a perfect sword-stroke by the first of the monstrous horsemen. In the bible there had been only four horsemen of the apocalypse.

***

Back on the now familiar ledge, William and Gilles clutched hold of one another, panting for breath. William slumped down against the wall with his head in his hands. Out of the corner of his eye, he sensed the whole plain in motion, as the crusader forces formed up and advanced towards the city gate, which was by this time no doubt firmly in their hands. Now that the city lay open to the crusaders with their huge superiority in numbers and weaponry, there could be no hope.

'Christ, what happened? How could they have…? And what did *we* do, Gilles!? We *ran*.'

Gilles was still standing, sickeningly near the edge for William's comfort, and shook his head. He looked close to tears.

'I don't know. What could we have done? Get our heads chopped off too?' And now he also slumped down against the wall, burying his face in his hands. William put his arms round him and hugged him tightly, but felt no response. Then they both sat back against the wall in silence for some time, sunk in their own despair.

Finally Gilles said: 'And my family, trapped in the city… What can we do?'

'Yes, we must do whatever we can… Of course, your father and his friends will be there to protect them, but, well…' His speech tailed off as he realised how hopeless it all sounded.

Gilles looked up, his eyes shining with unwept tears. 'No,' he murmured, 'no, there's no hope. What can we do? Did you see those fucking horsemen? A killing machine! They won't take prisoners. It's what my father feared if they once got into the city. And if we go back, we'll be slaughtered too.'

'What choice have we got?' William asked. 'There's no way out of the city except the gates and those are sure to be guarded. The whole citadel will be swarming with crusaders and *ribauds* in no time.'

'Actually, there is another way,' Gilles said very quietly, almost under his breath, so that William wasn't sure he had heard correctly. He looked up at Gilles, genuinely puzzled.

'What did you say? We couldn't possibly...'

Gilles nodded along the cliff-face to the east where the coastline stretched away into a blue haze, but William still didn't understand. Had the horror turned Gilles' mind?

'This isn't just a good look-out point. If we can get down the first fifty feet of the walls there's a goat-track that runs diagonally down the cliff-face and comes out in the woods at the eastern end of the city. The men down below probably won't notice a couple of tiny figures creeping down the slope this far round. If we stay in the city, we can do nothing. But if we could get out we would have a chance of fighting back, of doing something.'

William was shocked that Gilles was suggesting fleeing the scene, with his family still inside the city, but that wasn't why the blood drained from his face. 'Have you lost your mind? It's a vertical drop down there! No-one could scale that slope, you said so yourself. It would be certain death.'

'I said that an army could never get up that way, being attacked from above. Getting down won't be easy, I grant you, but I've seen it done. Not many people even know the path is there, but a boy I know did it for a dare a couple of years ago. We were up here, flat on our stomachs watching him, and I for one was sick with fear he'd kill himself and we'd all be held responsible for letting him do it. But he made it. He had ropes to get down the first stretch, though he reckoned afterwards that there were enough toe and finger holds that he could have done it without them.'

'Sounds like bravado to me.'

'Certainly – he's the sort. In fact I wouldn't be surprised if he wasn't one of the hotheads who opened the gates and charged down the hill. But we might be able to find ropes, and anyway, what are our chances otherwise?'

'But your family? We can't just leave them.'

When Gilles finally spoke, it was in a whisper: 'If we stay here, we die. I keep telling you, there's bound to be a massacre. It's what my father feared. Our people armed with rusty swords and pitchforks won't be able to stop them; you saw those horsemen! I love my family, but…'

The two boys stared at one another, stunned by the enormity of the unspoken words. William was shocked at how far Gilles had thought this through, and later he would wonder, guiltily, if it was only his presence which had led Gilles to this agonising choice. But then, if there were a possibility of escape – he shuddered again – it was now or never. They were sitting side by side against the back wall of the ledge now, looking out over the shimmering plain, but invisible from below. William put his arm round Gilles and squeezed him tightly.

'I don't want it all to end here either, and you must be right about what will happen if we stay. Maybe if we got away we could get to Carcassonne and join the fight-back. But, how would you feel, for the rest of your life, if we just fled, even if we could get down there?'

Gilles returned his anxious gaze, and shook his head dumbly. Then suddenly he was alert and holding a finger to his lips. From not far away came the sound of heavy footsteps running, and rough voices. Gilles raised an eyebrow to William who nodded in confirmation: the shouts were in the *langue d'oil*, the language of Paris.

Gilles held William by the shoulders and whispered urgently, his doubts thrown aside. 'There's another ledge, not much more than the height of a man below us and wide enough to sit on. I'll go first and help you to follow. We can hide there until they've passed, then decide what to do. They're coming this way. If we don't get off this ledge now we're as good as dead anyway.'

William shook his head desperately, but he knew Gilles was right. They wouldn't be able to help anyone, least of all themselves, if they were captured or simply killed now. But his mind was recoiling at the idea of dropping down to the lower ledge, with the precipice below. Then he realised Gilles was peering into his terrified face, holding him by the shoulders and talking to him in an urgent whisper: 'I know, you have the fear of heights; I'm not blind. Just don't look down, tell yourself you can do it and I'll help you all the way. There's nowhere else to hide!' William couldn't really take it in, but perhaps, if he kept his eyes fixed on Gilles and on the solid rock, and if he didn't look down or even think about what lay below. Maybe, just maybe.

Before William knew what was happening Gilles had turned round, lowered himself down feet first and disappeared. He heard a skittering of small stones, a crunch, then silence. He edged forward, looked down and could see an arm waving and Gilles' upturned face not far below. He sat back, fighting down the nausea for a moment, then turned round and lay flat on his stomach. It was now or never, and edging backwards he let his legs out over the void. He jerked as he felt Gilles catching hold of his ankles, then tried to focus on the whispered instructions coaxing him down. Above him, the shouts were getting nearer. He eased down further, desperately seeking handholds in the scrubby grass, feeling his weight pulling him down. There was a sudden lurch as a clump of grass came away in his hand, a sickening moment of freefall and a sharp pain in his left knee as his feet crashed awkwardly onto the lower ledge. Gilles pushed him roughly against the cliff-face and he held on, his heart pounding wildly, with fear but also with exhilaration. He almost cried out his relief but Gilles clamped a hand over his mouth, and pressed both of them into the rock face. William could taste the grit in his mouth, and he heard footsteps and a man breathing heavily on the grassy patch above their heads.

It seemed to William that the man was just standing there, perhaps regaining his breath, perhaps looking out at the wide plain and the encampment below, as he and Gilles had. Then he was joined by a second man, who roughly asked the first if he'd seen anyone. The first man replied that he had not, though he added that there were plenty of hiding places in the sheds and animal shelters along the path. The second man grunted and replied that they should probably search them for infidel survivors – and for anything worth having. Neither thought to look over the edge, where they could not have missed two such survivors pressed into the cliff-face and holding their breath.

After a period of silence the second man ordered the first to come with him to search the houses which backed onto the wall, but the boys' relief was short-lived, as the first man said that he would follow in a moment or two. They pressed themselves as far back into the rock-face as they could and held their breath. Was the man even now looking down at them and considering how to kill them? William gripped Gilles' hand tightly. For a minute nothing happened. Then a stream of glittering yellow arced out into the void in front of them and William could barely contain a snort of laughter. When the man had buttoned up and his footsteps had receded William and Gilles glanced at each other but still didn't dare to move or speak for several more minutes. Then, slowly, cautiously, they eased themselves down and sat on the ledge, their feet dangling, the great plain stretching away before them in the warm sunlight. They sat in silence, stunned by the horror of the last hour and sunk in their own thoughts.

Finally Gilles said: 'I don't think we have a choice now.'

William turned, his body still clamped back against the rock-face, and looked at his friend blankly.

'What about your family, how can you…'

'But what could we *do*…'

William hugged his friend as tightly as he dared on the narrow ledge. 'But…'

'I know, I know. But, there's a more practical problem now. Look up!'

William did so, cautiously, but he still didn't understand.

'The path is almost twice my height above us, higher than I thought, which is why you landed so heavily. And you brought most of the handholds down with you! There's no chance we could get back the way we came, and even if we tried more soldiers might come past at any time and we'd be sitting targets. Maybe God has settled the matter for us.'

William looked up and he could see that what Gilles said was true. Then he turned cautiously to his friend, and saw that his eyes were full of silent tears. He eased a hand round his shoulder but said nothing. William had no idea how long they sat like that, staring into the void. In the end, Gilles said: 'We should go. Sitting here won't do us any good.'

***

When William related the story of his and Gilles' escape from the city in the future he would say that he could remember nothing of the descent down the next fifty feet, but that was not quite true. The detail was lost, blanked out perhaps, but he remembered the gut-twisting terror well enough. And he remembered Gilles, totally focused on the task in hand, coaxing him on gently from one crumbling toe and finger-hold to the next, reaching out a supportive arm, reassuring him that they were nearly on the path, until finally they were. Better still, they were protected now by low scrub from any eagle-eyed crusader looking up from the encampment beneath them, though as they got closer it did appear to be largely deserted. The path, narrow, crumbly and precipitous but recognisable nonetheless, stretched before them down and around the city, getting further away from prying eyes in the main crusader encampment as it did so.

A couple of hours later they lay huddled in a shallow depression in the otherwise flat land outside the city. William held Gilles in his arms, trying to comfort his younger friend who, now that the immediate danger had passed, was sobbing uncontrollably; the cause of his grief all too evident. Across the reed beds the flames licked up from behind the walls of the once proud city, and a pall of smoke and ash drifted northwards on the gentle breeze blowing off the sea. The screams of the people of Beziers as the soldiers of God ripped their way through the city had fallen silent now, but they would echo through the boys' waking hours and recur in their dreams in the months and years to come.

'I should have gone back, I should have done what I could, I should have tried to save them!' Gilles wailed again and again through his sobs.

'Once we were on the ledge, we had no choice, you said it yourself.' William replied in a vain attempt to soothe Gilles' anguish, but he knew that his words counted for nothing. His own grief and regret tore at his heart. He may not have lived alongside these people for long, but he had come to love them, and now? Now in his heart he knew they had almost certainly all been slaughtered. As the pair had crept away on the northward side of the city they had not been able to see the movements of the crusaders, but once the main gate was in their hands surely nothing would have stopped them from flooding into the city and indulging in an orgy of killing, rape and plunder. Torching the city, most of whose buildings were built of wood and tinder-dry at this season, would have been the final punishment for the gentle *credentes* and their loyal Christian neighbours, and perhaps also meant as a "lesson" to the rest of the Languedoc. William shuddered to think what might have happened to the defenceless women and children, trapped in the church of the Magdalene. Surely the crusaders could not have been so depraved as to…

William suddenly felt an overwhelming sense of responsibility. It struck him like an axe-blow that if it had not been for him, Gilles would almost certainly not have fled Beziers. He would have stayed, fought – and died – alongside his own people, defending the city where he had grown up and the family whom he had loved. It would have been futile, but it would have been honourable, and Gilles would not be lying here now, inconsolable with grief for the destruction of his city and the almost certain loss of everything that had been dear to him.

Part II – Rome

Cast adrift: July 1209

In the immediate aftermath of the disaster William feared for Gilles' sanity, or even his life. His friend spoke little and when he did it was to berate himself for his failure to defend his family and his city. All William's reasoning that there was nothing they could have done to change the outcome made no difference. On the facts he was right, of course, but Gilles' grief ran deeper, and on that deeper level it was not about the facts. Attempting to protect what was most dear to him might have been futile, but it had been an absolute duty – and a spiritual duty – and he had been found wanting. In a split-second of selfishness and fear he had turned and run, when he should have stayed and fought, even against all the odds, even when there was no hope, even when it meant certain death. Sunk in despair, he seemed to care little what happened to him now or what they did next, and William understood that he was going to have to think for both of them in this world from which all certainty and safety had been swept away. Secretly, William vowed that his role, his duty now, was to keep his dear friend safe, and to bring him through his dark night of the soul.

That first afternoon, the two survivors had crept away and hidden themselves in a patch of scrubland a league of so to the north of Beziers. From their hiding place they could see the outline of the ruined city as the last flickering glow of the fire died down, the smoke was borne away on the breeze and an eerie silence fell across the sunlit plain. From where they lay the crusader encampment was out of sight, but now and again the sounds of drunken carousing drifted across to them in their hiding place. No doubt the soldiers were celebrating their victory and swapping exaggerated tales of their exploits in the all too brief battle. William kept to himself the grim thought that they were probably bragging too about their success in the plunder, rape and killing of survivors which had followed. He held his own horror and despair at bay by focusing on the task of bringing Gilles through, and diverting him from thinking too much about all that had happened during that dreadful day. The burned-out tower of the church of Saint Mary Magdalene, prominent on the ruined skyline, was reminder enough of the catastrophe.

As the sun moved lower in the sky, William suggested gently that they should find a safer place to rest. Bands of the crusader force might start to emerge from the encampment, looking for survivors or plundering outlying farms before nightfall. Gilles showed little interest, but he nodded blankly towards the low hills to the north.

'We could go up into the Minervois. Robert lived up there in a sort of shepherd's hut, just four stone walls and a thatched roof. I went there once.'

'All right, let's do that,' William agreed. It struck him that the remote hill country might be the best place to keep clear of crusader bands on the look-out for plunder, or more killing of heretics, and neither of them mentioned that Robert had almost certainly met his death in the city too. He gave Gilles a companionable hug and added: 'But we should set off soon; better not to be travelling after dark.'

Gilles said nothing, but got wearily to his feet. And so the two stricken figures made their way slowly across the flood plain and then up the gentle incline and into the foothills of the

Minervois, fragrant with the scents of early summer and warmed by the late afternoon sun. They spoke to no-one, although they noticed signs of life – a swirl of smoke from a chimney, a shadow within – from one or two of the huts. The local people who had remained in their homes were no doubt fearful of the crusaders even if they had no real idea of what had happened that day, and William and Gilles passed on by without stopping. In a matter of hours, caution and fear had become the watchwords in a land which had seemed so blessed when William had walked down from these same hills just a few short months ago.

Dusk was falling as they reached an area of denser woodland and it was soon too dark to see the way ahead. There seemed little option but to stop for the night and continue in the morning. Despite the failing light William found a small clearing a few dozen paces off the track where there was plenty of dry grass to bed down in. They had drunk from streams once or twice during the day, but had had nothing to eat since breakfast – how long ago that communal meal of bread, oil and wine round the dining-table in the fine house in Beziers now seemed! He shuddered, and put a comforting arm around Gilles once again. At times he himself just wanted to lie down in the grass and never get up again, but in those dark moments one thought gave him the strength to carry on. He would prove his love in this terrible time by comforting Gilles, keeping him safe as far as he was able, and – please God! – restoring his will to live.

Gilles had already curled up in the undergrowth, and William spread his tunic over him and lay down beside him with an arm thrown protectively round his body. In a few minutes he was relieved to feel the steady rise and fall of his friend's chest and to hear his breathing lengthen and deepen. The oblivion of sleep was surely the best thing for Gilles now, and already he could feel his own eyelids dropping.

***

William woke in the darkness from dreams which he could not quite grasp, though he knew they had involved fear, violence and danger. He dozed fitfully for another hour or so, and was fully awake first in the morning, hazily aware that something other than bad dreams had woken him this time. Immediately on his guard, he kept still for a moment, then eased himself up to look around cautiously – and came face to face with a young roebuck. It was a beautiful creature, light brown in colour with liquid black eyes and compact, lightly furred antlers. Man and animal looked straight into one another's eyes for a moment, assessing, questioning. Then the gentle creature turned and fled with a flash of its white rump. William felt strangely moved by the unexpected encounter.

Now Gilles was awake too, bleary-eyed and anxious.

'Was there…someone?' he asked.

'No, it was just a deer, nothing to be afraid of,' William replied reassuringly. 'But we should move on, there may be soldiers around sooner or later,' he added more briskly.

'Oh, let me sleep, I just want to stay here and sleep,' Gilles mumbled, turning over and burying his face in his hands. His voice was without emotion and William feared the grief would well up again, which was another reason to focus on what to do next.

'No, Gilles, we must go on,' he said firmly. He lifted Gilles up into a sitting position and looked into his eyes. 'Perhaps we can find a shepherd or woodsman with some food to spare in one of the huts.' Gilles said nothing but he nodded weakly and pulled himself to his feet.

They made their way through the silent woodland and then out into more open country again which stretched down into a valley of lush grass before rising higher to the next ridge of forested hills. It was still eerily quiet.

'I think I recognise where we are,' Gilles said after a while. 'We're not on the same path, but it's across that way I think,' and he pointed vaguely across the next gentle valley. 'Robert's hut is up there somewhere...' Gilles' voice trailed off, and William put his arms round him and held him tight, whispering in his ear: 'Remember you've got me; I'll look after you.' Then he looked across the valley and said more firmly:

'Good – we'd better get on! Robert's hut will provide some shelter even if he isn't there, and with a bit of luck there'll be some provisions. If not I can scout around.' He hoped inwardly that Robert would not be there.

Gilles nodded blankly and they set off again, across the open ground and then into the woodland again. It was darker and denser than the woods of holm-oak and olive they had passed through so far, but there was a clear track which they followed and which turned gently round the ridge of the hill, climbing slightly before falling again. It was further than Gilles remembered and they walked slowly and silently, both of them exhausted and numbed by the horror of the previous day and by the lack of food. Now water too was a problem. They had had nothing to drink that day and as the sun rose higher their need became ever greater. Gilles began to complain of feeling dizzy, and several times stopped and slumped down to his knees. Each time, William put an arm round him, waited a while, then urged him on, reminding him of the stream with fresh water which he had mentioned was nearby. The thought of clear, running water was the one thing that kept them going.

Finally, the trees started to open out and there, only a hundred paces away, was the stream. Even Gilles broke into a gentle trot and they both dropped to their knees and drank the clear, cold water greedily and noisily from cupped hands. When they had drunk their fill they lay back on the grassy bank above the stream.

'Robert's hut is just over there,' Gilles said, pointing vaguely across the stream.

William nodded his encouragement, and they found the hut exactly as Gilles had said. It consisted of four stone walls, roughly mortared, and a ragged thatch roof which wouldn't be much use if it rained. There was a wooden door with no lock, and one small opening to allow in a little light, with a wooden shutter. There was some grubby straw-bedding in one corner, a blanket or two, and a stone jar with a sealed lid which they prised open to find olives preserved in oil. They smelt odd but the boys couldn't resist eating several handfuls of them at once, before resealing the jar. William pointed out, wisely if a little late, that eating too many on an empty stomach might make them sick.

Exhausted, they fell back on the straw, curled into one another's bodies and were soon fast asleep. That was how Robert found them when he returned home some hours later.

***

'Well, well; visitors!' Robert sneered. 'Our two young heroes who were going to fight to the last to save their city? But of course, there wasn't much chance of that when it came to it, was there? So what did you do? Saved your own skins instead by the look of it!'

William gawped at Robert, who seemed unchanged and unmoved by the catastrophe which had befallen the city and its people. Before he could react or even speak he sensed rather than saw Gilles leap up and lunge past him at Robert. If the older man had any further sarcastic thoughts to share they were silenced as his young relative grabbed him by the throat and tightened his grip. Robert was grasping for breath, the veins standing out on his scrawny neck and sunburnt temples like fat red worms, and a strange gurgling coming from his throat. A few drops of blood-flecked sputum dribbled out of Robert's mouth, spurring William into action. He sprang forward, grabbed Gilles round the waist and struggled to pull him off.

'Let him go! Killing the bastard won't bring your family back!' he heard himself cry out, grabbing Gilles from behind. Gilles, his moment of uncontrolled fury over, released his grip and both boys fell backwards into the straw. Robert crumpled to the ground opposite them, groaning. William could hear Gilles sobbing quietly and put an arm round him, whilst keeping a wary eye on Robert, though the older man didn't seem to be in a fit state to try anything. For several moments no-one spoke.

'Mad buggers! Asleep in my hut and then trying to murder me when I get home!' Gilles just stared at him with blank eyes, and even Robert realised he had gone too far. 'All right, I'm sorry for your family, of course – only family I had too, come to that. I can't imagine there's much to hope for, except that it will have been quick.'

William, appalled at Robert's words, was tempted to set about him too, and stayed his hand only because he didn't want any more violence played out in front of Gilles. At the same time, the question of how Robert himself had survived the massacre was gnawing at the back of his mind.

'Mind you,' Robert continued, 'I should have known you had some fight in you after what you did to that crusader inside the gates. Finished him off with one blow, and no mistake!'

Gilles, who had lain back down on the straw stared at Robert silently, then turned over and curled up facing the wall. William put a hand on his shoulder before turning back to Robert.

'So you were down inside the gates, too, after the crusaders broke in? We didn't see you.'

'Oh, you wouldn't have. We were heading up into the city by then, not down amongst the action like you two!'

William's eyes narrowed.

'Heading up into the city? It doesn't sound as if you were doing much to protect it.'

'Of course we were. But there were too many of them, weren't there?' he replied sharply, then quickly changed the subject. 'You two boys must be hungry. There's nothing here to eat, I took everything with me when I came down to throw myself on my cousin's mercy before the attack. I lost the damned sheep down there too – some crusader rabble are probably feasting on those now!'

He obviously wasn't going to mention the olives so William thought it better not to do so either. Gilles wasn't saying anything.

'I'd better tell you now, so *he* doesn't get carried away again' – Robert nodded towards Gilles and rubbed the red weal on his throat at the same time – 'but I ran in with some fellows who'd been following along with the crusade. Not real fighting men like the one Gilles did for, just lads along for a bit of adventure. They saw enough fighting in Beziers and they're going to stay here until they decide what to do next. I don't suppose they care about the heresy one way or the other but you'd probably both do best to play the part of regular Christians when they get here.'

'So where are these "lads" now?' William asked, appalled at the idea of having anything to do with ruffians connected with the massacre, most of all for Gilles' sake.

'Foraging for food,' Robert replied, 'you must be hungry too?'

'Not hungry enough to accept food from crusaders,' Gilles snarled, jumping to his feet. 'Come on, William, let's get out of here before his new friends turn up. I'd rather starve than accept food from any of them! And any food they bring, they'll probably have stolen from other local peasants and farmers, maybe even killed one or two if they tried to protect what little they had. How *could* you?'

This last remark was spat out at Robert with a venom William had never heard from Gilles before. Robert glared back, a sudden anger in his eyes too, and he looked as if he might be about to strike Gilles. But in the tense silence all three of them could now hear muffled voices in the clearing outside the hut.

'Sounds as if it's too late for more talk about that,' Robert muttered, 'and there are half a dozen of them so you should keep your mouths shut if you know what's good for you.' Luckily only William caught the twisted smirk as Robert opened the door to his new friends. Presumably he was relieved that William and Gilles would be outnumbered now.

***

There were in fact seven of them, rough-looking types from their late teens to early middle age, mostly northern French, and they seemed on very friendly terms with Robert. William was still puzzling over how Robert had got to know them, and how he had escaped from the city in one piece, but he wasn't about to ask. Robert introduced Gilles and William by name without explaining who they were, and the new arrivals nodded but showed little further interest. The dried leg of pork and the flagon of wine a couple of them were carrying suggested that they were, as Gilles had said, happy to plunder food from the local population, and they seemed equally casual about accepting shelter and hospitality from potential heretics. Perhaps it really didn't matter to them one way or the other, especially now that the city had fallen. Robert added the tub of olives to the supplies and slung a couple of knives on the table for the men to hack off the meat. He cast a sideways glance at William and Gilles when he first opened the olive tub and peered into it, but he didn't say anything.

The two boys sat silently on a heap of sacks in the corner of the room as the gruesome supper progressed. Gilles pulled his knees up to his chin and stared blankly at the backs of the men as they ate, but William suddenly realised how hungry he was; he hadn't eaten all day. He helped himself to a hunk of pork and some olives, but when he offered some to Gilles – who must have been just as hungry – he shook his head blankly.

William listened to the conversation around the table. He couldn't follow all of the fast and heavily accented *langue d'oil* of the north, but he caught enough to pick up how Robert had got involved with these men. It seemed that they had cornered him inside the gates and weren't sure at first whether he was defender or attacker. When it had become clear that he was a local, they had put a knife to his throat and demanded that he show them a few houses nearby where there might be plunder. With a knife to his throat he may not have had much choice, but this seemed to be a bit of a joke now, and evidently he had more or less become part of the gang. Together they had grabbed what spoils they could find without venturing too far into the city, and had sneaked out of the gates again whilst the battle was still raging further up, and before there was any sort of formal guard in place. No doubt Robert had passed himself off as just another *ribaud* as he left the city, and if he had had any qualms about leaving his people to their fate he showed no sign of it.

The men's conversation turned briefly to what they should do next, but they seemed to have no firm plans. They evidently had quite a bit more booty piled up outside, in plate and coin. There was some mention of Carcassonne being the next target of the crusade, which sounded plausible given that that was Trencavel's stronghold.

Gilles seemed to be drifting in and out of sleep, although William roused him enough to persuade him to accept some scraps of pork and a few sips of wine. He was already planning how they were going to get away from such loathsome company, and Gilles would need to build up his strength for the days ahead.

The two of them sat propped against the wall in the darkest corner of the room, whilst the rest of the party finished off the wine and then started to argue about the division of the rest of the spoils, which were brought in from outside and ran to several bulging sacks of assorted valuables. Gilles soon fell asleep, slumped sideways against William's body for support. William was no less exhausted, both mentally and physically, but struggled to stay alert and listened quietly for any clues as to the intentions of the ragged band.

A pock-marked, rough shaven man, whom the others called Elmo, appeared to be the leader, as far as there was one. When he talked the others listened, and now he was busily claiming a larger share of the booty for himself on the basis that they would have got nothing without his cunning and leadership.

'We wouldn't have all this if you hadn't listened to me,' he was saying. 'I was the one who spotted the chance when we met our new friend with his knowledge of the city,' and here he nodded to Robert, who was sitting slightly apart on an empty barrel. 'In fact, I reckon he deserves an extra share more than you idiots!'

'I didn't do anything!' Robert exclaimed, casting a sideways glance in the direction of William and Gilles as he did so. William put an arm round Gilles, who seemed to be soundly asleep, thank God! At that moment he knew without a doubt the extent of Robert's treachery: Gilles' relation had betrayed his family and his people and helped these men to plunder the city, and ...God knows what else. William stared straight at him. Robert looked away.

The squabbling raged on, becoming more irritable as the wine loosened the men's tongues. William quietly gathered some old sacking for blankets, then lifted Gilles gently to his feet, and led him, still half-asleep, out to the rickety lean-to at the back of the hut to bed down away from the others. The older men were too busy with their argument to take much notice as the two of them left.

Outside, William laid Gilles down in a mound of straw behind the hut and arranged some of the old sacking over him as best he could. The night was not cold, Gilles had barely awoken and soon his breathing was coming deeper and longer. Sleep, oblivion, must be the best thing for him now. But William lay awake for a long time, distantly aware of the raucous voices inside the hut, thinking through what he and Gilles should do next.

***

William slept fitfully and woke before the dawn. His experience of many nights sleeping under the sky had taught him to judge the hour, and he reckoned that the first glimmerings of the new day would begin soon. The first-quarter moon which he could just see through the trees would give a little light anyway. He was clear what they must do.

He moved closer to Gilles, and whispered gently to wake him without alarming him: 'Gilles, it's only me. All's well. The others are still sleeping.' Gilles turned towards him with bleary eyes and William waited for him to surface. Then he quietly laid out his plan, without revealing the depth of Robert's treachery.

'I don't think we should stay here. I don't trust Robert's new friends, and I don't trust Robert. I know he's your relation, but he's hardly shown much loyalty, and…there may be more he's not telling us. My idea, if you agree, is that we should get up quietly and leave before they're awake in there. They were drinking until quite late last night so I don't suppose they'll be up for hours, but – if we're going – then the sooner we're away the better. Take your time and tell me what you think.'

Gilles was now fully awake and nodded thoughtfully as William finished speaking. Finally, in a flat but firm voice, he replied.

'William, I know exactly what Robert did. I was only pretending to sleep last night so that I didn't get drawn into the conversation, but I heard what those bastards were saying. I only managed to keep quiet because there was no telling what they mightn't have done to us too, with some drink inside them.

'But as I listened to them one thing became very clear to me. The city can't be much more than a smouldering ruin now, but I still can't leave without going back to look for any trace of my family. God knows, there's little enough hope, but I could never live with myself if I didn't do this.

'I'm not asking you to come too. There's probably some sort of guard around the city, and maybe still looters who'd stick a dagger through anyone they didn't like the look of. It might even mean getting back in the way we came out, if the gates are guarded. I can't ask you to take the risk, but I thought it all through last night. Did my deep breathing while we were still in there really fool you too?'

'Yes, it did,' William replied, staggered at Gilles' sudden clarity and determination. He was also relieved, though, that his friend was thinking for himself again, and immediately he knew that he had no right to question his decision. However dangerous it might be for both of them, they must do this, if only to allow Gilles the peace of mind that would come in the future from having some certainty about the fate of his family. He propped himself up on one elbow and looked Gilles straight in the eyes.

'You're right, of course. How can I even have suggested leaving here without having returned to the city first? You're right that there can be little hope, but of course we will go back. Thinking about it, the crusaders may have left some sort of guard, but I can't imagine they'll worry too much who's nosing around in what remains. It might be best to play the part of looters ourselves, and to talk in the *langue d'oïl* as far as possible.'

'As I said, I'm not asking you to come.'

'And as *I* said, I'm coming anyway!'

Gilles looked into William's eyes and threw his arms around him. After a few minutes William eased himself away, nodded towards the hut and murmured: 'We should leave quietly, now, before any of *them* wake up.'

Gilles nodded his reply, and silently they got up, piled up the sacking and brushed down their clothes. They checked on their few simple belongings and for the first time since the disaster, Gilles grinned as William opened his tunic and pointed to the sizeable hunk of pork he had secreted in the inside pocket the night before. Then they crept away from the hut and set off back towards Beziers, or whatever remained of it, by the same route they had come the day before. This time the journey was mostly downhill, and as so often with return journeys it seemed shorter. They were in sight of Beziers shortly before nightfall, though the city was now just a range of jagged stumps on the skyline from which wisps of smoke still rose. Rather than venture into the city in the gathering darkness they bedded down for the night in a small clearing surrounded by a thicket of thorn and bramble.

The following morning they ate the remains of the pork and drank from a stream, then descended the last slopes into the river valley, and rounded the city wall to the Porte de Carcassonne. There was, as they had expected, a nominal guard, apparently a detachment of regular soldiers who had been left behind to keep some kind of order, but they showed no interest in the struggle of civilians who were making their way in and out. Some might have been local people who had left the city before the attack, returning to salvage what they could, or perhaps the relatives of residents who had stayed, motivated by some forlorn hope.

William and Gilles, ragged and despondent, did not look out of place as they made their way through the great gate, and past the spot where Gilles had slain the *ribaud* just before the mounted crusaders had arrived. At this level the city appeared relatively intact, but as they followed the twisting street up towards the cathedral and the citadel the true extent of the devastation became clear.

The whole upper district had clearly been torched and the domestic buildings, most of which were timber-framed, had been almost completely destroyed. Bodies lay everywhere, mostly of townspeople though there were soldiers too, and even one mighty stallion whose corpse almost blocked the narrow street where he had died. The acrid smell of burnt timber failed to mask other, unmentionable odours which would no doubt soon increase as the heat started to build. Some of the people who had ventured this far were clearly looters, helping themselves to whatever they could find that had not been destroyed by the fire. William and Gilles saw no-one they recognised, and William had a sudden sickening realisation of what that meant.

The layout of the streets was still evident, and Gilles easily followed the route to where his family's house had stood. As William had feared, this too was almost completely destroyed. Some of the larger timbers still stood, blackened by the fire, up to the height of a man, and one jagged roof beam had survived, pointing into the sky like a crooked finger accusing God. The only recognisable piece of furniture was the great wooden chest which had stood in pride of place in the main hall. Its warm patina was gone of course, replaced by the same sooty blackness of everything else, and the lid had evidently been forced since the fire and the contents looted. William put an arm round Gilles, who was gazing blankly at the devastation. Then he murmured, to no-one in particular:

'All the family's valuables and heirlooms were in that chest. I only saw into it once. There was gleaming gold and silver-plate, documents rolled up and sealed with red wax, and beautiful silks and damasks which were part of my mother's dowry...' He fell silent for several minutes. 'Well, it's all gone now. And we can go, I've seen enough here.'

William looked tenderly at Gilles but his expression revealed little of what he must be feeling. Silently they made their way further up towards the church of Saint Mary Magdalene. Neither of them spoke as they approached the massive stone structure which had been meant to provide sanctuary and security for the women and children of the city. William secretly hoped that the building would be guarded, or still sealed shut, but as they approached they could see that the small side door which had been the usual means of entry and exit was open. He longed to suggest that they should not enter, but he doubted that Gilles would agree, and in any case if the point was to be sure of what had happened then they must go in.

Inside the blackened building the walls and the air were still hot from the fire which had raged the day before. The crusaders had evidently built some kind of pyre in the middle of the nave. The only small mercy was that the resulting inferno must have been so intense, and so enclosed in the narrow space, that it would have consumed almost everything very quickly: the wooden chairs, screens and other furniture, the rich awnings and, of course, the bodies. The floor was covered with mounds of grey ash, and here and there bones and fragments of metal clasps and buckles. William peered upwards through the stifling air to the only daylight, which shone down from the high windows. Those must have allowed the fire to be fanned by a massive updraft, perhaps aided by one guarded door being left open at ground level. No-one could have survived the inferno.

William was still gazing up when Gilles spoke: 'Go! Please go, I'll see you outside.'

William nodded and walked quietly out of the place of horror which the once austere but beautiful church had become. He waited anxiously in the shade of the building for perhaps a quarter of an hour before Gilles emerged. When he did, he made no effort to conceal that he had been weeping, but he was composed now and said simply: 'I've said goodbye. There's nothing more for me here now. We can go.'

Eternal City – April 1210

'Well, I didn't think they could surprise me any more, but today the Romans really aren't in their right minds!' William didn't reply at once but turned to Gilles and grinned; it was good to see him distracted. He himself knew roughly what was going to happen next, having picked it up in the tavern on the corner of their street the evening before, but he decided to keep Gilles guessing for a little longer.

'Yes, what *can* they be thinking of, filling wooden carts with swine and taking them up to the top of a giant rubble heap?' Recently he had noticed that Gilles could be diverted from his dark moods a little more easily, and was showing more interest in what was going on around him, but he still didn't notice when he was being teased.

'I've got an idea you're going to enjoy the spectacle, and maybe even the feasting that'll follow this evening!' he added.

Gilles didn't reply, and after a pause William returned to a regular theme. 'You know, it really is time you got out into the city and found out more about what's going on around you. Get some work, like I'm always telling you. You've seen how many bakeries there are in the streets around our lodgings, and I'm sure some of them must be looking for extra help. Especially someone who knows how to bake something better than those hard little rolls we seem to live off.'

'Well, maybe. I know it's not right that you're doing all the work, but…well, we'll see.'

'That's more like it. Think about it, you'd be pleased to get back to work, I'm sure!'

William noted with some satisfaction that Gilles' response had become a little more balanced, no longer a blank refusal. It wasn't just the money, though William only had to look at his own callused hands to remind himself how hard he was working in the carpentry workshop. Even so, he was more savvy than Gilles about money, and had soon learnt that the constant flow of pilgrims, refugees and tourists into the city meant that wage rates for casual labour were low. His earnings in the workshop just about paid for food and lodgings for the two of them, but that was all. There would never be enough spare cash to continue their journey at this rate, though that thought in turn raised the even thornier question of whether Gilles would wish to continue the journey at all. He sometimes pined for the Languedoc, though in an abstract way which avoided the awkward truth that he was recalling a land now utterly changed. They had heard enough reports along the road and on the ship which had brought them from Marseille to Ostia about the further course of the crusade there. They did not speak of it but they both knew that no more than vestiges could remain of the peaceful culture and faith with which Gilles had grown up. They had heard little of any kind of resistance or fight-back, but then word of that would be less likely to travel.

At the same time, in his heart William knew that Gilles had come with him to Rome because he had nothing and no-one else to hold on to. He sometimes lay awake at night asking himself whether it was right to have brought Gilles so far from home – or indeed to take him much further and into more dangerous territory if his own quest to reach the Holy Land was to be fulfilled. Was he taking advantage of Gilles' vulnerability?

Did Gilles really love him, or was that in the past and did he now simply have no-one else to cling to? William knew that the time would come when these questions must be answered, but in the meantime he reassured himself that persuading Gilles to get some work and to re-engage with life must stand him in good stead, whatever the future held for both of them.

For now he was dragged out of his reverie by Gilles, who had been watching the scene unfolding before him.

'What in God's name are they up to?' William didn't mention the unconscious blasphemy but grinned at his friend's excitement.

'Hah! Just what our friendly tavern-owner told me about,' he replied, 'rolling the cartloads of pigs down the hill! Watch out!'

There was no time for more words. William grabbed his friend by the arm and dragged him to his feet and out of the path of the oncoming carts as they careered down the hill, some of them already turning over, breaking up and tossing their hapless, squealing cargo onto the hillside where they continued their descent, slithering and bouncing down the steep incline alongside the splintering remains of the carts. The whole crowd seemed to have misjudged the route of the chaos and were scattering backwards out of the way, grabbing hold of one another, scooping up their children and laughing and shrieking. Several people were clutching bleeding wounds even as they ran.

William and Gilles scrambled onto a higher ridge and held onto one another, panting and laughing all at once. As they gathered their breath they looked down to the base of the hill where the waiting slaughter-men and butchers were already finishing off the pigs which had not been killed on the way down and skilfully dismembering them for the pot.

As they watched, William recounted what he had been told. This was just another of those strange Roman customs. On the last day before the traditional Christian period of fasting for

Lent, all the smallholders in the suburbs sold their mature hogs to the city butchers, who organised the descent of the Monte Testaceo before turning the carcasses into a pre-Lenten feast in each district the same evening. The local citizens, and resident visitors, were welcome to attend the feast for a small fee.

Like so much else in the city, the Monte Testaceo itself was said to date from the time of the Roman Emperors, though no-one really seemed to know, and although it was big enough to be a natural hill, closer inspection showed that it was not. The vast mound was in fact no more than an enormous rubbish-heap of smashed pottery, apparently mostly jars, which had simply built up over the centuries. The jagged shards of pottery made the descent lethal for most of the pigs as they were tossed out of the carts, and the few that survived could quickly be finished off by the sharp knives of the slaughter-men.

William had been concerned that Gilles would be offended by the brutal slaughter of the animals, and the crowd's laughing acceptance of it. But in fact he was used to the Romans' lust for life and their enthusiastic meat-eating by now, and he looked as animated as William had seen him since before the disaster some nine months ago. He had made little mention of his faith and of the simple life of the *credentes* during that period, and then only wistfully as of a world and a time he had left far behind.

***

A few hours later the two friends were sitting at the trestle-table which snaked its way all along the via Santa Catarina, only a couple of blocks from their lodgings; the evenings were already warm although the oppressive heat of summer had not yet begun. They had gone along to the feast with the first friend they – or rather William – had made in Rome. Geoffrey was also an Englishman, a few years older than William, who came from a tiny settlement called Kilpeck in the county of Hereford. Like William, he had left home at a young age, though for different reasons. He came from humble Saxon stock, though mixed with Celtic blood so that he was darker in complexion and shorter in stature than most Saxons. As the youngest of four sons of a tenant farmer he had soon realised that he had few prospects in life. He saw the drudgery of his father's life and dreamed of the wider world. Added to this – and in this respect much more like William – he had an adventurous spirit and his dreams of adventure had been heightened by the travelling minstrels and troubadours who brought their vision of distant lands even to the remote and lawless Welsh marches. Recruiting officers had visited too, offering healthy young men the chance of adventure and glory, by joining the forces stationed in Anjou and Poitou to defend the English possessions against attack by the French king.

Geoffrey had talked openly to his parents about his plans to join up, and they had been resistant at first though they recognised their youngest son's determination. His father knew too, though he kept the thought to himself, that with one son off his hands he would be able to offer a little more to the others, and he recognised the honour and respect which the family would earn for having one of their sons serving the King, even if John was not well-regarded. Geoffrey's mother was not at all happy with her husband's decision, but she had little choice but to bow to his will. She sought to comfort herself with the idea of his returning soon from France covered in glory, but had wept bitterly nonetheless the day he left home.

Geoffrey had indeed seen some ragged fighting on the borders between the English and the French lands, but King John's clumsy diplomacy and tactless treatment of the English barons in Anjou and Poitou had soon undermined his cause, and led to an indecisive and uneasy truce. John's nickname swiftly changed from 'Lackland' to 'Soft-sword' and Geoffrey, disillusioned with the life of a soldier but with his taste for foreign lands and adventure undimmed, had deserted and tagged along with a group of like-minded fellow-Englishmen. Together they had resolved to travel on as pilgrims to Rome, the fabled city of the ancient world which was now packed with renewed life as the centre of the Christian church. They had amassed a certain amount of plunder in the fighting, which they supplemented by picking up short-term work in their respective trades along the road.

In this way Geoffrey and his colleagues had spent six months travelling by the land route to Rome, but soon after they arrived there the group had broken up. Some had set off to return home once they had had their fill of what the city could offer, and others had returned to soldiery. Indeed, Geoffrey had mentioned one evening that some of the last had left little more than a year ago, to join the crusade against the heresy in the Languedoc. Gilles could not let this pass, and had described the brutality of the crusaders in general, though without revealing his own family's beliefs or their fate. Geoffrey had replied that he couldn't imagine his former comrades taking part in such brutality and the moment had passed, but William heard Gilles sobbing quietly to himself for the first time in several months after they had settled down to sleep that night.

Geoffrey himself had chosen to stay on in Rome. He had done odd jobs at first, picked up a smattering of the Italian dialect and after a while landed regular work in the kitchens of the Lateran, the *palazzo* of the Popes and at the same time the religious and bureaucratic headquarters of the Holy See. He was also courting a local young woman, who was pretty and charming but shy of her husband's new English friends. William smiled when he saw the great joy that Geoffrey's relationship with Catarina brought him, though it evoked a sadness in him as well which he tried to put out of his mind. He and Gilles had a tacit understanding that no-one should know about their own closeness, though in practice their crowded accommodation and William's long hours of work meant that there was little for them to be discreet about. Their stolen afternoons on the sunlit beach seemed so far away now, part of another life which had been swallowed up by the intervening horror. William sighed softly to himself at the memory of those innocent days, then brought himself back to the crowded Roman bar and the present.

Geoffrey was deep in conversation with a couple of new arrivals from somewhere in Saxony, advising them on the best places to look for accommodation, and Gilles was leaning against William, eyes half-closed, almost asleep. He seemed to tire much more quickly these days, though William thought that more wine than usual might have contributed on this occasion.

Left to himself, William's thoughts drifted back further in time, to his journey from England, to the death of his dear friend Edwin and to the pledge he had made to him to protect the casket containing the lock of his beloved Emilia's hair. He felt inside his jacket, as he often did, to ensure that the casket was still safely secreted in its hiding place deep in the lining. He thought too of his simple expectation then that his journey would take him all the way to the Holy Land to fulfil his promise in full by seeking out Emilia, and the recollection was bittersweet. It brought back the youthful confidence of those days, the simple belief that everything could be made right again in time. But even though he was recalling events less than two years ago, he had come to think of himself as older, wiser and more realistic about the chance of earthly happiness than the callow youth who had set out to cross the Channel from Romney on a distant, cold dawn.

Of course, his love for Gilles, and his duty now to support him in the face of the catastrophe that had befallen him, gave him an inner strength and a different purpose in life, though at times his natural restlessness and his promise to Edwin came back to him too. Recently William had had a recurring dream in which he and Gilles walked together through a city of whitewashed houses and domed churches under a burning sun, but when he woke he was still in the stuffy dormitory with the sounds of the Roman street drifting up from below. Naturally he had said nothing of this to Gilles, who didn't speak of the future at all.

Gilles, who seemed to have come to, dragged him back to the present.

'Hey, William, are you nodding off?'

'No, no, just thinking…and you're a fine one to talk!' William replied.

'Well, yes…I think I've been asleep, and…I feel so tired…I might go back to the hostel…'

'Shall I come too?'

'No, I can find my own way!' Gilles muttered, almost aggressively. William noted the change of tone but put it down to the tiredness and the wine.

'I shan't be long,' he said, gently.

Gilles stood up abruptly and William watched as he disappeared through the crowd, swaying slightly. Geoffrey, who had finished his conversation with the Saxons, asked quietly: 'Will he be all right?'

'Yes, I think so, he's just tired,' William replied. Then, after a pause, he added: 'Gilles had a tough time, back in the Languedoc, when the crusade came…'

Geoffrey nodded: 'I had guessed that much.' He sighed. 'The proclamation from His Holiness said only that the crusade had wiped out a minority of heretics, and those Christians who had sided with them, returning the peace and love of Jesus Christ to lands which had been filled with foulness, *et cetera, et cetera*. But in the corridors of the Lateran the talk was that Arnaud Amaury, the Papal legate who was really in charge in the Languedoc, had overstepped the mark. "Kill them all; God will know his own," he's supposed to have said! A madman...'

William shook his head wearily. 'That certainly tallies with what happened, but please, don't mention it in front of Gilles.'

Geoffrey nodded. 'Of course not.'

They sat in silence for several minutes, then William looked up. 'I shouldn't tell you this, but I have to share it with someone. Gilles lost his whole family at Beziers. Everyone in the city was massacred in the most horrible way. Pure chance allowed us to escape. There can have been very few survivors.'

Geoffrey put an arm on his shoulder. 'Truly a cross to bear – for you as well as Gilles.'

William nodded, grateful for the understanding. 'It hasn't been easy; it *isn't* easy to know what to do next.'

'Well, if there's anything I can do to help...'

'Thank you, it's a relief just to be able to talk about it with someone.' He smiled weakly and the two Englishmen sat silently for several minutes in the midst of the noisy crowd. Finally Geoffrey spoke again.

'It may not be the moment, and after what you've just told me it may not be of any interest, but there was something else...'

William looked up. 'Oh! What's that?'

'Well, I heard during the usual kitchen gossip in the Lateran a few days ago that the *scriptorium* is looking for people with knowledge of the English tongue to work as scribes and translators. Relations with King John may be at an all-time low but the flow of pilgrims from England is greater than ever, and when they turn up seeking audiences or whatever most of them can't speak enough Latin to be understood. I just thought it might be good for you, with your knowledge of the English and French tongues, and it'd be less tiring than working in the carpenter's workshop, sawing and planing all day! I hear they pay quite well too for brain-work.'

'Oh, I don't know if I'd be up to it,' William replied, 'I had a little schooling with the monks in Rochester and can read and write Latin well enough, though it's probably got a bit rusty. I'm much better at the sort of French you hear in the ale-houses, but I don't suppose that'd be much use!'

'I wouldn't be so sure of that. Some of the work those fellows do seems to be sorting out arguments over bills and compensation for damage between travellers on the one hand, and innkeepers and brothel-owners on the other. The disputes were getting so bad, ending up in stabbings and all sorts, that the Church started to get worried. They thought trade might suffer if word got out and the flow of visitors dried up. The city in general and the Church in particular make a lot of money out of all the people who come to cleanse their souls!'

'Somehow that doesn't surprise me,' William said quietly. 'I could probably live with it, and we could certainly do with some more money coming in, but you're right to think that Gilles is likely to see it differently. He's the one who's suffered directly from the works of the Holy Church. He seems to have put the horror out of his mind somehow, but I don't know how he'd react if I proposed, well, working for them.'

Geoffrey nodded. 'Yes, I can see that. I almost didn't mention it at all after what you told me about Beziers, and of course it's entirely up to you. You can think it over and decide whether to follow it up. Then if you're still interested let me know and I could put you in touch with someone there; otherwise I won't mention it again. Now, another glass?'

***

When William got back to the dormitory Gilles was asleep, though his breathing was laboured and uneven. William took off his outer clothes and lay down next to him in the straw; Gilles had wrapped most of the bedding round himself and he didn't try to retrieve it.

William lay awake for some time thinking about the events of the evening and in particular Geoffrey's suggestion. In most respects it was the right thing to do. It sounded as if it would bring in quite a bit more money and would be less tiring, and perhaps more interesting. Unlike in Beziers, where he had been learning new skills in the carpentry shop, here he spent most of his day preparing the raw wood to the point where it could be handed over to the apprentice carpenters who were all locals. He had soon understood that pilgrims and other travellers who turned up seeking work were not expected to stay long and were taken on only for repetitive piece-work at the lowest rates.

Of course, he was not enthusiastic about working for the Church, but he was prepared to hold his nose and take their money if that was what it took to be able to move on. Simply being in Rome fulfilled a long-held dream for William, and in the short-term at least the experience seemed to be taking Gilles' mind off his loss and the puzzle of where their lives were going. But he couldn't imagine any sort of long-term future for either of them here.

William had drunk more wine than usual himself that evening and sleep was creeping up on him. But before he drifted off he resolved that sooner rather than later the question of their future must be raised with Gilles.

***

The following day Gilles slept on, and when he finally woke he seemed refreshed and made no reference to the previous evening. William was the one who was preoccupied now, to the point that his overseer at the carpentry shop noticed that one of his best casual workers was distracted and not producing work up to his usual standard. Gilles too noticed that William was not his normal self and in the end it was he who brought the issue out into the open.

They were sitting out on the street after supper, finishing off their mugs of the weak ale that was served with the meal. Without turning to catch William's eye, Gilles broke a long period of silence between them.

'Is anything wrong? You haven't seemed yourself these last few days.'

William nodded thoughtfully but didn't look round either. This was the moment.

'Well, yes,' he said, 'I've been thinking things over. Maybe it's time for a talk. How about if we walked down to the river where it'll be quieter?'

Gilles nodded and together they walked through the narrow noisy streets where the people were making the most of the few hours of rest between work and sleep. William glanced up, as he often did, at the makeshift upper stories which had been constructed out of wood above the stone houses below, to cope with the shortage of living space in the city as it drew in ever more workers, pilgrims and exiles from impoverished or war-stricken regions. Sometimes he wondered if it was just faith that kept most of these improbable structures from tumbling down again – as one did every now and again.

As he and Gilles approached the Tiber, the buildings thinned out and there was a degree of solitude. Rome's so-called river was actually made up of a tangle of rivulets which meandered their way towards the sea, some fifteen leagues distant at Ostia. The mass of shingle banks, dotted with olive trees and scrub, made a good place for trysts or discreet conversations, for which there was little scope anywhere else in the city. William and Gilles found a suitable spot where they sat in silence for a while, both sunk in bitter-sweet memories of another, distant shore and putting off the impending conversation a little longer. A tang of sea air drifted up on the breeze. Again it was Gilles who spoke first:

'You want to move on, don't you, William?' he said, quietly.

'I didn't think you knew.'

'I see more than you think. I see that you're frustrated working long hours for not much money in the carpentry shop. I see you checking on the casket in the lining of your jacket in odd moments. I see the faraway look in your eyes when you don't think I'm watching.'

'You're right: you do see more than I realise!'

There was a long silence, broken only by the gentle lapping of the river and the clumsy flutter of a nesting-pair of storks rising up from the reed beds.

'Yes,' William went on after a while, 'I do want to move on, sooner or later, though in the short-term I need to earn more money to pay for the journey. There are boats from a place called Brindisi two hundred leagues south of here, but they're expensive.'

'So you're serious about this. You're thinking about the route.'

'Yes.'

'Are you expecting me to come with you?'

There was a long pause. Then, out of the gathering darkness, the reply:

'I think that should be your decision.'

'I don't know. I've feared this moment and I've thought about it, but I don't know what my answer is. I couldn't bear to lose you, but I don't want to go on the road again. I followed you here, because of what we have, and… because you were all I had. But I'm not a traveller at heart, not like you. If I'm to have a future I need to settle, perhaps build a family of my own to replace…what I've lost. We can't go on as we are.'

'It sounds as if you're ahead of me on this,' William said ruefully. 'But we don't need to settle anything right now. As I said, before I could go I would need to get some better-paid work and save up enough money for the boat.'

'Yes, I understand that, and it's good. It means we have at least a little more time…'

Gilles reached across and put his arm round William. They sat in silence, holding on for a little longer to something precious which they could both feel ebbing away. Gilles was thinking of the troubadours' songs of the transience of love, and of earthly happiness. William was thinking that it would be too much for Gilles if he raised the matter of working for the *scriptorium* as well now. But once again Gilles was one step ahead and after a while it was he who broke the silence again.

'What better-paid work are you thinking of?'

William sighed. 'You won't like it, but I only see one option if I'm to save up enough money for the crossing to the Holy Land on one of the pilgrim ships; the passage isn't cheap.'

Gilles looked him in the eye sadly. 'I know, the Church. I've heard enough people say that they're the best payers in Rome. Geoffrey could put in a good word for you.'

So Gilles had worked it all out for himself. William had feared a bitter argument, anger and tears, or quiet desperation, which would have been worse. Perhaps he didn't know Gilles as well as he had thought. Perhaps a stronger, harder Gilles was now emerging again from the tragedy he had gone through.

'Actually, he already suggested it. He didn't know about my plans for further travel, but just thought I might be interested in some less tiring work. Apparently they take people on as scribes and for translation, so my knowledge of the English and French tongues might be useful to them. He's said he'll find me a contact if I want to follow it up.'

'But you haven't done that yet?'

'No, I didn't want to until we'd talked about it. I can see how difficult it would be for you, having me working for the Church.'

When Gilles finally replied it was so quietly that William had to strain to hear.

'Well, it can't really make any difference now.'

William cast an arm casually round Gilles' shoulder, and Gilles nestled closer. They sat in silence for a while, each pondering the difficult decisions that lay ahead. Then Gilles murmured: 'Should we move a bit further off the path?' William turned to him, kissed him briefly and nodded. He had been holding back his own unspoken desire, unsure how Gilles would react.

Some time later the two young men walked arm in arm back into the city together. A new moon was rising, and the spindly pines cast eerie shadows across the dry scrubland.

***

A few days later William dropped in to Geoffrey's hostel. He told him that he'd discussed the question of working for the Church with Gilles, who had not been surprised and was resigned to the idea. Geoffrey nodded and said he would see what he could do. Then he put an arm on William's shoulder and looked him in the eye:

'This must be a difficult time, with some hard decisions for both of you. If there's anything I can do…'

'Thank you, I appreciate that,' William replied softly, turning away.

Geoffrey had seen enough of life to have a fair idea of the nature of his new friends' relationship, but he didn't pry further. A few days later he called in at William's workplace and passed on the name of a man in the Office of Secular Works who would be expecting a visit from him. William let his overseer know that he needed a morning off and the overseer agreed easily; there was not a lot of work at the moment and it would save him four hours' pay. That evening William told Gilles where he would be going, and was relieved when he just nodded his agreement. William smartened up his worn clothes as best he could and presented himself the next day just after the tenth hour.

***

Brother Aldhelm was a mild-mannered young Englishman whose clean-shaven face made him look even younger, though he told William he had been in Rome for five years after first serving God at Dereham Abbey in Norfolk for two. William guessed he was only four or five years older than himself. They sat on one of the stone benches around the echoing entrance hall to the Lateran Palace, which was dark and forbidding. They spoke in their own language, though Aldhelm also tested William's northern French briefly and questioned him about his knowledge of Latin. He raised an eyebrow when William said he could get by in the Occitane speech of the south too, adding that that might prove useful though he didn't ask him how he had come by such arcane knowledge.

Aldhelm explained that some of the work would be routine translation of documents, mostly from English into Latin and *vice versa*, but that William might expect to be called on now and again to translate for English speakers who turned up seeking an audience or because of a dispute. He added with a grin that some of the latter could become quite lively and would require skills of diplomacy as well as language. William replied dryly that he had had some experience of such situations during his long journey overland from England.

Aldhelm went on to explain how much William as a novice would be paid for his work, and William nodded sagely, barely disguising his surprise at how generous the money sounded compared to carpentry rates. In barely more than an hour he would be earning more than he could expect for a half-day in the carpenter's yard. The hours were long: from the ninth hour to the sixth, six days a week, with a one-hour break in the early afternoon, but William was already calculating in his head how quickly he would be able to save enough for the journey to Brindisi and beyond. The two young men then chatted more generally for a few minutes about their respective upbringings in England and the astonishing scale of pilgrimage to Rome, and William left with a note confirming that he should be admitted to the offices to start work at the eighth hour on the following Monday.

William told Gilles the news as soon as he returned home, though he was careful not to sound as pleased as he felt. Gilles nodded and smiled.

'I'm glad for you William,' he said, and gave him a hug, but William saw the sadness in his eyes too. Even so, he still felt sure that he was doing the right thing, and the following morning he gave notice at the carpentry shop. The overseer shrugged and said he would sorry to lose him, adding that he would be paid to the end of the day.

***

When William presented himself for work at the Lateran at the appointed time there was no sign of Aldhelm, but he was greeted by a solidly-built young man from the city of Colonia in Saxony. His hair was almost as fair as William's and he was perhaps in his mid-twenties. Johannes welcomed the new arrival in Latin, though they soon found that they could communicate on day to day subjects in their native tongues; the English and the Saxons shared a common heritage. They sat for a while on the same stone benches in the main entrance hall where William had talked with Brother Aldhelm, and Johannes explained that he had worked in the Lateran for almost two years. This made him quite an old hand in this city where the turnover of foreigners was rapid. As overseer he would familiarise William with the work and generally help him settle in. William felt an immediate affinity for Johannes, as a fellow northerner amidst the maelstrom of the sometimes overwhelming southern city.

When they had finished their discussion Johannes led William along echoing stone corridors lit by flaming torches fixed to the walls at regular intervals and busy with clerics and clerks hurrying to and fro, then up a narrow spiral staircase to the second floor. The scribes' room was large and relatively well-lit by high windows on all sides, though it struck William that it must get cold in winter. Johannes showed William to one of the twenty or so high desks set up in rows. One or two of the other scribes, though already busy at their work, looked round curiously or with a conspiratorial grin to the new arrival.

William's own desk was at the end of the third row, and like all the others its surface had been rubbed to a pleasing smoothness and rounded at the edges by centuries of use. It made William think of the generations of clerks who had sat in this place before him, which he found a rather reassuring thought amidst the constant change and movement he had lived through in the last year. Once the interest created by William's arrival had passed, the other young men were again all apparently absorbed in their work. Johannes had brought William a pile of documents to translate from the English tongue into Latin or *vice versa*. He said that William should ask if he had any problems before seating himself at his own desk at the front facing the rest of the room, and getting down to work.

William took the first document from the pile of cheap parchment, dipped his quill into the ink-pot and was soon absorbed in the work. William found that the texts were fairly straightforward and, as he had expected, were mostly concerned with day to day disputes over such matters as unpaid bills, ownership of property or advance payments for onward journeys which were then delayed or cancelled. The majority of the documents seemed actually to have been written down by scribes on behalf of the parties themselves, who were presumably illiterate. William had seen these scribes seated on stools on street corners around the city, copying down as well as they could the stream of words flowing from their often angry customers. There were separate locations for scribes able to understand Latin and the main languages spoken by the pilgrims and other travellers.

As he read and translated the documents it struck William that he would pick up some useful information about the pitfalls and sharp practice which he should watch out for as he made his own arrangements for travelling on. One or two of the disputes were juicier though, and one in particular caught his interest. The letter came from a Roman inn-keeper – one educated enough to write his own letter, though his Latin was difficult to follow and seemed to include a lot of the Roman dialect. Even so, it was clear that the inn-keeper was accusing a young English lodger of having got his twelve-year-old daughter into a "delicate condition". This had to be translated into Anglo-Saxon to be put to the lodger when both men came in to settle the matter, and William spent some time finding the right words. Somehow the whole business sounded more sordid in Anglo-Saxon than it did in Latin.

William was pleased when the bell rang for the lunch break, during which the scribes went out into the courtyard, ate whatever lunch they had brought with them in the cool of the colonnades and then chatted or snoozed for the remaining time. William had not brought anything, but Johannes shared some of his bread and cheese with William who promised to return the favour, and they chatted about their respective backgrounds in Rochester and Colonia, though Johannes noticed that William avoided saying too much about his reasons for leaving home or his life since. The hour passed quickly and they returned to their work. The time passed more slowly now, but towards the end of the afternoon Aldhelm appeared to check on progress, deal with any problems and take away the completed documents. He looked more closely at William's work than that of the other scribes, but seemed satisfied with it and nodded approvingly at one or two of the turns of phrase.

'You write a very clear hand, William,' he said.

'I had a good teacher, sir, a chaplain to the Bishop of Rochester.'

'Indeed! Well, it shows in your work. But you can call me Brother Aldhelm; we are not so formal here!'

'Thank you, Brother Aldhelm.'

Aldhelm leafed through some more of William's completed work.

'Ah, I see you've been working on the case of your unfortunate countryman!'

'Well, if he is guilty of what the landlord claims…'

'*If* he is, William. This landlord is well-known to us. He's a dubious character who's made accusations against people lodging in his inn before: failure to settle bills, theft of household goods, that sort of thing. I wouldn't be surprised if he isn't responsible for his daughter's condition himself! As you've seen, the boy simply denies the charge, but he may be too afraid of the landlord to say what really happened, if he knows. Given the seriousness of the accusation, I've asked the two of them to come in to settle the matter in person. I'd like you to take on the interpreting at the meeting; it should be a lively discussion!'

'Well, if you think I'm ready, sir …I mean, Brother Aldhelm.'

'Oh, I'm sure you will be, William, quite sure,' he replied, and with a friendly smile he moved on.

The rest of the afternoon passed uneventfully and William, absorbed in the report of a tavern brawl, was surprised when the hour chimed for the end of work. After saying farewell to Johannes and exchanging a friendly word with one or two of his other new colleagues he headed back to the lodgings, tired but pleased with his first day of work in the Lateran. As he made his way through the crowded but now familiar streets he felt a renewed sense of purpose.

***

William arrived home that evening eager to talk about his first day of work, but he soon picked up that Gilles' polite questions did not come from the heart. He turned the conversation around to ask about Gilles' day, though there seemed to be little to tell.

If William had hoped that his own example would spur Gilles into seeking work too, so far he had been disappointed. Of course, William had had no comparable loss to bear, but he could see that he must encourage Gilles to get out of their lodgings where he was still prone to spend his time brooding on those horrors. Ever since their final departure from Beziers William had seen it as his role, his duty even, to help him find a renewed purpose in life. Now that the idea of his own departure from Rome was taking shape, the matter was simply more pressing. Gilles must have some future here to look forward to.

William's first idea, that Gilles might seek work in the private bakeries which thrived in every quarter of the teeming, food-obsessed city, had fallen on stony ground. Gilles had not actually rejected the suggestion, but somehow he never actually got round to going out to seek the work, though it seemed to be readily available. William had wondered if the thought of working in a bakery would remind Gilles too much of his former life in Beziers and his own family's business, but was hard-pressed to come up with other practical suggestions.

Now it struck William that he should encourage Gilles to think more widely. He had seen in the early days in Beziers that his new friend could turn his hand to most kinds of practical work: repairing furniture, hammering out dents in the family's pots, pans and silverware, helping his mother with the cooking and even carving small ornaments and presents for family birthdays. The most obvious lead from all this would be to see if Geoffrey could put in a good word for him in the Lateran kitchens, which were said to produce the best meals in the city, but William immediately ruled this out. Gilles might be prepared to accept the fact of William working for the Church, but to do so himself would be quite another. So William called in at Geoffrey's lodgings one evening to ask him what he thought were the chances of Gilles finding suitable work elsewhere in the city.

Geoffrey, who by now understood Gilles' predicament quite well, not least that he might need to fend for himself in Rome sooner or later, was keen to help. He said he thought that the best source of work would be the larger hostels and lodging houses which employed kitchen staff to provide supper and sometimes breakfast for their guests. The problem would be that these jobs were much in demand and experience of work in a busy kitchen might be expected.

But, as William already knew from personal experience, breakfast and lunch could equally well be purchased from street vendors who offered delicious rolls filled with fried tomato, egg or cured ham, flavoured with the rosemary, basil and other herbs which seemed to turn up in all Roman food. There was even a tasty alternative, said to have been invented by the poor peasant-farmers in the lands further to the south, where tomato, cheese and herbs were smeared over flatbreads which were then baked in the oven, chopped into portions and sold as handy snacks.

Geoffrey explained that some of the street vendors were self-employed, selling food prepared in their own family's kitchens, which was obviously not an option for Gilles. But others were paid a small percentage by restaurant owners to sell the street-food which they themselves prepared in their kitchens in the early part of the day. This last arrangement was apparently the least lucrative, but the work was easier to find and might be a way for Gilles to get started. William thanked Geoffrey for his advice, which seemed sensible, though privately he wondered whether Gilles would be cut out for the work in his current state of mind. After he and Geoffrey had chatted for a while of other things, he walked home through the still warm streets wondering how best to raise the subject with Gilles, or whether he should look into the possibilities further himself first.

***

A few days later, before William had had time to take the matter of a job for Gilles any further, it was completely and unexpectedly overtaken.

When William returned from work on the Saturday, tired but satisfied at the end of his first week, Gilles greeted him with an excited gleam in his eye which William had not seen since before the catastrophe. He grabbed William by the arm and sat him down on the bench outside the lodgings.

'There's something I must tell you!' he began.

'Gilles, calm down! I've had a long day – a long week in fact! – and I need an ale first. Here, get us a couple of glasses,' and he handed him a few coins from the weekly pay which he had just received.

Gilles grinned: 'All right, all right, I'll fetch the poor, exhausted worker his drink!' and he hurried across to the tavern on the other side of the street. William waited, dog-tired but also on tenterhooks to hear what had got Gilles so excited. He felt vaguely anxious as Gilles returned with two tankards of the light Roman beer and sat down on the bench beside him. William took a deep draught, wiped his lips with the back of his hand and put the tankard down.

'That's better! Well?'

'Well, I could hardly believe it! I was sitting out here after breakfast this morning, when a couple of young chaps not much older than us came past, talking in the Occitane tongue. It's the first time I've heard my mother tongue here and I called out to them at once. They seemed surprised to hear their own language too, and joined me straightaway. They introduced themselves, Pierre and Philippe are their names, brothers from Toulouse! When I said I was from Beziers they looked shocked, and mumbled something about how bad it must have been. I…I just agreed and changed the subject; I didn't want to talk about it to strangers and they didn't ask any more.'

'That was tactful of them,' William said and Gilles nodded silently before continuing.

'Anyway, what they did talk about was what's been happening since. It seems that after Beziers, the crusader army moved on to Carcassonne, and these two certainly knew all about that, probably because there were more survivors to tell the tale. I just hope I can remember it all as they told it. So, it seems that at first everyone settled in for a long siege, expecting that Trencavel – you remember him, the Count of Carcassonne and Beziers who abandoned us – well, expecting that he and his forces, well-protected by the city walls, would be able to hold out for a long time. But the crusaders were clever – oh, they were clever! – and they started by attacking two suburbs of the city, partly fortified but outside the main defences. They quite quickly succeeded in picking off the first one, Bourg, on the north side. It wouldn't have mattered so much, except that it contained the main source of fresh water for the city, and that of course was a major blow to the people trapped within the walls.

'Next, the crusaders moved on to Castellar, a bigger suburb to the south. That was better protected and it took them longer, but they had the better weaponry. They attacked with siege engines, Pierre said, catapulting burning brands, and rotting animal carcasses into the city. Then what? Oh, yes! At the same time they had teams of men undermining the main city walls until they were left only shored up with wooden beams. They knew what they were doing, all right! When they were ready they set fire to the beams, the main wall collapsed and the crusaders took Castellar too. So now all the defenders, and the elderly, the women and children, were trapped in the core of the city, with no access to fresh water and under constant siege. It must have been terrible…

'Well, in just a matter of days people were dying so fast that Trencavel had no choice but to surrender. The end seems to have come very quickly. Trencavel himself was taken prisoner and led away in chains, and some of the other leaders were killed or taken prisoner. There wasn't a total massacre this time, but the rest of the survivors were banished from the city, if they hadn't already fled. Then the leaders of the crusade appointed an Englishman called Simon de Montfort as the new Viscount of Beziers and Carcassonne. I don't know who he is but he must be a man with an eye for the main chance!'

He stopped talking at last, and William put an arm on his shoulder. 'This must all be a terrible shock,' he said, uncertain about Gilles' mood, which seemed to verge on hysteria, though he seemed strangely elated too.

'Yes, but there's more,' Gilles went on, and now there was

a fresh urgency in his voice. 'Listen to this! When Philippe and Pierre left, this man de Montfort and his forces were still holed up in the city, and very unpopular in the countryside all around. But out there, ordinary men – and even some women – were forming into militias and launching surprise attacks on the crusaders if they ventured out for supplies. Apparently, my people, the *credentes* I mean, are building defensive settlements to protect themselves from further attacks. There are some already in the foothills of the southern mountains. D'you remember? The snow-topped peaks you first saw on the horizon from the hills above Beziers. It's a fight-back, a new beginning!'

Gilles finally sat back and took a generous swig of beer. William suddenly grasped the reason for Gilles' elation.

'Yes, I see,' he said quietly, 'and you want to be part of that fight-back!'

Gilles looked up. The excited gleam was gone, replaced by a much more serious expression. He spoke more quietly.

'Yes, William, I do. It's where I belong. I've been thinking about this all day, ever since talking with Pierre and Philippe.'

'And what about them? Are they of your faith? What are they doing in Rome if there's a fight-back going on?'

'No, they're not of our faith,' Gilles replied. 'They're Roman Christians though they said they were on good terms with their *credentes* neighbours until the crusade came. They're just a couple of mates who wanted to get away from the troubles in their own lands for a while and settled on the pilgrimage to Rome as a way to do it. I expect they'll go home when they've seen enough of the city. You can judge for yourself; they're staying in some lodgings round the corner and I've invited them to come and join us later.'

***

When Pierre and Philippe arrived soon after sundown William liked them at once. They were solidly built and swarthy, and William guessed they were a few years older than him. He couldn't help thinking that they'd be more useful in a fight than Gilles. The new arrivals greeted William cheerily, commented on his Anglo-Saxon appearance, especially his hair, and went straight across to the tavern, returning with more ale. They had been in Rome for barely a week and were still exhilarated by their arrival in the largest city of Christendom. They praised William's fluency in their own tongue but were clearly being careful not to ask too much about William and Gilles' own story, even though they must have been wondering how the two of them had survived. William was grateful for their discretion. One evening when Gilles had turned in early, he had privately told Geoffrey the tale of his and Gilles' escape from the city, but he still avoided the subject as far as possible in Gilles' presence.

The new arrivals showed more interest in William's childhood in England, perhaps seeing it as a safer topic. They were particularly interested to know if William had any knowledge of de Montfort, the new Viscount, and were disappointed when William replied that although he had heard mention of the de Montforts as one of the noble families of England, with lands somewhere in the north, he knew little more about them. He did entertain the new arrivals though with stories of his upbringing in Rochester. He told them about the Royal progress he had witnessed, the hunting parties for boar and stag in the forests of the Weald of Kent, and the travelling players who seemed to be a common feature of life across all of Christendom, even if most of the traditional stories and legends they performed were different.

As he talked of his upbringing in far-off Kent he felt a pang of nostalgia for the home and the family he had left behind. These feelings caught him out once in a while, but as usual he put them aside, gently feeling for the tiny casket in the lining of his jacket to remind himself of the commitment he had made to Edwin. All thoughts of what he would do next, and where he might one day put down roots, must be put aside until that sacred trust had been fulfilled.

Back in the present, he shared some tales too of his journey from England across the French lands, mentioning that he had set off with an older companion who had fought in the crusade to liberate Jerusalem, but glossing over his murder, saying only that 'sadly his friend had died along the way', in a tone which invited polite sympathy but no further questions.

Pierre, the more inquisitive of the two new arrivals, asked if William didn't miss his home and his family. William replied that he did think of them sometimes, and dreamed that one day he would return, but that England seemed like another world now. He mentioned too that he intended to travel further, and he could see the new arrivals were intrigued. At this point Gilles, who had not spoken for some time, intervened softly.

'Yes, it seems as if we may be going our separate ways soon.'

He and William looked at one another, without emotion but as if fully recognising the truth of what Gilles had just said for the first time. Philippe, sensing the tension, brought the discussion back to the practicalities of life in Rome, which William and Gilles were always pleased to talk about with newcomers, and before long the four of them were chatting like old friends.

Towards the end of the evening William sat back and noticed Gilles laughing and smiling in a way that he had not seen since the early days in Beziers. He thought ruefully that his friend's high spirits reflected his renewed sense of purpose in life, now that he had a plan for a return to his own people. He himself, on the other hand, if he was to continue his journey all the way to its destination, would soon be back on the road again, alone.

***

During the following days William and Gilles avoided too much talk of the future. William's work continued to absorb him during the day, and Gilles saw more and more of Pierre and Philippe. The latter had asked William for advice on getting work, confirming Gilles' hunch that they needed fresh funds to pay for their passage back to Marseille and on to their homeland. William had passed on Geoffrey's suggestion about reselling street food, and the pair had taken it up with enthusiasm. They had decided to seek work separately, thinking that potential employers were unlikely to have more than one vacancy at a time, and Philippe had struck lucky almost at once, finding a job selling breakfast rolls on a street corner in Trastevere for a local tavern which also served food. The pay was modest but it was regular work and a generous breakfast was also provided for the vendors. The tavern-owner, a jolly man who looked as if he ate too much of his own food, soon saw that Philippe was reliable and found work for Pierre too.

Gilles, newly motivated and encouraged by their example, went out searching for something similar and before long was selling bread and savoury rolls from a bakery in the same district. He seemed to have lost any inhibitions about the bakery trade now that he knew exactly what he was earning and saving the money for. William was pleased to see Gilles' new enthusiasm, though it filled him with sadness too. Without a great deal more having been said, he knew that the die had been cast and the thought of separation, though it remained mostly unspoken, loomed ever larger. Even the newly established habit of an evening walk down to the banks of the Tiber, where they had found a hidden clearing surrounded by dense laurel and oleander, was an increasingly bittersweet pleasure.

***

When William had been at work for an hour on the following Monday, Aldhelm came to the scriptorium and invited him back to his own room for 'a short discussion'. The other scribes looked up curiously as William followed Aldhelm out of the room.

Aldhelm led him along twisting corridors and up a narrow flight of stairs to a small but comfortably furnished office. There was even a carpet on the floor, with a beautiful flowing pattern picked out in gold around the edges.

'You've noticed the carpet, William! It is beautiful, isn't it? Don't admire it too much though, it's an infidel carpet, apparently one that someone brought back from the crusade twenty years ago. It shouldn't really be here at all, I suppose!'

William immediately recalled Edwin having spoken of the beautiful carpets with intricate gold script which he had seen in the markets of Acre, and he was briefly transported to another world. Then he pulled himself back to the present as Aldhelm came to the point.

'Well, William, your work is proving very satisfactory,' he began. 'Are you enjoying it?'

'Certainly, Brother Aldhelm,' William replied, 'though I am very tired by evening!'

'Oh, that's quite usual!' Aldhelm replied with a slight smile. 'You'll soon get used to it. Now, the reason I asked you up is that the landlord and lodger whose case you've worked on are coming in at the tenth hour tomorrow for a short hearing at which we will agree what is to be done. They have two different versions of events, as you know, so it's likely to be lively and I'd like you to be ready to interpret for us. I thought it would be a good idea if you read the earlier letters which have built up so that you're prepared for what they'll be talking about tomorrow.'

'Of course, Brother Aldhelm,' William replied, thinking that it would be an interesting break from more written translation. And...'

'Yes, William?'

'Thank you for offering me this task – I hope I can live up to it.'

'I'm sure you will, William; I wouldn't have asked otherwise. One of the messengers will bring the papers down during the afternoon. Now, can you find your own way back through the maze of passages?'

'Ah, that may be a harder task, Brother Aldhelm,' William replied with a smile.

∗∗∗

William found his way up to Aldhelm's office reasonably confidently the next morning, feeling rather important as his footsteps echoed in the dimly-lit corridors. A cardinal in scarlet robes and beretta, gliding by in the other direction, murmured absent-mindedly: '*Deus tuus tecum, filius meus*'. William, taken by surprise, belatedly mumbled what he hoped was the correct response, but the cardinal was already gone. He arrived a few minutes early, but Aldhelm was already there, scanning some notes he had obviously prepared in advance.

'Good morning, William – I trust you're looking forward to whatever little drama our visitors may play out for us! Remember, your role is simply to interpret what people say: Anglo-Saxon to Latin when the lodger speaks; the reverse for my or the inn-keeper's words. If the inn-keeper speaks more in Roman dialect than in Latin, I should be able to help out.' Then he shook his head and added: 'Perhaps our Lord uses Rome to remind us how completely He confused the languages of the world at the Tower of Babel!' William was not used to the biblical stories being treated lightly and wasn't sure how to reply, but he was saved from any embarrassment by a knock at the door, and a messenger who ushered in the parties to the dispute.

The inn-keeper looked exactly as William had expected; he was a man in his middle years, running to fat and with a tousled head of dirty hair. He wore a stained leather tunic and baggy breeches and had several days' worth of black stubble on his face. If he had tried to smarten himself up for the encounter it was a poor effort. William could see he was a bully from the defiant stare he directed at Aldhelm. The boy barely looked his stated age of fifteen, with fair hair which suggested he was of Saxon stock, but only the faintest shadow on his upper lip. He fiddled anxiously with the cap which he was holding.

Aldhelm invited both of the visitors to sit down, which they did, the one heavily, and the other tentatively, on the edge of his seat. William felt sorry for the boy at once, and wondered what he was doing so far from home.

Aldhelm introduced himself and William, adding that they were both familiar with the written statements. He said that it was unusual for the parties to be brought in, but then the charge in this case was a serious one, where such a young man was accused of something which was not just a serious crime, but a mortal sin. The boy twisted uncomfortably and gripped his cap even more tightly. Then Aldhelm asked both parties to restate briefly their version of events. The inn-keeper immediately leant forward, pointed his finger at the boy and launched into a torrent of Roman dialect. William could understand almost nothing and turned anxiously to Aldhelm, who signalled to him with his hand not to worry.

'Sir, sir,' he interrupted, 'not so fast, please, we aren't so familiar with the spoken tongue of the city!' The man glowered and started again, a little more slowly, so that William was able to follow the gist of what he was saying. Even so it was left to

Aldhelm to pick up when the tirade of angry words and finger-pointing had come to an end.

'So, if I understand correctly, you are accusing this boy of carnal relations with your daughter, who is – let me see – only fourteen years old, such that she is now with child?'

'Yes, sir, that's the measure of it,' the inn-keeper replied in a surly tone. 'And 'er at such a young age, too, sir!' he added as an after-thought.

'Hmm, quite, quite...' Aldhelm said quietly. 'And you say you saw them, er, perform the deed?'

'Yes, sir, I did, sir.'

'And how did you see it? Where did this take place? Surely the act you accuse the boy of would have happened somewhere... private?'

The inn-keeper glared but he had his answer ready: 'It 'appened in the loft above my kitchen, where the boy slept. I came in, 'eard a noise up there, crept up the ladder and saw them with my own eyes, sir!'

William found it hard to imagine such a big man creeping up a loft-ladder without being heard, but then the boy broke in with a rapid burst of English. Aldhelm could see the surprise on William's face and asked him to translate.

'Yes, brother Aldhelm,' he said, taking time to phrase what the boy had said in Latin. 'He says that what the inn-keeper said is not true. He says it was the other way around. He himself came in from his work in the abattoir and heard sounds in the loft, and when he went up the ladder, he saw this man and his daughter – '

The older man broke in with a torrent of angry dialect, though it was clear he was denying the charge and at the same time berating the boy. The poor lad burst into tears, but through his sobbing he was speaking again too.

'What's the boy saying now, William?' Aldhelm asked.

'He's saying that Matilda is a lovely girl, but he's insisting again that he never did what he's accused of, though the inn-keeper told him to say that he did. He says he can't lie to you, sir. Now he's repeating that it was her own father – and he says he can prove it!'

'Really! What is his proof?'

'There was a further whispered exchange in the guttural English tongue, then William turned back to Aldhelm with an embarrassed expression on his face.

'Well, Brother Aldhelm, he says that he saw the two of them, you know, and that the inn-keeper has a large purple birth-mark…on his backside!'

There was a moment's silence whilst the parties considered this new information. Then Aldhelm, with a hint of amusement in his blue eyes, turned to the inn-keeper and said mildly:

'Well, that could be proved easily enough one way or the other.'

The inn-keeper blustered that it was a bloody lie and it was nobody's business where he had a birthmark, but it was clear to everyone present that the game was up.

Aldhelm put a reassuring hand on the boy's shoulder. 'Young man,' he said, 'James, isn't it? Don't be afraid. You were brave to speak up and I believe everything you have said.'

The inn-keeper cut in defiantly: 'Well, I've had enough of this. I'm off!'

'No, you aren't,' Aldhelm responded calmly. 'William, go and fetch the nearest guard. The gentleman can be a guest in our cells overnight. It will give him time to repent of his actions while we find somewhere else for James to stay. I don't suppose you want to return to your current lodgings, do you, boy?'

William translated briefly for James, who looked as if he might have kissed Aldhelm's hand if he hadn't stopped him. Then William slipped out to fetch one of the Lateran guards who stood at arms in the lobbies or patrolled the corridors. In fact one was standing right outside, presumably posted there by Aldhelm in case he was needed. When they came back in the inn-keeper glared at the guard aggressively. He put up some token resistance but the guard was too strong for him. He let himself be escorted out meekly enough, with the burly guard gripping his arm firmly behind his back.

'His sort are usually cowards at heart,' Aldhelm murmured when he was gone, and William and James both gave a sigh of relief. The boy almost smiled.

***

For the next couple of months, through the oppressive heat of the Roman summer, William and Gilles' life continued its settled course, on the surface at least. William worked six days a week at the Lateran, mostly hunched over the writing desk. His days were sometimes lightened by further opportunities to translate in discussions about the more serious disputes, though none were as entertaining, or had such a satisfying outcome, as the first. In the end the inn-keeper had been kept in the Lateran for a couple of nights whilst arrangements were made for the two young people involved. The guards reported that he banged on the cell door and demanded to be let out periodically, but Aldhelm had sent someone round to the inn where the man's wife was evidently keeping the business running and caring for her daughter, and was not in any hurry to have her husband back. William himself had suggested that James could move into the lodgings where he and Gilles stayed; that way they could keep an eye on him and help him find work somewhere other than the abattoir. Aldhelm knew of the lodging-house and that it was cleaner and more honest than most, and immediately agreed.

Some months later Aldhelm passed on to William the news that Matilda, now living with her aunt and uncle outside the city, had miscarried, but that she was well in herself, and they agreed that it was the best outcome for all concerned. Aldhelm, of course, saw in this the will of God, though William asked himself if that would not mean that the landlord's act had been the will of God too. Lying awake in the dormitory that night, he wondered if there wasn't some truth in the *credentes*' simple belief that this world was ruled by the devil, and the only hope was to reach the better one beyond the grave.

William's hard work was rewarded by a regular income, of which he used only about a third for living expenses in Rome. The balance went into a growing reserve for the planned continuation of his journey, which Aldhelm had agreed could be deposited for safe-keeping in the Lateran's locked and guarded treasury. At this rate, he calculated, he would be able to leave in another eight or nine months, in the spring of the year 1211, with enough funds to cover most of the journey. He was already starting to research possible routes, of which the boat from Brindisi seemed the safest and most practical.

Gilles' job as a street vendor had led, as Geoffrey had suggested it would, to more regular work in the same bakery where the goods he sold were produced. His previous unwillingness to return to the business his family had pursued in Beziers was now forgotten, and he came home in the evenings white with flour and cheered by the camaraderie of the bakery. He had earned plaudits for introducing some of the southern French techniques of bread-making, including a lighter dough which had proved successful with customers. His standing in the bakery had enabled him to get work as a vendor for James who had taken to the job and was doing well.

William smiled ruefully to see Gilles' new confidence and purpose. He was relieved that Gilles was able to stand on his own two feet again, but the relief was tinged with sadness for the loss of his own role as Gilles' protector. In the early days in Beziers he had lived for the present and without a thought of the long-term; during the hard times after the fall of the city he had been motivated and rewarded by his role in bringing Gilles through; now he understood that nothing lasted for ever, in this world at least. He thought sometimes of Edwin in those days on the road in northern France, world-weary but unaware of the closeness of his own death. For his sake too he must continue with the quest on which he had so willingly embarked and which had already led him so far. He could not break his vow to Edwin to seek out his former lover, however slight the chance of finding her might seem after so many years.

***

One evening, as William, Gilles, James and Geoffrey sat outside the tavern in the last of the early autumn sunshine with a tankard of ale each, the story of James' own journey to Rome came out. He had gained greatly in confidence since getting away from the inn-keeper and finding a circle of friends, but until now had said little about his past except that he had grown up in London, the son of a blacksmith. It was Geoffrey's natural curiosity which finally drew him out.

'James, lad, you've heard our stories, isn't it about time we heard yours? Only if you want to, but we're all friends here.'

James looked at him for a moment, then he nodded.

'You're right. I'd like to tell you the tale, though it starts badly, but I feel I can trust you fellows. Especially after William helped get me out of that business with the inn-keeper.'

He paused for a while, thinking where to begin. The others waited expectantly.

'Well, my father was a blacksmith in the city of London,

just inside the walls at Cripplegate. His father before him too, though by the time I knew him grandfather was a wizened figure sitting more or less motionless in the old wooden armchair in the corner of the kitchen… He still had a twinkle in his eye, but God had confused his mind and I never heard him speak.'

James stopped briefly, unused to being the centre of attention, but his listeners nodded sympathetically and encouraged him to continue.

'But mostly it was a happy home, and all was well – until last summer. It was a hot year and it brought a fresh outbreak of the pestilence which had already swept London several times in my parents' memory. They had survived when they were younger, but now it was their time, and… they both succumbed within a few days of each other.'

He stopped again, and was visibly on the edge of tears. William put an arm round him and murmured:

'It can be a cruel world, James; let the tears come if it helps.' Sure enough, the boy slumped forward and sobbed, with William cradling him.

When he sat up, his eyes were red but he continued, almost smiling as he did.

'Yes, it was terrible, but…in one way we were lucky. My uncle and aunt took us in, me, my older brother and my younger sister that is, and grandfather too, though he faded away and quite soon he passed over.

'Our uncle and aunt were kind to us, but I could see how difficult it was for them. They had two sons of their own, and there wasn't enough room, or enough money coming in, to keep all of us fed and clothed. They had sent Henry out to work already and I knew I would have to start soon.'

James looked down, composed again now, but evidently moved afresh by the memories brought forth as he retold his story.

'Then, one day, a way out turned up quite by chance. I was down in the food-market which ran along the city walls on the north side of the Tower, running a few errands for my aunt. There was a big crowd gathered round, and I stopped to see what it was all about. A band of troubadours from the Low Countries had set up a temporary stage and were juggling, telling bawdy jokes and playing traditional tunes on the flute. It was magical, and I sat down in the front of the crowd and watched the show until the end. Then they announced that this was just a taster for their main performance which would take place that evening on the hillside which overlooks the city to the north. It was to be a retelling of part of the Chanson de Roland with music and mime, and I immediately resolved to be there, of course.

'Well, the show that evening was wonderful – you must know the story? Roland and his boon companion Oliver fight with Charlemagne's army to help save Christendom from the Moslem infidels swarming up from Hispania. *"Rollant est proz, e Oliver est sage!"*, that's to say: "Roland is bold, and Oliver is wise" – a perfect pairing! You must know the ending too; Roland and Oliver lead the defence of the pass of Roncesvalles which is the turning point in the campaign. Christendom is saved, but Roland and Oliver and most of their men are killed – they die as martyrs and go straight to Heaven, of course!'

The listeners did all know the story, which was a staple for the troubadours who criss-crossed all of Christendom. For William the memories were bitter-sweet, taking him back to the greensward outside the castle in Rochester where he had heard a similar performance several times. Something in the story of the two faithful friends had always struck a chord with him. He had spoken of the story to Gilles, too, but for him it had darker resonances: the armies of Charlemagne were crusaders, mercilessly smiting a religious enemy. He had never met a Moslem and he suddenly wondered if their armies could really be any worse than the Christian crusaders who had come to Gilles' peaceful homeland intent on wiping out the gentle *credentes*. It was an impious thought and he put it aside.

James had stopped speaking and was looking round to see if his audience was with him. They were and they encouraged him to continue.

'Well, that night, after the performance, I lay awake for a long time thinking about the troupe and whether I might join them. I'd been playing the flute for several years. My uncle said I showed some talent, and I'd performed in nativity plays at Christmas. I knew that my uncle and aunt wouldn't like the idea, not least because I was only just fourteen, but at the same time it'd mean one less mouth for them to feed…

'The next morning I was down at the troupe's camp-site early in the morning, and got chatting with a couple of the players. They were friendly and praised my flute-playing when I gave them a few tunes, and they took me along to talk to the leader of the troupe. He was an older man with a pock-marked face, but friendly too, and he said they could always take another willing lad with some musical knowledge, an interest in learning more, and a readiness at first to turn his hand to whatever needed doing! He added that he would need to talk to my uncle, as my guardian, to be sure he was happy with the arrangement, and that I must be ready to travel to France as they intended to try their luck there next.

'The idea of travelling beyond the shores of England scared me and excited me at the same time, and I was anxious about my guardians' reaction to the whole idea. In fact it was much as I'd foreseen. My aunt in particular was unwilling to let me leave home at such a young age, given the promise they had made to my parents that they would care for their children. On the other hand, my uncle said little and I guessed he was thinking of the practical benefits for his immediate family.

'So my uncle spoke with Jeroen, the troupe leader, and the thing was agreed. When the troupe left London a couple of days later to make its way down through Kent, I went with them. The parting from my family was painful – little Helen especially cried and begged me not to go, but I promised I would come back before too long, full of stories of foreign lands! It didn't help them or me much on the day we left, though.'

'And you weren't planning to come as far as Rome!' Geoffrey said.

'No, I wasn't, but I'll come to that. Well, we travelled down through Kent, performing in Rochester and Canterbury on the way.'

'Rochester! You must have performed outside the castle walls!' William exclaimed.

'We did, William, though I was only helping behind the scenes at that time. Perhaps your family were there; most of the people were. It seemed a fine place, though we only stayed one night.'

William was sunk in his own thoughts for a while after this, but James, now that he could see that his audience was interested, pushed on with his story.

'We gave a couple of performances in Canterbury, and prayed at the shrine of Archbishop Thomas, before going on to Dover where we had to wait a few days for a boat to make the crossing to France. Then we headed towards Paris, performing along the way. I was playing the flute in the choruses and for the musical interludes, and loving the life on the road with the troupe. They were a young and happy crowd and we had some fun! I could tell you some of their stories another time.

'We reached Paris after a couple of months – a rougher city than London and such a melting-pot of different people and languages! But after Paris the group was planning to return to the Low Countries, which as they described it sounded flat and wet and, well, a bit too much like England! I'd developed a taste for more travel by this time and I fell in with a group of English pilgrims who were intending to journey all the way to Rome. They made it all sound so exciting: heading south every day towards the sun, crossing the Middle Sea from Marseille and reaching the greatest city in Christendom. Well, it has been exciting, and here I am now in Rome...' His voice tailed off, and he peered up at the rickety three-storey tenements which loomed in the darkness above them, noisy with the sounds of Romans making the most of their brief hours of relaxation at the end of the working day.

'And what are your plans now?' William asked, after a long pause.

'Oh, to return to England, sooner or later. I think I've learnt enough skills along the way to survive and find work in London, without being a drain on my uncle and aunt, and I reckon I've had enough adventures – one too many perhaps!' He paused and grinned at William before continuing more softly.

'I'm very fond of Matilda, of course, but, well, there are plenty of fair maids in London too. The truth is I'm ready to go back to my home and my people, knowing I shan't be a burden to my uncle and aunt.'

'Sounds like a good plan,' William commented wistfully, and everyone fell silent, sunk in their own thoughts of travel and home and family. Then Geoffrey downed the dregs of his ale and thanked James for his story, and the party broke up soon after.

***

William lay awake in the dormitory under the eaves for several hours that night. He envied James his simple certainties. The boy from Cripplegate had seen something of the world, had some adventures, grown up, and now he would return to his people, marry some pretty girl and have a family of his own. It all sounded so simple.

But for William, it was not so simple. There was the promise to Edwin to be fulfilled, and there was still the restless urge to travel further, to see more. There was, too, the mystery of his enduring love for Gilles, which had mellowed and changed into something deeper. The two young men had sometimes gone down to the scrubland along the banks of the Tiber in the evening, and relived the passion of those long-lost afternoons on the shore in Beziers. It had been good, but it had not been the same. The innocent happiness of those days was over, haunted by too many ghosts, and overshadowed by the forces which were pulling Gilles back to his people, and William ever onward to the fulfilment of his promise. Their different fates were drawing them apart, and perhaps the truth was that a love such as theirs could not survive for long in the world such as it was.

As William finally drifted into sleep that night, listening to Gilles' deep, calm breathing from the adjoining bunk and with his own hand clutched around the casket containing the lock of auburn hair, he could feel the end of their time together drawing ever nearer.

Part III – Palestine

Piraeus to Acre: late Spring 1211

On the sixth day out from Piraeus, William woke early and knew at once that something was wrong. On the journey so far he had been sleeping the deep sleep of a young man, lulled by the motion of the ship and the reassuring creak of the timbers, but now, in the stuffy darkness, there were flashing lights and his ragged clothes were sticking to him, hot and damp. He groaned quietly. He had seen others on the journey fall sick, fade away and die within hours.

Perhaps if he turned over and curled up and drifted back into sleep he would feel better when he awoke, or if he awoke… or perhaps it would all end here, dying of the sweating fever in the Middle Sea, with no-one to mourn him…Gilles, Edwin, the girl he had to find, what was she called: Eleanora, Emilia?… None of it made any sense. None of it meant anything, except the fever and the throbbing in his head. Rest, he wanted to rest, he wanted to sleep…

***

'I think he's coming round! Quick, fetch fresh water!'

William tried to focus his eyes and remember, but it was too hard. The face before him seemed familiar, yet everything was moving and floating in the strangest way. Gilles, was it Gilles? No, it couldn't be. He had stayed in Rome, hadn't he? A last embrace and tears on the dockside, then Gilles standing at the very end of the harbour wall, waving, waving, waving, the red cloth he had brought specially fading to a tiny dot and then disappearing altogether as the sails caught the wind and the ship picked up speed and the land faded into the haze.

And he was on the ship, going to… where was he going to? And who was…?

'William, lad, drink this! It'll make you feel better.' A callused, sunburnt hand was held out bearing a mug of water. William went to take it but was too weak. The hand brought the water forward, tipped it gently and held it up to his lips so that William could drink. It didn't taste right, but he gulped at it clumsily.

'Don't let him take too much at once!' another voice advised, further off. 'Just sips.'

The first face started to come into focus. The face had a name, if only he could remember it…

'Albrecht?' he mumbled.

'Yes, William! It's me, Albrecht. We thought we'd lost you; you've been in a high fever for three days and three nights. It would have killed an ox. You bloody Anglo-Saxons must be made of stern stuff!'

William nodded slowly.

'Yes, Albrecht, I remember. Thank you, thank you…' He slumped back on the straw, exhausted.

Albrecht looked round at the others, and shrugged. The lad was strong, or he had been. But even so…He leant over again and felt William's damp brow and his still feverish breath on his face.

'We're nearly there, William! Hold on another few hours and you'll be on solid ground. You'll pull through, strong young fellow like you! Oh, we'll have some fun when we get to Acre!'

Acre. The name seemed to mean something to William. He opened his eyes a little wider and focused on Albrecht more. His high forehead and flowing blond hair made him unmistakable.

'We're really nearly there? Acre, wasn't that where Edwin went years ago? Where he fell in love with... the girl? Or was that somewhere else? It all seems so long ago...'

He drifted off into silence, and Albrecht offered him the water again.

'I'm afraid I don't know who these people are, William. But don't you worry yourself with that now. You need to get your strength back first.'

William lay back, mumbling something inaudible. Albrecht looked round at the others with a resigned shrug and whispered:

'Still in the hands of God, I'd say...'

***

William was too weak to be taken off the ship for the first few days after they docked, so Albrecht and a couple of others formed a rota to sit with him. On the third night he slept soundly and long, and when he finally awoke the fever seemed to have gone. He smiled weakly at the young man who was sitting on the end of the bunk, half asleep himself, and said: 'I'm very thirsty, is there anything to drink?'

With tears in his eyes, Jerome came to, clasped his hand and smiled at him.

'Of course, of course, take some of this water first, then I'll fetch you a hot drink they have here and bring the others! Thank God you've made it, we thought we'd lost you.'

'No such luck!' William replied with a weak smile.

Jerome was back in a few minutes with Albrecht and one or two of the others from the journey; most had dispersed and found lodgings in the town by now. He also brought a steaming mug of some dark brown liquid with a rich aroma.

'Drink that,' he ordered. 'We don't really know what it is,

but the traders who bring the beans it's made from say it comes from Africa and call it *kahwa*. It certainly wakes you up in the morning! Don't drink too much at once though; the vendors on the dock make it strong!'

William took the brew and sipped cautiously; he'd never tasted anything like it but it was good.

***

Sustained by kahwa and the weak local ale which Albrecht brought him so long as he remained on the ship, and by a gradually increasing diet of solid food, William was strong enough after a few days to get up and leave the gloomy darkness where he had lain for almost a week. The ship was in any case due to sail on its return voyage the following day. Guided by Albrecht with a steadying hand, he made his way carefully up the rickety wooden staircase, and felt briefly dizzy again as he emerged into the blinding light of Palestine. As he got used to the glare, he gazed round in amazement at the creamy white and ochre skyline of the city, its towers and domes and battlements clustered together in profusion, and at the colourful chaos of morning life laid out before him on the wide dockside promenade.

Men in flowing robes of white and crimson, russet, purple and green, gathered round to trade the glistening fish and other unfamiliar seafood that was being brought ashore in great wicker-baskets, laid out on trestle-tables under protective awnings and sprinkled with water to keep it looking fresh and appetising. Hawkers strolled through the crowd, each endlessly repeating his guttural sales-pitch. William noticed that some of them were offering kahwa in tiny terracotta cups which their customers drained in one gulp before dropping the cups underfoot to be crushed back into the flagstones and trodden earth of the dockside. There were women too amongst the crowd, though for the most part they remained separate from the men, moving calmly amongst them, modestly dressed in flowing garments in sombre colours with their heads covered and their eyes averted.

William would later learn that the infidel women lived more separate lives from the men-folk than their Christian counterparts; for now he just marvelled at the melting-pot of cultures and races which swirled around him as Albrecht led the way through the throng. He had known from discussions on the ship before he fell sick that the crusader armies had retreated and most of the fighting men had melted away again after the failure to recapture Jerusalem twenty years before, though some had remained and now they, and new arrivals from the West, controlled a crusader foothold in the Holy Land. Of course, it was that crusade which had brought Edwin to this place and which he had spoken about on the early stages of William's own journey with him in distant France – but even after hearing Edwin's tales he had never imagined anything as exotic as this!

'Bit different from the markets in Saxony or England!' Albrecht said with a grin, interrupting his reverie. Then he put a protective arm round his younger friend as he looked slightly dizzy again. 'Do you need to sit down?'

'No, I'm fine. It's…it's astounding,' was all William could think of to say.

'Oh, you haven't seen anything yet!' Albrecht grinned, guiding his friend into the maze of narrow streets which made up the heart of the town behind the port. Here too, market stalls were set up wherever there was enough room for them, laden with fresh produce brought in from the surrounding farms and orchards. There were vegetables and fruit which William recognised, and many that he did not, nuts and dried fruit too, and unfamiliar grains. The smooth flagstones underfoot were slippery with discarded waste and the air was dank and humid, but here and there the alleys opened out into irregular squares where William gazed up in wonder at graceful spires, so much slimmer and higher than the stumpy church towers in England! Albrecht drew his attention back to ground level, pointing to a stall selling great mounds of a tiny pale-yellow grain, alongside a contrasting display of shiny red and green vegetables shaped like gnarled fingers.

'You'd better hurry up and get your appetite back; the food here is delicious when you've got used to the stronger flavours!'

He waved aside an old woman whose wrinkled flesh dangled from her outstretched arms as she thrust samples of a round orange fruit out towards him imploringly. Then he turned back and offered her a couple of coins from inside his cloak which she grudgingly accepted in exchange for two of the fruit. He tossed one of the fruit to William.

'Here, try this!'

Following Albrecht's example, William broke open the hard skin with his thumb-nail and tried one of the segments. It was tangy, sweet and refreshing all at the same time.

'They grow wild on the trees in the hills outside the city,' Albrecht explained, 'but you can't get a good apple!'

They ate the fruit as they strolled deeper into the city, finally emerging into the central square, also filled with traders' stalls at this hour and overlooked by the tallest and slimmest of the tower-like structures. Albrecht said that they were called minarets, and that five times a day a Moslem priest recited holy words calling the infidels to their prayers. 'They're not bad people you know, William, their God is just a bit different from ours – and a bit more warlike, it seems. Oh, and you'll curse the call to prayer when the first one starts before dawn!'

'That must have been the wailing I heard from the ship – it sounded like someone mourning the dead or the loss of a battle!'

'That will have been it. But it's utterly sacred to the Moslems, so be careful what you say. There are plenty of the local population who understand French, and some know the rudiments of the Saxon tongue too. They're nobody's fool!'

William looked into Albrecht's blue eyes.

'It's good to have found a friend who speaks my own language – or something like it!'

'Hah, exactly what I was thinking about your curious English speech!' Albrecht replied, mimicking the Anglo-Saxon accent.

He grinned and put a friendly arm round William's shoulder to lead him across the square to a busy tea shop. They sat in the shade of awnings on low, wooden stools sipping from tiny glasses of mint tea, and watching the world go by. A group of old men sitting on a bench opposite observed them silently through clouded eyes.

***

Albrecht had found lodgings in the attic dormitory of a house deep in the old town which belonged to an Armenian trader, and he introduced William to the same establishment. Aram was tall and wiry with sleeked back hair and a glint in his eye which suggested a sharp mind, and he was certainly a canny businessman. The dormitory was just a sideline to his trading interests, but it also provided work for his wife and three unmarried daughters, and brought him contacts and gossip. He was fluent in many tongues, and William was soon familiar with the tale of his first journey from his distant mountainous homeland to the shores of the Middle Sea, and how he had run away from home with a group of the traders who plied the old routes from the east. He had made the journey again many times until he was rich enough to bring an Armenian bride back with him and settle in Acre as middle-man, trader and general fixer.

Albrecht had warned William: 'Oh, he's charming all right, but check what extras he's charged you for when you settle up!'

William had grinned, but he had been struck by the significance of Aram's story too, and the idea began to form in his mind that there was scope for making money here, in this crossroads of peoples from all over the known world. His early experience of trade as apprentice to his father when he was growing up in Rochester might come in useful after all!

He soon learnt too that Acre was effectively the capital of Outremer, the Christian territory which had been brought under Frankish control after the crusade. Jerusalem itself remained in the hands of the Saracens, and the result was an uneasy peace, with neither side strong enough to take on the other. The Franks seemed to form the biggest group in the population of Outremer, but they were supplemented by a fluctuating population of Anglo-Saxons, German-Saxons and Austrians, by people from Rome and the surrounding kingdoms and principalities, by Hispanics and Greeks, not to mention the Armenians and others from the east who came in on the trade routes and some of whom settled.

This melting pot of peoples, languages and lifestyles fascinated William, quite apart from the elation he felt at finally reaching the Holy Land – the place where Edwin had fought and had his brief but passionate love affair with Emilia! The casket was still safely sewn into the lining of his jacket, and he had quickly established through casual questions that Jaffa, where she had lived, was only a couple of days' journey down the coast from Acre. The route was constantly plied by camel trains of traders and pilgrims since it lay on the road to Jerusalem. As soon as he was fully recovered he intended to go there, fulfilling the promise he had made to Edwin before he died, though he kept reminding himself that the chances of finding the woman were slim. She might well be dead, and even if she was still alive she would almost certainly be long-since married, and would probably not want anything to do with a stranger who arrived from the other end of the world with tales and even a memento of a long-lost passion.

In the short term, William concentrated on regaining his strength. He progressed to more solid foods, and developed a taste for the yellow grain *kuskus* and the spicy vegetable stew that accompanied it, supplemented with lamb if you could afford it, or other, unidentified meat if not. He had learnt to pick out some of the stronger-tasting ingredients which stung his throat and made his eyes water, though Albrecht ate everything with relish. Perhaps when his own stomach was stronger…

He had enough savings from his work in Rome to pay for his board and lodging for a month or so, but not enough for a further period of travel. He would need to replenish his funds before he could continue the journey to Jaffa; there was no telling how long he would want or need to spend there, and from the accounts he had heard it was a smaller town where it would be harder to find work. Albrecht had already landed a job as a porter with one of the wealthier merchants, who seemed to employ a small army of the travellers who arrived in Acre needing to replenish their funds before moving on. William still intended to speak to Aram as soon as he felt sufficiently recovered to take on work if it was offered.

In the meantime he revelled in the novelty of everything in Acre, and was constantly astonished at the number and variety of travellers who thronged the narrow streets, conversing in a dozen languages, wearing all manner of outlandish clothes, motivated by religious quest, fleeing from troubles at home or simply in search of adventure. For most, reaching Jerusalem was the ultimate goal, and William had already picked up that although the Holy City was under the control of the Saracens, they allowed pilgrims to make the journey.

William had paid his one and only visit to London as a boy of nine or ten years, when his father had taken him to Westminster Abbey and shown him a meticulously drawn map of the world displayed on the wall. A great city had stood out in the centre of the map and William had asked him if that was London, but his father had laughed and said, no, of course not: that was Jerusalem, the true centre of the world. Then he had pointed to a much smaller place squeezed onto the edge of the map: *that* was London! Now William understood why the map had been drawn as it was, and marvelled that he had come from a remote corner of it to within striking distance of the centre…

***

Once his fever had receded, William's health recovered rapidly and after a week or so of recuperation and a steadily increasing intake of the new food he felt as if he had been reborn. The gruelling sea journey and the period of sickness were a distant nightmare from which he had awoken into a bright, new day, and he began to think more practically about the future.

His first approach was to his landlord. Aram always appeared busy, but William had noticed that he sat first thing every morning for a quarter of an hour or so outside the house, with a supply of mint tea in a finely beaten silver tea-pot, checking his order lists and accounts, and chatting amiably with passing acquaintances.

Aram invited William to sit down and offered him tea, but laughed at first when William enquired about work, replying that he himself would be a rich man (as if you weren't, William thought!) if he had a dirham for every young traveller who'd asked him the same question. But then he relented, looked William in the eye and challenged him to tell him what new trading opportunities he'd spotted since he'd been in Acre.

'Well, sir,' William said thoughtfully, pausing as if to think the question through, though he had in fact prepared his answer. 'I've been keeping an eye on the prices for the silks which the traders bring on the eastern route from Tartary and Cathay, and I've noticed that they always have some lower quality rolls. They're mostly sold for local use, but I think they could open up a wider market in England. At the moment only the richest Lords in London can afford silks for their ladies, or so my father always used to say!'

'That was probably said for your mother's benefit!' Aram chuckled.

'Maybe, sir, but I think there was some truth in it. I still remember the glow of the ladies' veils and shawls when my father took me to London and we saw the court processing to the great abbey at Westminster on Easter Sunday. But the lower nobility and even the richest merchants could not afford silk. It seems to me there would be a market for the lower quality silks which sell in the bazaars here for much less than the price of the best pieces.'

Aram half nodded, half shook his head with the practiced ambiguity of a merchant, but then he smiled at William and asked:

'You speak the English tongue, of course, and French also?'

'Yes, sir, and I understand the Saxon tongue and the Occitane speech, and some Latin of course!'

Aram raised an eyebrow.

'Really? Well, French would be the most useful as the general language of trade here, but no doubt the others would come in handy.' Then he paused before continuing and William wondered if the discussion was ended. But finally he spoke again.

'How about if you worked for me for a while, and we'll see where that leads? I need a bright lad who could do some of the preliminary work when a new caravan comes in from the east, finding out what's available, how much and at what initial price, before I get involved. I have good contacts of course, but it can be useful to have someone they don't know so well go in first.'

'I'd be honoured, sir.'

'Aren't you going to ask me how much I'll pay you?'

'I'd do it for the experience, at first, sir… but I hope that you'd find my work of value.'

Aram smiled. 'Well answered, boy! We'll work out a commission basis when I've seen what you can do.'

William thanked him, confident that Aram would pay him fairly when the time came. Then some of the trader's friends joined him, and as the conversation drifted into the Armenian tongue William politely moved away.

***

A few days later, William, Albrecht and two other friends of his from the ship went out to celebrate William's recovery. It was well understood that Moslems did not take alcohol, but equally that there were ale-shops outside the city walls to the east, where the drinking of beer and wine by non-Moslems was permitted, or at least a blind eye was turned. Everyone also knew, however, that public displays of drunkenness could end in a night in the dungeon of the citadel, which by all accounts was a very unpleasant experience and so discouraged over-indulgence. William, who recalled the damage caused to some families in Rochester by their men-folk's drinking, thought that the Moslem attitude was not all bad. All the same, he looked forward to a mug or two of the weak local ale.

Soon after sunset, Albrecht led the way confidently through the maze of streets east of the centre, finally ducking under a low arch and along a dark alley before knocking on an unmarked door. The door was opened at once to admit the four young men, and William was surprised by the pleasant surroundings: there was one large room with several cosy alcoves, dimly lit by sconces in the walls which left sooty residues on the domed brick ceiling. A large, florid man in a stained leather apron greeted Albrecht and the rest of the group in the Saxon tongue, showed them to a table and brought mugs and a flagon of ale. They sat down and took their first sip, and William looked around curiously.

'This could be a tavern in Rochester!' he exclaimed.

'Or in my home town of Osnabrück,' Albrecht countered, 'and as our friend the innkeeper comes from Münster which is not far away, that's more likely.' Thomas and Matthias, brothers who were also from Saxony, cheerfully agreed.

The conversation quickly turned to the options for finding local work, which preoccupied most of the travellers, except the few who were wealthy enough not to have to worry. As Albrecht pointed out, the rich had their own concerns, in particular how to keep their coin or gold or other valuables safe. He told the story of a Flemish trader, a big man and a famously hard-bargainer who was said to be far wealthier than he ever admitted. No-one had been too sorry when he reported to the city council that he had been robbed of a vast amount of gold coin, and soon everyone had learned his secret: he had carried his wealth around with him at all times sewn inside the linings of his clothes. Relieved of all his wealth by robbers whilst walking home through the backstreets one evening, he was much less of a big man in all respects.

The other young men had all laughed, but they agreed that it was a problem. William recounted how he had worked for the church in Rome, and had been able to deposit his savings securely in the vaults beneath the *curia*, but no-one was aware of any such options in Acre. Small amounts of money could be entrusted to the lockable storage-chests of boarding-house owners and innkeepers if they seemed trustworthy, but still you heard stories of money going missing or arguments over how much there had been in the first place. Traders turned coin into goods as quickly as possible and paid to store them in locked warehouses. They recruited armed guards, mostly ex-crusaders, for journeys.

William took the opportunity to share the gist of his discussion with Aram and his plan to raise some funds as his agent. It seemed that others had toyed with similar ideas, but had not taken them further, and William was pleased to see how interested they were. Then Matthias asked about his long-term plans.

Albrecht sat back thoughtfully as William told his new friends about Edwin and the pledge that William had made to him to find Emilia, though he kept half an ear on the tale in case any extra details emerged. He himself had set out from Saxony on a pilgrimage, and also for whatever adventures befell him along the way. His final objective was to reach Jerusalem itself, though he had heard different reports along the road about whether this was possible or not. In any event, he hoped that William, who was already a firm friend and who struck him as a smart and resourceful fellow, would be his travelling companion as far as Jaffa, and perhaps on to the Holy City itself.

Sunk in thought, Albrecht had lost track of William's tale, but now he turned his attention to his friends again as Matthias, the more outspoken of the two brothers, exclaimed:

'Perhaps Emilia will have a daughter of your own age by now and you will settle down in Jaffa!'

William laughed and his face reddened. 'Oh, I don't know about that. I don't seem to be the settling kind!'

'Just a matter of finding the right girl!' Matthias responded, slapping William on the back.

William smiled ruefully but didn't respond, and Albrecht watched him closely, again wondering what really went on in his new friend's mind. He sensed some deeper sadness but didn't want to pry, certainly not until he knew William better.

'Well, I'm sure we're all hoping to do that!' he exclaimed, and everyone laughed. 'Now, how about some more of this excellent ale?'

***

The weeks went by and William settled into his new life in Acre. Rome already seemed a distant memory, and though the horror of the destruction of Beziers haunted his sleep in strange and surreal dreams, the earlier days in the city seemed a long-lost idyll, barely more real than the tales of the troubadours. He often thought of Gilles, especially as he lay in the dusty loft waiting for sleep. He hoped that he had kept safe on the sea crossing and overland journey back to his homeland, and wondered what he had found when he got there. He had spoken wistfully of joining whatever survived of the kindly community he had grown up with, perhaps in hideaways in the hills if life in the cities had become too dangerous. But he knew that he could do no more than speculate on what Gilles' life was like now, and mostly he tried not to dwell on those memories too much. The pain of their separation, and of not knowing what had become of his dear friend since, still ached within him.

During the day William was kept from brooding over the past by his new role working for Aram. When a fresh shipment arrived from the east, the camel trains gathered in an area of scrubland outside the Eastern Gate of the city and the traders sent runners into the central markets to announce what products they were offering. The runners' wailing voices reminded William of the town-crier in Rochester in his youth, who would announce forthcoming events or pass on news of the doings of the King or the local Lords, though here the announcements were in heavily accented French, which as Aram had said was the common language of trade.

When a caravan came in, Aram would brief William on what kind of goods he was interested in, and at what price, as they hurried out of the city to get the best pick. It was Aram who negotiated the final deal, though increasingly he asked William to approach a dealer first to express a general interest and to explore what the price might be. Then Aram would join him, embrace the trader as an old friend, sit down and accept a glass or two of tea and proceed by indirect routes towards the final deal. William was under instructions not to interfere at this stage, but to attend closely and to keep notes of the prices and quantities which were finally agreed. Later he would be responsible for collecting the goods, checking the quantities and quality and arranging porters to deliver them to Aram's warehouse in the city. When the goods were all safely stored in the warehouse, Aram would invite William for more tea, and would then question him to see how far he had followed the negotiation. He did not give much away, but mostly he seemed content with the young man's answers, embracing him in the local manner when the discussion was over.

***

And so the months passed. As the blazing heat of summer built up, people rose earlier to visit the markets and get their chores done before it was too hot to do anything but retire to whatever shade they could find and doze through the afternoon. In the late evening, life returned to the streets, the men-folk gathered outside the tea-shops, whilst the women chatted indoors and the children played under awnings on the flat roofs of the houses. William marvelled at the boys' skill with the brightly coloured kites which swooped and dived in the sky all over the city like mythical birds. Sometimes they attached tiny blades to the strings and engaged in elaborate "battles" where each side attempted to cut down the other's kites.

William settled into his working routine with Aram, and felt that the older man was pleased with him, whilst he himself was pleased with the payments which Aram handed to him at the end of each week. Thomas and Matthias had found work of their own in the kitchens of a large boarding-house outside the walls. They liked Acre – and the friends they had made there – and they intended to stay until the cooler weather came, building up their funds so that they could make the short final journey to Jaffa and Jerusalem and back without the need to seek work along the way.

It struck William that the local people here seemed contented enough with their life, certainly compared with the squalor and casual lawlessness he had experienced in Rome. He loved the way the city opened straight onto the sparkling sea, refreshing the air and whispering of the wider world. He understood why Edwin had reminisced about Outremer with such fondness, quite apart from his encounter with Emilia.

***

As the heat began to recede and the flow of traders from the east resumed, William's thoughts returned to the next stage of his journey – maybe the final stage! Enquiries about the possibilities of travelling to Jaffa had quickly confirmed that it was a well-established route. Guarded camel trains left every few days in the cooler season, led by local guides who provided the animals and basic food and drink along the way in return for what seemed a reasonable fee. The journey took two days if there were no difficulties along the way. "Difficulties" seemed to mean ambushes by robbers, though the guides of course played down the risks, pointing out that there would be plenty of regular travellers on the road in the cooler autumn days, which created better security.

It was agreed one evening that William, Albrecht, Thomas and Matthias would travel together, at least as far as Jaffa, if not on to Jerusalem itself. Jaffa was a key staging-post, from where the last leg of the journey could apparently be completed in a single day's travel, provided permission was forthcoming. William's initial objective was to reach Jaffa and find Emilia, but Albrecht had slapped him on the shoulder and said: 'I don't think you'll want to miss out when the time comes, even if the lady in question has a very beautiful daughter – you're a traveller at heart!' William had smiled as they raised their glasses of tea to the shared journey ahead.

The next few weeks were spent in preparations for and eager anticipation of the journey. William let Aram know what he was planning, and was relieved when the older man nodded ruefully. He embraced William, saying that he would miss his assistance, and would gladly take him on again if he decided to come back to Acre. Then he looked at William from under his hooded brows and added that he understood he had "personal business" in Jaffa and might not be coming back. William had already marvelled at the reach of Aram's personal grapevine, which was a key resource for a successful trader, but he hadn't imagined that it stretched to knowledge of his own personal affairs. He grinned, and replied that of course Aram was well-informed as ever. Then he had a sudden thought, and asked if he could speak privately to Aram for a few minutes. Aram raised an eyebrow, glanced at the sun to judge the hour, and said: 'Why not? Come in to my lair!'

When he spoke of his 'lair', Aram meant the dark little space at the back of the house where he retired for an hour every evening to record the day's business and complete his accounts; normally it was kept locked and Aram had the only key. Aram led the way, and they sat uncomfortably close across the small wooden table piled with lists of goods and rows of meticulously recorded figures.

William described the situation as briefly as he could.

'I ran away from home three years ago, following an older friend, Edwin, who had travelled to Palestine before, with the crusade, when he was barely my age now. Along the way, Edwin confided in me the story of a youthful adventure: he had got to know a young lady in Jaffa, by the name of Emilia, who would now be in middle-age.'

He had not expanded on this point but had glanced significantly at Aram on the words "got to know a young lady" and Aram had nodded.

'After telling me this tale, Edwin asked me to take on a sacred trust for him. He explained that he hoped to reach Jaffa again and seek out this woman, whom he had never forgotten. I promised him that, if anything happened to him along the way, then I should take on the task of finding Emilia, and hand over to her a keepsake which he had treasured all those years.

'Of course, I embraced him and cried out that nothing so bad would happen to him. But he was older and wiser than me, and knew the cruelty of the world better than I did then. Not long after he was…he was killed by common robbers.'

Aram reached out a hand and rested it on William's shoulder, seeing how upset the young man was by the memories he was sharing. He murmured: 'That must have been very hard for you.'

'It was, sir, it was. But I vowed over Edwin's dead body to carry out his wishes. If I myself reached Jaffa I would seek out this lady, if she was still alive and could be found. I would tell her that Edwin had never forgotten her, and I would pass on to her the keepsake of his love.'

William paused, his story told, sunk in thought. Then he pulled himself back to the present, and added:

'Of course, Edwin knew – and I know – that the chances of finding this woman after so many years are very slim. And even if she is still alive...'

Aram waited for some time before completing the sentence.

'...she may not want to be reminded of what happened then. Well, you will only know the answer to that if she can be found, and approached discreetly. It seems to me that it's a fine thing you are doing, and if it was a sacred trust to your unfortunate friend then it must be respected. I imagine you're interested in contacts in Jaffa who might help you to track her down?'

'That's exactly what I was going to ask you, sir.'

'So what further details do you know about Emilia, beyond her name?'

'Well, I know that she was of Frankish origin, had auburn hair and was very beautiful – in Edwin's eyes at least! If she was roughly the same age as Edwin she would be in her early forties by now – and...'

'And?'

'...and at the time he met her she was working in a brothel!'

A momentary expression of surprise crossed Aram's usually inscrutable gaze, then he pressed his fingertips together and thought for a moment before responding. Finally he said:

'Well, what an intriguing story, though that last detail probably reduces the chances of... well, no, we must wait and see. In any event, you promised to fulfil your friend's wishes, and so this woman must be found if it is humanly possible. Leave it with me, William. I have a few contacts in Jaffa, and I will think who might be able to help you.'

And with that he pushed back his chair to make clear that the matter was closed for now. William thanked Aram for his help and backed out of the room respectfully.

***

Meanwhile the four friends' preparations for the journey continued. By the beginning of the ninth month they had built up sufficient funds and turned their attention to finding a reliable agent to book their journey as far as Jaffa. The expectation after that was that they would separate, with the three Saxons continuing to Jerusalem, where William would follow them when his personal task in Jaffa was fulfilled one way or the other.

Once he knew that his young assistant would be leaving soon, Aram had invited William into his lair once again. This man whom William had come to admire and respect, firstly thanked him for his work over the previous months, then presented him with a final payment, which was generous, even when his accommodation costs had been deducted. Aram had waved aside William's thanks.

'Better to have enough funds for a journey – but keep them close to you at all times!'

Then, brushing aside William's further expressions of gratitude, he turned to the more personal matter. He took a piece of parchment from the pile in front of him, closely inscribed in Aram's meticulous hand, folded it over and sealed it with a blob of wax from the candle which provided a little extra light on the desk. Then he wrote something on the outside and pushed it across the table.

'This is a short recommendation for you to give to the man whose name appears on it. He is a distant cousin and an old friend of mine, who might be able to help you find the woman you seek, if it is possible after so many years. I've summarised the situation for him but I leave you to fill in the details. Please give him my heartfelt regards and my best wishes for his interests when you meet him. Anyone involved in business in Jaffa should be able to direct you to his house.'

'Thank you, sir. I am very grateful for everything you have done for me. If I have the good fortune to return through Acre I will of course stay here, bring any news of your friend, and tell you the outcome of my search.'

'And perhaps I will tempt you to stay on and do some more business for me!'

'I hope that will be possible, and it would be a pleasure, sir.'

So, with due formality, William took his leave of Aram, and embarked on the final stage of his long quest.

To Jerusalem and back

The camels were gathered outside the southern gates of the city, where the well-worn track, hammered flat by the regular traffic, stretched out into the rough scrubland to the south. The four young men from far-off England and Saxony felt pleasantly cool for the first time in months as a fresh breeze blew in off the sea at the early hour. The cameleers were preparing the animals and loading up the provisions which boys were carrying out of the city in boxes and in water-pots balanced on their heads. There were a dozen camels for the travellers, plus three more for the supplies, and four guides who would lead them on foot and prepare the food for the evening meal and a light breakfast the next day. The other travellers seemed to be mostly local people, making visits to family or friends in Jaffa now that the summer heat was receding, although there were also a few pilgrims travelling on to the Holy City. Everything seemed well-organised, and the train set off shortly after sunrise.

The newcomers to camel travel had been observing the creatures which they were to ride for the next two days: up close they were intimidatingly tall with a scornful gaze which was turned on anyone who ventured too close. Scraggy tufts of fur sprouted here and there, between bare patches of pale leathery skin. They had an odd, musty smell.

One of the guides gave a short introduction to the riding technique: mount the beast while it's sitting down, and be sure to lean back as it stands up because the camel straightens its rear legs first. Once the beast moves off, simply go with the flow of the gentle bouncing motion. William found it surprisingly easy at first, though his muscles would be aching by the end of the day because of the odd motion of the animal – truly a ship of the desert! He sensed that his mount was a little ill at ease too, looking round at him testily once or twice with its great glassy eye.

The heat built inexorably during the day, and William and his friends were all relieved when a brief lunch stop was called in the shade of a small clump of scrubby palm trees. Bowls of dried fruit and nuts were handed round, and gourds of warmish water which were nonetheless quickly drained. William noticed that the local travellers drank more sparingly than his own party, and resolved to hold back a little more at subsequent stops. He noticed too that people spoke little and moved around no more than was necessary, out of respect for the heat in the middle of the day. He reflected that a Kentish upbringing prepared you to protect yourself against the cold and rainy seasons, and simply to make the most of the summer warmth!

The call to remount came sooner than he would have wished, and the afternoon ride was somewhat longer but otherwise similar to the morning. There was only a brief mid-afternoon stop at a shady oasis with a trickle of running water diverted into a basin from which everyone took a few mouthfuls. The guides were clearly eager to remount and get to the day's destination before the sudden nightfall, when the danger of attack or robbery would be much greater. The last couple of hours as the sun gradually edged towards the horizon were the hardest; William felt faintly sick from the constant jogging motion of the beast below him, and his leg muscles were screaming by the time they finally reached the tiny settlement where they were to pass the night.

Simply stopping and dismounting was a great relief. There was a natural spring which provided cool, clear drinking water and also fed a small pool in a thicket of palm trees where the male travellers stripped off their sweaty clothes and splashed around in the water, which was tepid and brackish but a delight nonetheless. By the time they returned to the encampment the guides were cooking over two or three open fires, and the mixed aromas of wood-smoke and spicy stews were wafting deliciously on the cooler evening air. The meal lived up to the expectations of all the travellers, and by the end of the dinner the men at least were chatting amicably in a mix of French, sign language and the smattering of polite expressions in the local language that William and his friends had picked up. The women of course ate separately, before slipping away quietly, presumably for their own turn in the pool.

Sleeping mats and blankets had been laid out in a row of rough stone huts, but the atmosphere inside was stuffy and oppressive and most of the travellers brought their bedding out into the cool night air to sleep under the stars. William lay awake for some time, dog-tired from the exertions of the long day's journey but unable to take his eyes off the myriad stars which twinkled like silver dust in the moonless sky. When he finally gave up the struggle and drifted off, it was into dreams of white-clad angels swooping across a skyline of sandstone palaces and graceful minarets.

***

The guides ensured everyone was awake just before dawn on the second day, and had already prepared breakfast of freshly-baked bread, green and black olives and strong, black kahwa sweetened with honey. The travellers ate silently, still wrapped in blankets against the chill morning air. The most talkative of the guides at this early hour, a younger, fresh-faced man with a red and white check head-cloth, explained that the cooler breeze was blowing down from the mountains inland. He himself came from a village in those hills, but had had to move down to the coast in search of work. He welcomed the flow of foreign travellers and pilgrims for the cash they brought into the region.

Within the hour everything had been packed up and the travellers remounted. William's thigh muscles were aching from the unaccustomed motion of the camel the day before, but the pain actually eased somewhat as they set off and got back into their stride. Ashraf, the young guide who had chatted over breakfast, pulled alongside and grinned: 'Not too painful this morning, William? It gets better after the first day; you'll be riding like one of us by the time you get to Jerusalem!'

William grinned back: 'I'm not sure I'll get used to the way they stare at you, though.'

'Ah, for that you probably need to have grown up with them! Are there no camels at all where you come from?'

William grinned and shook his head. 'In England? No! Ponies and donkeys for the common people, and horses for the rich, but nothing which rocks like these camels do.'

'Well, you're riding well already – for a *ferengi*!' Ashraf replied, and with a skilled flick of the reins steered his camel away and back up to the head of the group.

The guides had assured them that the ride would be shorter than on the first day, with only a brief pause for lunch, but in the event there were a number of unexplained delays, and a long pause for lunch and a doze in the shade of the palm-trees at a cool oasis. In the end the sun was already sinking towards the horizon when the weary party crossed a low pass over a stony line of hills and had their first sight of the citadel and city of Jaffa. It dominated the stretch of coastline before them, rising up in the form of an upturned bowl on a low hill overlooking the sea.

William took a deep breath as he caught his first sight of the city he had heard so much about from his dead friend – was it really two and a half years ago when he had heard that story in a tavern in the French plains one cold, dark evening? He wondered whether Edwin had had this same first view of the city when the crusader army had reached it twenty years ago, and where they had made their encampment. He wondered too where in the maze of little ochre houses which covered the hill-top Emilia had lived then, and whether she was somewhere down there even now, sitting quietly in a shady courtyard or preparing food at the end of another day.

Sometime before sunset the tired but relieved group reached a dusty open space outside the main entrance to the city, where they dismounted gratefully, collected their baggage and were immediately surrounded by local boys trying to grab the bags from them and offering to show them to the best lodging houses: 'Really very best – clean and safe!' William made a point of thanking Ashraf and embracing him in the local way, and even gave his trusty camel a friendly slap on the flank, though he got only a haughty stare in return. Then the four friends picked up their bags and made their way in through the city gate, elbowing aside the would-be touts and porters.

They made their way into the crowded warren of steep and twisting alleyways which formed the centre of the city, keeping their eyes open for a simple lodging-house. There were plenty of choices and they soon found what they were looking for in a simple but clean attic dormitory run by a gruff old Syrian called Mohsin. Despite the excitement of arrival in a new city, the new-arrivals were all too weary and sore after two long days of camel-riding to do anything but fall into bed.

***

Next morning the four woke well after sunrise and had a late breakfast of fresh flatbreads and olives, washed down with several glasses of piping-hot kahwa, outside a simple eatery just along the street. The other customers ignored them completely, Jaffa seeming less open to the wider world than Acre despite also being a port. But then William recalled something Aram had said: his own city would always have the advantage over Jaffa as the main entrepot for trade with the East. He tried nodding in a friendly way to the old men sitting on a bench opposite, but got only blank stares in return.

William's three friends were eager to explore the options for making the final stage of their own planned journey, the last short leg over the hills to Jerusalem. It seemed impossible to mention the Holy City without rolling its exotic name around on your tongue: 'In two or three days we could be in *Jerusalem*...' They urged William to come with them; the return journey would be by the same route and he could deal with his "other business" when he got back.

But William shook his head; the other business was more pressing to him, a deeply personal matter, and now that he was so close to the long-imagined encounter even the Holy City must wait. His reply was clear and simple: 'Jerusalem will still be there next week or next month. I must seek out the person I came here to find first.'

The others could not miss the seriousness in his voice and in his expression, and Albrecht took his hand and murmured: 'Of course you must do what is right for you. Would you like me to stay and help you to find the woman?'

William could feel the tears welling up as he looked his new friend in the eye – friendships formed so quickly and easily amongst travellers in foreign lands – but his resolve was firm.

'Thank you, Albrecht, I really appreciate the offer, but there's nothing two people could do that one could not. In any case, the whole thing may be settled one way or the other in a day or so and then I can follow you to the city at the centre of the world!'

'We'll look out for you there, then!' Albrecht replied. 'You'll probably come across us sitting in the street somewhere drinking kahwa!' and they all laughed.

***

William's friends set off straight after breakfast to enquire with the agents and touts who gathered just outside the city walls on the eastern side about the costs and frequency of travelling to Jerusalem, leaving William feeling bereft once they had gone. He drank another kahwa and decided that he would try asking their host, Mohsin, if he knew of Aram's contact. Despite his gruffness the evening before, he seemed a better choice than the fat camel-owner, and probably had more contacts in the city. William downed his glass and hurried back to the lodging-house, to find Mohsin before he had got involved in other business or gone out.

He was still there when William returned, engaged in an irritable conversation with another resident of the dormitory, seemingly over the cost of his stay. William waited politely out of earshot on the other side of the alley until things quietened down, which they did in due course but with neither side looking pleased. William strolled across and Mohsin acknowledged him with a brief nod.

'Well, I hope *you*'re not dissatisfied!'

'No, no, everything's fine,' William assured him, 'I just wanted to ask your advice about finding a man I need to get in touch with here in Jaffa.'

'Well, what's his name?' He snatched the proffered envelope and studied the script, which William could not read.

Mohsin looked impressed and murmured: 'Hmm, Fayad al Hannad, a very big man in Jaffa. You won't find the house by yourself, but if you head down to the *souk* one of the lads down there will show you the way for a few coins. Oh, one more thing: like I said, he's an important figure, so make sure you show respect and call him *effendi*.' Then he turned away almost before William could thank him.

The advice was good. A boy with a stunted arm but a cheerful grin showed William the way to the house he was seeking in the maze of unnamed alleys, and left him standing outside an ornate doorway in an otherwise blank wall. He tapped the brass knocker tentatively on the ancient wood and waited for several minutes. William was about to try again when the door was opened by a servant, and he again showed the envelope as evidence of his *bona fides*. The young man raised a sceptical eyebrow, but showed William into a cool colonnade running along the side of a fishpond full of plump carp, and told him to wait. After a few minutes a stocky man of maybe forty years appeared, deep in conversation with a younger man. As Fayad al Hannad wished his previous visitor farewell, William had time to note his rich robes and the rings encrusted with gemstones on his plump fingers.

He then turned his attention to William, who greeted him in French as respectfully as he could and handed over his letter of introduction. Al Hannad looked at it, sliced it open and studied the contents, and his manner at once became friendlier.

'So,' he said, 'my dear friend Aram Bakshan recommends you and writes that you are trying to find a long-lost acquaintance here in Jaffa. I am always pleased to help a friend of Aram!'

'I worked for him for a while, *effendi*, and found him an excellent master and a kind man,' William replied with what he hoped was appropriate formality. Al Hannad nodded.

'Indeed, a clever businessman and a fair one too, which is a rare combination!'

He pointed to a cushioned divan set against the wall under the colonnade and they both sat. The servant reappeared with a tray bearing a finely-wrought pewter pot and tiny engraved tea-glasses which he set down on a side-table. Al Hannad poured a glass for each of them and invited William to explain his request.

'Thank you, *effendi*. The lady I seek is not exactly an acquaintance of mine, but of a dear friend of mine who is sadly no longer alive.'

'I am sorry to hear that. Aram has given me the gist in his letter, but please tell me the story in your own words.' William felt increasingly intimidated, and that he was going to feel somewhat embarrassed telling the less savoury aspects of the story, but there was no going back now.

Al Hannad listened carefully as William recounted the tale, nodding thoughtfully here and there but without giving away any reaction, though he too raised an eyebrow at the mention of Emilia's previous role in life. When William had finished he thought for a moment, then delivered his verdict.

'It's quite a story that you tell, young man! But I respect the effort you are making to fulfil the trust your late friend put in you – that is admirable! – even if some of his conduct was less so! I do not believe I have met this lady myself,' and here he smiled ironically, 'but I shall make a few enquiries and if you come back tomorrow at the same time, well, we shall see what those enquiries have turned up. Feel free to take some more tea before you leave.'

With that he swept out, acknowledging William's thanks with a gracious wave of his hand. William relished another few minutes of the cool courtyard before downing the remains of his tea and obediently following the servant to the door. It was a shock to emerge into the crowded alleys and streets of the city, but he made a point of noting the way back to the central square so that he could find his own way tomorrow. As he did so, he reflected that Aram certainly seemed to have some influential friends.

***

This left William with the day to himself. He walked north along the shore for an hour or so before the full force of the sun would make it too hot, then stopped at a deserted spot, stripped off his ragged clothes and strode strongly out into the sea for a swim in the warm blue waters. He swam idly first on his front, then on his back, parallel with the stony beach, staring up into the cloudless sky and recalling his stolen afternoons with Gilles at the shore outside Beziers. Mostly he blocked out the memories of those times, though he could not resist indulging in them once in a while, and reliving all the joy that had preceded the pain. Not for the first time, he played with the thought that maybe, when his promise to Edwin was fulfilled and his travelling days were over, he would return to the source of his happiness.

He turned into the shore, waded out of the water and walked thoughtfully back along the beach. In the few minutes it took to get back to his clothes he was completely dry and he quickly covered up against the strengthening sun – it was a standing joke that new arrivals from England and the other northern countries could be identified by their red and peeling skin, and he didn't want to make that mistake.

Back in town he returned to the lodging-house, changed into the cleanest of his limited stock of clothes and took the rest to wash at the communal fountain at the end of the street, where it widened into a small square lined with orange trees. The gaggle of veiled ladies who were performing the same chore and chattering happily as they did so glanced at him now and then and were obviously enjoying a joke at his expense. He nodded to them in what he hoped was a respectful way, but they only turned away and giggled even more.

As he pounded his shirts in the water-trough, wrung them out and hung them over the low tree branches, he wondered about the women's lives. The women here did not seem in the least downtrodden, despite their restrictive dress and limited role outside the home, and William concluded that the relationship between men and women was not so different from England. In both societies men sat in council and ran the cities, worked as butchers or blacksmiths, merchants or farmers, went off to war when called upon and generally regarded themselves as being in charge. The women stayed home – the Moslem women rather more rigidly than their Christian counterparts – but they still ran the household and brought up the children, and no doubt influenced their husbands in all sorts of subtle ways that the men barely noticed. Listening to the babble of the women's talk in some local patois, he concluded that they had a whole existence from which the men would always be excluded.

While his clothes were drying he went back to the lodging-house and dozed through the scorching heat of the late afternoon, despite the oppressiveness of the dormitory. Hovering between waking and sleeping, visions of what the future might hold flickered through his mind: a meeting with Emilia, a middle-aged woman by now, embracing the emissary of her long-lost lover, or screaming at him in embarrassment and rage; a vision of the Holy City, rising up on the skyline like a scaled-up version of the intricate image on the map in Westminster Abbey; and, most disturbing of all, Gilles' dear face, looking again into his with those laughing brown eyes and that mop of unruly hair.

***

William was awoken from his doze by Albrecht, Thomas and Matthias climbing the steep wooden stairs noisily and bursting into the dormitory, flushed with the success of their mission. They had found a merchant who made regular trips from Jaffa to Jerusalem, the main purpose of which was to transport goods imported from east and west to the Holy City. But he was willing to take travellers along for what seemed a reasonable fee, in return for some help with loading and unloading the baggage camels at the start and end of the journey, and leading the animals through the narrower defiles along the way. It seemed that the route, though shorter, was more challenging terrain than the coastal journey which they had all already made. The three of them had arranged to depart at dawn the following morning, so as to reach their goal by nightfall.

Again they urged William to join them (they had already mentioned this possibility to the merchant who had readily agreed to take one more strong young man for the same price) but again William shook his head. He recounted his discussion with Fayad al Hannad, and said that he must wait and see what he could unearth, and if that led nowhere then he would explore other ways of trying to find the woman. Finding Emilia, if humanly possible, was the priority, though he certainly intended to make the journey to Jerusalem when that had been achieved. The others nodded sadly and said that they would miss his company. They understood the seriousness of his quest, but equally they did not intend to delay their departure. For them, reaching Jerusalem had always been the ultimate goal of their long journey and, more practically, they had paid in advance for the following morning's departure.

The four friends ate that evening at a nearby street-side stall offering the usual spicy vegetable and grain dishes, and turned in straight afterwards in preparation for the early start that three of them would be making the next morning. Before getting into his bunk that night, William embraced each of them, wishing them well for the journey and assuring them that he would follow them just as soon as his mission here had been accomplished, one way or the other.

***

William was aware of the others getting up, as quietly as possible, the next morning but feigned sleep to avoid a hurried or awkward repeat of the farewell scene of the night before. Once the creaking of the wooden stairs had subsided he turned over and drifted back into sleep for another hour or so before the first light of dawn, and with it the muezzins' wailing call to the faithful spreading across the city. He felt lonelier than he had for some time when he awoke fully and saw the three adjoining bunks cleared of their bedding. He was on his own again.

There was no sign of Mohsin this morning, and since al Hannad had asked him to call again at the same time as the day before he had a couple of hours to fill. He got up, washed as best he could at the pump in the courtyard and breakfasted on freshly baked rolls and kahwa, before strolling down to the port. As often happened, a few local lads sidled up and squatted down near him, asked him where he came from and whether they could practice their French with him. William already understood that, for local Arabic or Syrian boys who hoped to do more in life than take over from their fathers as herdsmen or landless labourers, gaining some knowledge of the language of trade was the first step.

These lads seemed friendly enough, and William whiled away an hour or so chatting with them about his childhood in far-away England, and recounting tales of his long journey from there to Jaffa. He omitted the most personal and painful episodes, of course, though harrowing images still flashed through his brain as he did so. He described the simple lessons in reading, writing and arithmetic that he had received from the monastery school attached to the cathedral in Rochester. There was evidently something similar here, though he guessed that the schooling the boys received in the local script using texts from the Moslem holy book would be of less use in daily life.

So the couple of hours passed pleasantly enough, and just after the tenth hour William again knocked at the ornate doorway, and was politely admitted to the cool colonnade to wait. The tea tray was already on the table, and Fayad al Hannad appeared in due course and greeted William graciously. They both sat down.

'Well, young man, I have some news for you,' he said in a business-like voice, then paused tantalisingly before continuing. 'But I mustn't keep you in suspense too long, must I?' He smiled and continued in a kindlier tone: 'I have identified the woman you are seeking, and she is alive and well and living in the city with her husband.'

William's heart was suddenly pounding but he tried to sound calm: 'That is indeed good news, *effendi*.'

'It is, of course it is. But, young man,' he went on sternly, 'it is only a start. She has been married for some seventeen or eighteen years to a man of French origin who is himself established in trade. His name is Dominique de Dompierre and I believe I have met him once or twice. I don't know him well, but I understand him to be a good and reliable man.'

Al Hannad's calm brown eyes glittered with amusement as he fixed William with a stare.

'You will have to tread carefully!'

'Of course, *effendi*, I understand,' William replied, trying to control the excitement in his voice – Emilia was alive and well!

'I'm not sure that you do. Wives here, even Christian wives, are more tightly controlled than wives where you come from.

There is also the question of how much her husband of many years knows of her past – he may be entirely ignorant of it. I can give you the man's name and the location of his house, but that is all. I would not wish you to mention my name in connection with this matter to him or anyone else. I have done as much as I have only because you came with a letter of introduction from my old friend Aram. From here you are on your own!'

'I understand, *effendi*, and I will of course respect your wishes entirely,' William replied, looking al Hannad firmly in the eye.

The older man nodded and pressed into William's palm another neatly folded fragment of parchment.

He murmured the formal Moslem farewell, which William returned, and swept from the room, leaving the same supercilious servant to show William out. Suddenly William was on the hot and crowded street again, clutching in his hand the parchment which brought him one step nearer his goal.

***

William returned from his second meeting with al Hannad straight to the dormitory, which was open for paying guests whenever they wished, but generally deserted at this time of day. In fact, only one other person was there when William returned, a taciturn Saxon, older than most of the other residents and who seemed to have few friends. He was rumoured to spend all his evenings in the underground ale-houses, and was often back in the dormitory during the day sleeping off the consequences. At least he wasn't snoring too loudly on this occasion, though William cautiously assured himself that he was indeed sleeping before unfolding the scrap of parchment which al Hannad had given him. Sure enough, it contained the man's name, Dominique de Dompierre, and a location in the local fashion, consisting of a district and a house number. The district was not far away.

William slid the parchment into his pocket and lay down on his own bunk to consider what to do. Knocking on the door of the house and asking to speak to either the man or his wife was clearly out of the question. The only possible approach William could think of was to take a walk around the area, which was central enough to have traders of various sorts selling produce and household goods from impromptu trestle tables. He hoped that he would be able to assess the location and keep an eye on any comings and goings while discussing the goods and making a few purchases. There was no point in going now, in the full heat of the day. Rather he would rest here for a couple of hours and undertake his reconnaissance later when the streets were more crowded, and of course when there were more likely to be comings and goings from the house. He would simply have to wait and see where that led, and take it from there. The next couple of hours were some of the slowest of his life, though he finally drifted off into sleep, and was woken by the early evening call to prayer.

***

The district where Dominique de Dompierre and his wife lived was close to the centre and most of the frontages were fairly wide, suggesting largish houses behind, though in the local fashion there was little to see from the street but a heavy, sky-blue painted door in an otherwise roughly plastered wall. Most of the numbers were marked in the Arabic script, but William had become familiar with the numerals from the markets – it always helped to know what the quoted price was before you started to haggle! There was a tea stall on the opposite side of the street where William could sit in the shade, apparently taking a break from the afternoon heat but with a clear view of any comings and goings.

He was soon drawn into conversation by a young Armenian who turned out to be a distant relation of Aram, which provided further cover for his presence. The late afternoon drifted by pleasantly enough with no sign of activity from the house. As the streets started to get busier again William's casual acquaintance drifted off on business of his own, and William buried his nose in some old documents he had found in a corner of the dormitory and brought with him as cover for his presence. Hopefully no-one would challenge him on his understanding of the Arabic script, which to him was just a pattern of elegant swirls and dots on the faded parchment.

The blue door was opened once to allow a delivery boy in, and again a little later for him to leave again, granting William a brief glimpse of a shady patio and a splash of purple bougainvillea within. After another, longer wait the door opened again, this time allowing a woman to emerge. William, immediately alert, noted that she was dressed in the usual modest robes of the local women, and though her face was not fully covered it was angled away from him. She was accompanied by two much younger women, barely more than girls, who carried baskets and were apparently maid-servants – a woman, and a household, of some importance, then! As the little party turned towards William, no doubt on their way to the markets, the woman's clear blue eyes briefly caught his, before she and her entourage moved swiftly on and away down the narrowing street.

William felt his heart pounding in his chest. The brief but direct glance as she passed had marked her out from the local women, who mostly lowered their eyes, but it was not that which had struck him most. Although her head was covered with an elegant silk scarf it did not fully hide her hair, her auburn hair, which despite the passing of the years still matched the curls in the casket bequeathed to him by Edwin. William sat motionless, aware of the pounding of his heart as it slowly stilled, and of the retreating figure of the woman as she disappeared into the crowd. He waited for a few more minutes, then, as if released from a trance, he picked up the parchment which had slipped, forgotten, from his hands, stood up and walked briskly back to his lodgings.

***

William felt lonelier that evening than he had at any time since the early days on the journey from Rome, deprived of confidants with whom to share the initial success, and to discuss what he should do next. Left to his own resources, he walked the streets for a while, then ordered supper in a part of the town he had not visited before, and pondered what to do.

He had little to go on. The brief glance the woman had given him as she left the house seemed hopeful; at least she had not averted her eyes automatically as most other unveiled women did. But that was a long way from thinking she would be prepared to speak with a man she did not know. Al Hannad had said that he didn't know the husband well, though he understood him to be a good man, but William reflected wryly that he would need to be more than that – he would need to be a saint – to take calmly any remotely accurate account of William's reason for approaching him or his wife.

As he expertly picked the spiciest ingredients out of the fiery goat stew which was the only dish on offer, another way of approaching Emilia occurred to William. He would write her a note, saying only that he bore news of a friend whom she had known at the time of the crusade, and deliver it via one of the messenger-boys who performed such tasks for a few dirhams. But supposing she could not read – which was likely – and gave the note to her husband? Or the messenger-boy might deliver the note direct to the head of the household. He in turn might well destroy the note, or become angry with his wife, demanding to know what the message could be about, perhaps beating her or confining her to the house. That would ruin everything.

He mulled the matter over some more, pushed his bowl aside and ordered mint-tea to justify staying a little longer. Then he thought of another variation. He would find a reliable messenger-boy who would deliver a message by word-of-mouth, though getting such a message to a woman would be especially sensitive. It occurred to him that Mohsin – a man who probably transacted some delicate business deals without too much being written down – would be able to recommend a suitable boy.

Reassured that he had at least some kind of plan in mind, William drained his glass, settled up and walked back to the lodging-house. As he made his way confidently through the tangle of dark lanes it struck him that he had begun to feel comfortable in this fascinating city, which was in fact so far from anything he could think of as home.

***

It was not until after supper-time that Mohsin returned to the lodging-house, and he disappeared into the private quarters looking tired. Disappointed, William had little choice but to fritter away the rest of the evening until he was tired enough to sleep, and put off speaking with Mohsin until the following morning. He knew none of the other lodgers, and felt lonelier than he had at any time since the early days on board ship after leaving Rome, but at the same time excited by the idea that very soon he might finally be about to fulfil the promise he had made to Edwin. That evening huddled round the fire in a draughty tavern somewhere in the wide plains of northern France seemed a world, and an age, away, but the presence of the casket hidden in his jacket made it real enough.

The following morning William slept on, and when he finally emerged into the early warmth of another day he was relieved to see his landlord still sitting in the shade at his usual table. He had a pewter jug of kahwa in front of him and, when William asked if he had a few minutes to spare, invited him to pull up a stool and poured him a glass. 'I think you appreciate our *kahva* as much as your own ale!' he smiled, and William wondered how much he knew about his residents' preferred haunts. Mohsin seemed friendlier this morning, and William suspected that his gruffness was simply a front for driving a hard bargain when he first met new arrivals or for dealing with difficult customers.

'Yes, sir, the kahwa is very good first thing in the morning!'

'Quite, quite! Well, your friends have all gone off to Jerusalem, in search of the Holy sites, no doubt,' he said with a wry smile. 'But you have stayed behind. Perhaps you have some business which you wish to transact, following your visit to your powerful friend...'

'Indeed, sir, a powerful man, who was easily able to identify the person I seek, though he made clear he could not put us in contact.'

'Ah, well, he is a man of discretion, like all successful men!'

'I don't doubt it! But it is particularly sensitive matter... because the person in question is a lady.'

'Ah! A lady... A *young* lady, perhaps?'

William could feel himself blushing and hurried on: 'Oh no, sir, not young, rather past forty years of age...and happily married, as I understand.'

'Hmm, how intriguing! And you would like to get a message to this lady in some way, but that would be risky, of course. She is unlikely to be able to read and might well pass a note straight to her husband, if she is a *respectable* woman...'

William looked down, relieved that Mohsin had grasped the nub of the problem, and hoping that he would continue his musing.

'Well, on the basis of as much as you've told me...'

William felt the rebuke and mumbled: 'It is a delicate matter, sir.'

'Yes, yes, I have understood that much! Well, given the delicacy, I should say the best thing would be to send her a spoken message. Perhaps one of my daughters – both bright girls – would be able to pass a short message to someone in the household to pass on to the lady herself, for instance via a maid-servant...'

'I saw the lady leave the house with two such servants yesterday, sir!'

'Good, good – you have done your reconnaissance! Well, you must think of a short message which will interest this lady enough for her to arrange to meet you. It seems to me she will be running quite a risk.'

'I think she will be prepared to do that, sir, when she has heard the message.' Then he thought for a moment and went on: 'The message should be: "A friend from England who knew Edwin is in Jaffa and wishes to speak with you." He hoped that this would be enough for Emilia to take the risk of meeting him, without creating the impression that Edwin was still alive. Mohsin repeated the message slowly in his heavily accented French, checked that he had it right, then made a note of the lady's name and the location of the house.

'Good, I won't ask you any more, though I can't say I'm not intrigued! In any event, leave it with me and I'll see what can be done. You seem an honourable fellow to have carried your friend's message all this way!'

'It has been a long journey, sir!'

'But now very near its end! You must continue to Jerusalem,

of course, when your purpose here is done. A holy city to all of us.'

'Indeed, sir, I shall.'

'Good, and in the meantime I'll see what I can do about the other matter here on earth.'

'Thank you, sir!' William replied, backing out and bowing respectfully at the same time in the way of the local people. He felt that Mohsin had changed from gruff landlord into a confidant and perhaps even a friend.

***

William continued to explore the city early and late, and to doze his way through the heat of the middle part of the day in the dormitory. He supplemented his dwindling funds by running a few errands for Mohsin and some of his friends and contacts, but the city seemed to offer fewer opportunities for work than Acre. During the long hours of inactivity he mulled over the possible outcomes of his mission here, and what he should do when it was settled, however it turned out, though without reaching any firm conclusions.

On the second morning Mohsin stopped him as he was leaving the house and led him into the cluttered den which served as his office. The usual glass of tea was placed in front of him and Mohsin fixed him with an amused expression before speaking.

'Well,' he said finally, 'my daughter passed on your message to the lady's maid-servant yesterday morning, and we have an answer already. It seems your message has struck a chord: the lady wishes to speak with you!'

Again William could feel his heart beating in his chest, but he merely nodded and tried to retain a calm expression.

'It seems she is cautious about the encounter, but apparently her husband is away on business in Ascalon for a few days, and she has suggested that you should come to their house tomorrow morning at the tenth hour. Her maid-servant will be waiting for you and will escort you to a room where the lady will be waiting. The maid will remain in the room throughout and will escort you out again afterwards. No-one else should even be aware of your visit.'

Mohsin paused and looked William in the eye: 'The lady is taking quite a risk. It seems she must be very eager to hear what you have to tell her!'

William nodded and measured his words carefully before replying.

'Thank you for your help, sir. It is a sensitive matter, and I hope she will not be too distressed by what I have to tell her. It was the last wish of my friend that I should do this.'

'I think I know enough already, William. I wish you well in your venture tomorrow.'

It was clear that the discussion was at a close, and William expressed his thanks again and withdrew politely.

***

The following morning William made his way again to the house where she lived, the woman he did not know but whom he had been inching his way towards for so long. When he reached the house he waited opposite until he heard the hour chime from a nearby church. He left it another few minutes before knocking at the door. It opened almost at once as if the maid-servant had been waiting for him on the other side. She signalled that he should come in, and shut the door behind him. She cast him a quick, enquiring glance before lowering her eyes, then turned with a rustle of her gown and led the way down a narrow corridor. She stopped outside a door at the far end and held it open for him to enter. He heard her slip into the room behind him and close the door almost noiselessly.

Emilia was a more imposing figure than William had expected, as she stood up from a finely upholstered couch which glowed crimson and gold in the half-light. She pointed an elegant hand to a chair positioned behind him, waited for him to sit and then sat down again herself, smoothing out her robe as she did so. The maid stood discreetly beside the door.

When Emilia finally spoke it was in the French tongue with the local, slightly guttural, accent.

'So, young man, you bring me news of the long-lost Edwin of Rochester. That is how I knew him, at least.'

'I do, madam, though I think of him only as Edwin, a dear friend from my own home-town.'

'Indeed! He was, yes, let us say, he was a friend to me for a few, short weeks some twenty years ago. A few short weeks only, though I recall it as if it were yesterday. For twenty years I have heard nothing, nothing. Then a young man arrives from out of the west with news. It is very…unsettling.'

William had imagined this interview many times over the last two years, had dreamt about it even, on occasions. He had imagined bitterness for her abandonment, though she could not know all the circumstances that had prevented her lover's return. But he had not imagined this cool and controlled sadness. It flashed across his mind that she had found true happiness with her husband and family and had put this past episode behind her. The awful thought came to him that it was perhaps better that Edwin had not lived to be here himself today…

'Madam, it may have seemed to you that Edwin abandoned you, but there were – circumstances.'

'Oh, I have always known that! The deserters who came into the city, and consorted with the likes of me, were rounded up and dragged away under armed guard to return to their soldiering. I presume Edwin told you about…my life then?'

William could feel his face reddening and looked down in his confusion. He was shocked by her directness but managed to mumble: 'Yes, madam, I believe Edwin was entirely frank with me, but I would never –'

'No, no, of course you wouldn't!' she interrupted with a half-amused glance. 'And in any case, my husband knows everything, if that's what you are worried about!'

The surprise must have registered on William's face, but Emilia only smiled, confident in her control of the situation.

'But perhaps, madam, you do not know what became of Edwin after the attack on Jerusalem was abandoned?'

She sighed.

'No, we never found out. We presumed he found passage on some ship which was returning to the west and made his way back to England. Most of the soldiers did.'

'That is what happened, up to a point, but Edwin had a further misfortune. On the journey from Jerusalem down to the coast, when the so-called deserters were still under armed guard, he fell very sick with the fever and almost died. By the time he had recovered enough to know what was happening and where he was, he was on board a ship somewhere in the Middle Sea, and still very ill. He only survived the journey back to France at all because he was tended by loyal fellow-soldiers on that ship.'

'No, we didn't know that,' Emilia murmured. 'What more can you tell me?'

'Well, madam, I can assure you that Edwin never forgot you over the last twenty years. In fact, two and a half years ago he set off from England once more, planning to return to this city and to find you again, and I came with him on that journey… for reasons of my own. I suspect Edwin felt in his heart that it was almost certainly too late. On the road he confided in me, as fellow-travellers do, the story of his time with you, with such tenderness, but then...'

'But then what...?' she asked gently, though William could see in her eyes that she had already guessed.

'I am so sorry to be the bringer of such bad tidings, and I will tell you it plainly. Edwin was killed by common thieves at an inn where we stopped for the night in our journey across France.'

Instinctively William reached out to put a hand on the woman's shoulder. He heard the maid shift uneasily behind him, but Emilia did not push his hand away as he had expected she might. Instead she sat very still, staring into nothing. Finally she spoke.

'All these years I have imagined that one day, perhaps, he would return. Now you tell me that he meant to, was on the way indeed, and now he is dead.' After a pause, she murmured, almost inaudibly: '*Requiescat in pace.*'

'His needless death grieves me greatly too, madam.' William responded.

'I am sure it does; you and he were clearly close friends,' she murmured distantly.

William waited but the woman seemed to have nothing more to say, and he spoke to fill the silence.

'Madam, I know it will be little comfort, but Edwin entrusted something to me before he died, in case he did not complete the journey. I have wondered since whether he had some kind of premonition of his own death. He made me swear that if he did not survive the long journey this time – he was no longer a young man, of course – I would complete this sacred trust.'

William reached into the inner pocket of his jacket, brought out the casket which he had carried for so long and held it out to her. She took the small package, slowly unwrapped the silken cloth, fingered the casket and then opened it. She looked at the lock of hair, looked up at William, but still there was no sign of the grief he had been expecting. Finally she said:

'A lock of my hair! Yes, I do recall exchanging these. There was a similar casket with a lock of Edwin's hair, it must still be here somewhere.'

***

When William got back to the lodging-house he went upstairs and lay down on his bunk in the corner of the dormitory. He gazed up at the cobwebbed rafters with unseeing eyes and thought over Emilia's reaction. She had placed the casket with the lock of hair on a shelf amongst some other ornaments. Then she had taken one of his hands in both hers, a rare gesture between a man and a woman in Palestine, and he thought back over exactly what her parting words to him had been.

'Thank you for coming, William of Rochester. Please do not think I am ungrateful. You have done a fine thing in fulfilling your promise to your friend – and mine. But you must understand it was all a long time ago, in a different world, and I…I was a different woman.

'A great deal of water has flowed under the bridge since then. For nearly twenty years – as both you and Edwin seem to have foreseen – I have been a loyal wife.'

She had paused, as if lost in a reverie of the past. Then she had said the most surprising thing of all.

'You must come again, and meet Dominique, my husband. He knew Edwin too, in that long lost time. He is away for a few days, but when he returns we can contact you through the young woman who brought your message and arrange a time. Now my maid will show you out.' Then she had thanked him for his visit, and held out the back of her hand for him to kiss formally, another rare sign of friendship between a man and a woman.

The loft was unusually quiet at this time of day, and as William lay there, still musing on the long-imagined encounter, he drifted off into a light sleep, filled with confused dreams which merged Edwin's journeying then and his own now, though no-one ever seemed finally to arrive…

***

The next few days passed slowly. Albrecht, Thomas and Matthias had only been gone four days, though it seemed much longer, and they would certainly not return for some time. Indeed they might well be waiting for him to join them in Jerusalem, but he could not leave while he was expecting a further message from Emilia. So each morning he walked along the coast and swam in the clear, blue sea before it got too hot, then retired to the dormitory or sat at shady kahwa stalls during the midday heat. Later in the day he explored the remoter corners of the city, before idling away the evening in one or other of the local eateries where he had come to be recognised and greeted. He sometimes chatted with other travellers from England, France or Saxony, but although most of them were around his own age he felt lonely and old, isolated from their naive excitement at finally having reached the fabled Holy Land.

Of course, he still marvelled at the strangeness and colour of Palestine, but he felt a tiredness too, an unnamed longing for something more stable, more secure. He found himself thinking back to his earliest memories: to the troubadour performances on the greensward in front of Rochester Castle; to meals around the family table where he would often drift off to sleep amidst the endless talk of the grown-ups and be carried to his bed; to days spent with Edwin at his simple cottage in the woods, learning carpentry skills or tending the vegetable patch.

But there were darker memories too from his childhood: the

frightening sermons of the priests, looming down from the pulpit of the cathedral and preaching eternal damnation for those who broke the commandments and displeased God. Surely he himself would be found wanting before them, and Him, for having left his family without a word, for all the little transgressions of daily life which he had not confessed over the years, most of all for his forbidden love for Gilles? Then he recalled the planned marriage and shuddered... Yes, he had been right to leave that behind!

If he had not done so he would never have had those truly joyous months in Beziers, before the city and its people were torn asunder. But there, perhaps, lay the key. He should have sacrificed more to hold on to Gilles. He had not separated from him willingly, of course. He had done so finally because he had been bound by his first real friendship to continue to his goal, to find Emilia, to assure her that Edwin's love had never weakened – even if her response had not been what either of them could have expected. And what of Gilles himself? The parting in Rome, surely driven by loyalty to his own people, can have been no less painful for him? Not loyalty to his immediate family of course; he could have been left in no doubt that they had perished after the dreadful final visit the two of them had made to the ruins of Beziers and the church of Saint Mary Magdalene. But to his people, to the gentle Cathars, with their thoughtfulness and compassion, and their lives of devotion to a simple belief in goodness beyond this fallen world.

For now, of course, William had unfinished business here in Palestine. He must wait for the further message from Emilia, though it found it hard to imagine that the encounter with her and her husband would be anything other than awkward. When that was done, he would be free to follow his friends to Jerusalem, fulfilling the more usual pilgrimage which brought travellers from the west on the long road to the east.

But the germ of an idea had begun to take shape in his mind

of what he should do when both these quests had been fulfilled. He found that he slept more soundly if he played with these thoughts last thing at night before drifting off.

***

On the third morning after the meeting with Emilia, Mohsin called William into his den after breakfast, offered him a glass of kahwa, and told him that a further message had come from the lady. She invited her young friend to visit again, an hour before sundown on the same day, when her husband would also be present. Having imparted this news, Mohsin fixed his young guest with his intelligent eyes and added: 'It seems the whole family wishes to make your acquaintance.' It was not a question, but William nonetheless felt a reply was expected.

'Indeed, the lady did tell me she would invite me again at a time when her husband was there.' He paused, then added: 'It seems he knew my friend Edwin too in those days.'

Mohsin's eyebrow rose marginally. 'Well, well, the tale becomes more and more intriguing!' Then, seeing William's concerned expression, he made a reassuring gesture with his hand and grinned. 'Don't worry, William, I won't pry further, and a merchant always knows how to keep a secret!'

William's expression relaxed. He thanked Mohsin for all his help in the matter and left him to his accounting. He spent the rest of the day as he had the last few, and was ready resting on his bunk by late afternoon. He had smartened up his appearance as far as possible for someone who had been on the road and lived out of a knapsack for longer than he cared to remember, but he still felt nervous at meeting the husband of his own dear friend's long-lost love. Dominique de Dompierre had no reason to look kindly on this intrusion into his evidently settled life with Emilia.

***

When William knocked once more on the solid blue door there was a slightly longer wait and then it was opened by a man-servant dressed in a crisp white robe and turban. He invited William in and led the way further into the house, which was larger than William had realised on his first visit, ushering him into a wood-panelled room where a finely dressed man in early middle-age stood up to greet him. Dominique de Dompierre was an imposing figure, but he held out a hand in the Christian manner and smiled encouragingly at William, who relaxed immediately.

'I am honoured to meet you, sir!' he murmured in French.

'And I am delighted to meet you too, young man, please take a seat,' de Dompierre replied, signalling to one of two chairs which had been set up in a corner as if expressly for a man to man discussion.

'Though, of course,' he continued, 'I understand from my wife that you bring us sad news of dear Edwin.'

William was taken by surprise, both by the older man's relaxed manner and by the easy and affectionate way in which he spoke of Edwin. It seemed that Emilia and her husband had few secrets from one another, but nonetheless he reminded himself that he must tread carefully.

'Indeed, sir, but before Edwin died he spoke to me of the lady who is now your wife, and asked my to seek her out should he not complete his own journey…'

'Quite, quite!' de Dompierre murmured. 'But you look somewhat uncomfortable, young man. There is no need – I wanted to meet you separately in order to reassure you of that, man to man! My wife and I have no secrets from one another. How could we, given that dear Edwin and I both visited the house where the woman who is now my wife had the misfortune to find herself in those days? Though I should say she found herself there through cruel circumstance rather than any fault of her own.'

William's mind was reeling: what could he mean? Was Emilia's husband saying that *he* too had visited the house where…

'You look shocked, young man! Perhaps Edwin did not tell you everything? You see, he and I went together into the town on those long-ago nights, when we were still young men! Ah, how young we were; we could not imagine then how quickly youth would fade!'

'But, sir… I am all at sea!' William mumbled. 'Edwin told me he went to… the house… with a soldier friend of his called Oliver, whom he lost track of after he was rounded up and forced to return to the army. He never found out what…' But de Dompierre interrupted with a great guffaw and slapped William on the shoulder.

'Dear boy, did he speak of me as Oliver! My middle name is Olivier and that's what he always called me. In return I called him Roland, like in the Chanson de Geste, surely you know it? "Roland is bold, and Oliver is wise." It was our little joke!'

And he sat back in his chair and chuckled, clearly taken back to this adventure of his youth. William was trying to catch up and put the pieces together. The Oliver of Edwin's sad story was in fact Dominique Olivier de Dompierre, the happy and successful man who sat before him now, the husband of Emilia! He could only suppose that after Edwin had been rounded up, Oliver had somehow avoided the same fate, and had rescued Emilia from the brothel, fallen in love with her and married her. Edwin had always thought of his friend as Oliver, and he had referred to him as such when he had told William the story. He had not mentioned that Oliver was French, but of course the crusader armies had contained men from all over Christendom.

De Dompierre sat back and looked more serious. 'Dear boy – may I call you William? – you have brought sad news to both me and my wife, but at the same time you have cleared up a mystery. My wife explained to me the reasons which made Edwin unable to return and, well, perhaps in the circumstances it is good that he did not turn round in Marseille and come back to find her. Even the friendship of Oliver and Roland might not have survived that! But I am equally grateful, as is my dear Emilia, that you have come now, a voice from the past, however much the news of his tragic death grieves us both. I like to think that if he had completed his last journey, after the passing of the years we could all have become great friends and rested easy with the past…'

He paused and both men sat sunk in thought for several minutes. Then de Dompierre looked up and spoke more briskly.

'And now, William, my wife and I would be pleased if you would join us for dinner.'

'I would like that very much, sir!' William replied.

***

When the evening finally drew to a close, William and Dominique embraced as friends, and the younger man shyly kissed Emilia's hand. She smiled at him and expressed the wish that they would meet often as long as he remained in Jaffa. The generous couple had offered him a room in their house for as long as he wished to stay, but William, after a moment of hesitation, had replied that in the short term he was planning to make the pilgrimage to Jerusalem, joining three friends who were already there. But he willingly accepted the invitation to visit again when he returned, and to share more stories of his childhood, his travels and his time in Rome.

He walked home, feeling strangely at ease as he made his way confidently through the darkened maze of streets and alleyways. He mused on the delightful evening he had spent, the warmth of the welcome he had received and the relief he felt that he had, at last, fulfilled his pledge to his much-lamented friend. He caught himself once or twice, instinctively reaching to feel for the casket sewn in the lining of his jacket, before realising that, of course, it was no longer there. He had noticed it at once, placed centrally on the mantelpiece above the fire in the comfortable dining-room of Dominique and Emilia's fine home. Alongside it stood another, similar casket.

William's thoughts returned also to Emilia's strangely cool reaction when he had first imparted the news of Edwin's untimely death. It seemed to him now that her muted reaction may in fact have been signs of her shock and grief, and perhaps also of embarrassment at the sudden arrival of an unknown person, bearing such dramatic news of long ago. She and her husband must have thought of those events as closed for ever, and in that light he could only marvel at the courtesy and kindness with which they had welcomed him into their house and into their hearts. Now that they had had time to absorb the news, the casket bearing the physical symbol of their continuing affection for his memory had been given its rightful place, alongside its pair.

One other thought occurred to him, which was that there had been no mention of children, and no sign of other people living in the house, apart from the servants. Dominique and Emilia de Dompierre clearly led settled and affluent lives, and were respected figures in the city, but William had noted a sadness too, at odd moments later in the evening when the conversation faltered and the couple sat side by side and gazed silently into the embers of the fire, sunk in their own thoughts. No doubt he would get to know them better on subsequent visits, but for now he was in sight of the lodging house door, which to his relief was still open at the late hour, and his comfortable bunk was calling him.

***

The next day, as William sat over his morning kahwa and one of the fresh rolls smeared with spicy paste which the street vendors sold, his thoughts turned to the future. His immediate plans were clear: he should continue to Jerusalem and join his friends. They had already been gone a week and if he left it much longer they might already be on the return journey. He knew that the camel trains left at first light to complete the journey during the day, so he would walk out to the departure point outside the east gate after breakfast and see if he could book a place for the following day. It should be possible to keep an eye open for returning travellers on the road in case his friends were planning to come back the same day, though he was not sure what he would do if they met on the road.

Mohsin joined William for a few minutes before retiring to his den. His role in helping him contact Emilia had turned the landlord into something approaching a confidant, though William was careful not to betray too many secrets. He didn't say much more than that the woman and her husband had been hospitable and courteous, and had invited him to visit again. He repeated his own gratitude to Mohsin for his role in helping him fulfil his pledge to his dead friend. Mohsin held up his hand and murmured that it had been but a trivial thing. He was still curious, of course, but he understood that William felt honour bound not to tell him too much.

***

Reserving a place on a camel-train leaving at dawn the next day turned out to be a simple task. There were a number of ticket-sellers who crowded round William as soon as he emerged from the gates, and he had selected the most respectable-looking one and taken him aside to negotiate a price. After some discussion he had agreed a rate which seemed to tally with what his friends had paid. He was assured that there would be no more than a dozen travellers in the party, which held out the promise of a quicker journey than in a larger group where there would be more people to arrive late or cause delays. He paid the fee in advance, and was given a copper token inscribed with some illegible script. This should be presented next morning to the leader of the group, who would be wearing a blue turban. With this business done, there was little for William to do for the rest of the day other than to take his usual walk along the beach, swim for a half-hour or so, and return to the lodgings in the heat of the day. In the evening he would have to settle up with Mohsin, pack his few belongings and arrange to be woken two hours before dawn to be outside the city walls in time for the departure.

As he walked out along the coast, William put Jerusalem out of his mind for now. It would of course be wonderful to visit such a famous city, to see the sights he had heard tell of and imagined since childhood, and the travellers who must come from all corners of the world for reasons of religion or trade. He would not miss it now he was so close, but his mind was more and more taken up with the longer term. He had travelled enough, seen enough wonders, found friends and lost them again and now he longed for stability, for a sense of belonging, of being on the inside not on the outside. He asked himself again where he had been happiest. In the blithe days of childhood when everything was strange and new and exciting? Yes, of course he had been happy then, and he was grateful for that, but he shuddered when his thoughts returned to his father's expectations and the plans for marriage to Agnes. His first true friendship had been with Edwin, but the older man had been thwarted and disappointed in life, and – as William now knew – if he had completed his journey to Palestine, the reunion would have been at best bittersweet. And yet, the further thought came to him that perhaps Edwin, gentle soul that he was, would have taken comfort in the happiness which his lover and his dear friend had found together...

The half-year spent in Rome had been an exciting time, when he had had a real sense of being part of the city through his work. But he could not forget that it was the same Church he had worked for which had unleashed the whirlwind of the crusade on the kind and gentle Cathars of the Languedoc. It was the same church which, only a generation ago, had led the fight against the so-called infidels here in Palestine, some of whom he had got to know in the final stages of his journey, and who he now knew for the most part to be good men and women seeking to follow their God, to live out their lives in peace, to bring up their families.

So, as always in these times of reflection, William's thoughts finally looped back to the few, wonderful months he had spent in Beziers, before that peaceful city and its good people had been swept away in a whirlwind of destruction and hate. In his mind's eye he saw again the city of yellowed stone, huddled within its encircling walls and backed by a sparkling sea. It shimmered before his eyes just as it had on the warm spring evening of his arrival, which now seemed so long ago. Most of all, his thoughts returned to the kindness and gentleness of the people who had lived there, and to his time with Gilles.

He dozed under a clump of ragged palms during the heat of the afternoon, then strolled back into the city, ate a light supper and returned early to the lodging house which had quickly come to feel like a sort of home. He settled his bill amicably with Mohsin, then thanked him with all the formal language of politeness and gratitude he had picked up during the last few weeks in the city. Mohsin dismissed his role in helping William find 'the woman he had been seeking' and they embraced in the local manner. William explained that he would be staying with his new friends when he returned, and felt a sudden pang of sadness at being on the move once more. He would make the final pilgrimage, to Jerusalem itself, and then…well, then he knew what he must do.

***

It was pitch black outside when one of the lads whom Mohsin employed as night-watchmen woke William in the cold hour before the dawn. He threw on his clothes, washed his face at the pump, sealed up his pack and gratefully accepted the parcel wrapped in a palm-leaf which Mohsin had left for him and which he guessed would be a tasty breakfast. He shook the boy's hand, asked him to thank his master again for all his kindness, and set off through the dark lanes. The city had not yet woken, though a few figures huddled in blankets glided past him in the gloom. When he emerged from the city through the crumbling East Gate, he was relieved to see lights, a crowd of ticket touts and would-be travellers, and slightly further off several trains of camels being prepared. The final approach to Jerusalem was clearly a busy route.

The man in the blue turban was easy to find; he greeted William gruffly, took his token and grabbed his pack to be loaded on the pack-camel. There was a crowd gathered around the food-stalls and William was grateful that he did not need to join them. He bought a terracotta cup of kahwa and drifted across to the group of camels which the man in the blue turban had pointed out. There was still some time to go before the dawn departure, and no sign of the baggage being loaded, so he sat down on a scrubby dune and unwrapped his breakfast, which as he had guessed consisted of flatbreads smeared with a spicy vegetable paste; along with the kahwa it made a good and warming start to the day. From here he had a good view of the camels being loaded and the others travellers arriving, so that he could stroll down as soon as there was any sign of the camels being allocated. A large beast standing slightly apart from the group looked the least restive.

The party finally left half-an-hour after dawn, but William was content because he was comfortably mounted on the large camel which he had picked out. The last arrivals, two irritable Saxons with an excessive amount of baggage, were having to share an equally irritable-looking camel, which already seemed to be trying to shrug off its double-load. William smiled to himself and felt like an old hand.

***

It was a long day's ride, with only a brief stop for lunch in the searing heat of midday. By the time their destination came into view the sun was dropping towards the horizon behind the weary travellers, lighting up the massive ochre walls which towered over them as they approached the Holy City. William already knew that those walls had been rebuilt by the victorious infidels at the end of the crusade in which Edwin had fought and the Christians had been defeated. He knew too, that as part of the peace treaty which King Richard and the other leaders of the crusade had negotiated with Saladin, Christian pilgrims were granted access to the city to visit their holy sites. It seemed a strange situation, even if his own simple assumptions about the rightness of Christianity and the falsity of other beliefs had been broken by the experiences he had gone through: the horrific massacre of the simple, devout people of Beziers by the armies of Christ; and the kindly and generous Moslems he had encountered in Palestine, who lived in peace alongside the

Christians who had come as invaders and occupied much of their land.

As the camels drew up in the corral outside the great Jaffa Gate into the city, snorting and eager to be free of their burden, there were more practical matters to attend to. William collected his pack, thanked the guides who had remained cheerful throughout, and sighed as the two Saxons approached them and started to argue about some supposed theft from their bags. If it was true it served them right! He shouldered his own pack and made his way through the gate into the teeming western districts. He was immediately struck by the size of the city and the limited chance of running into his friends, though they had agreed they would seek lodgings as centrally as possible, and that one of them at least would be outside the Church of the Holy Sepulchre at the tenth hour each morning. For now, William's priorities were to seek out lodgings for himself somewhere nearby, to have something to eat and then to fall into bed for a good night's sleep after the long and tiring day. He turned into the bustling alleys, in what he hoped was the right direction. Immediately, he was caught up in the excitement of the city.

William had already heard plenty of reports from returning travellers. He knew that this was a city unlike any other, and although it had its traders and business-people its primary role was as a city of God. Or rather, a city of Gods, sacred not just to Christians, but equally to Jews and to Moslems. Even so, the impression that the ancient, yellowing stone, twisting alleys and sudden imposing vistas made on him that first evening was overpowering. Jerusalem, the centre of the world!

Lodgings would clearly not be hard to find, though he turned down the first place he was shown which looked overcrowded and dirty. The second was better, and he was offered a bunk in at attic dormitory where the air was a little fresher. The other guests seemed mostly to be pilgrims like – or maybe not quite like – himself. He paid for one night, then went out to a simple eatery for a plate of lamb stew, and a glass of mint tea which was the only drink on offer. If ale was available here at all it would no doubt be more hidden than elsewhere. The cheerful buzz of the other customers, apparently of all faiths and races, was sufficient company, and he ate alone and returned directly to the lodgings. He wrapped his valuables securely inside his pack which doubled as a pillow overnight, curled up on his bunk and fell straight into a deep slumber, undisturbed by dreams.

***

William slept late the following morning, and when he finally surfaced the sun was shining obliquely across the attic. The only other guest who was still there told him that the ninth hour had long since struck, and William hurried to get dressed, rinse his face at the pump in the courtyard and make his way to the meeting place where he hoped to find the familiar face of Albrecht, Thomas or Matthias waiting for him. He had to ask the way to the Church of the Holy Sepulchre several times; each time an arm was waved in one direction or another, along with some garbled instructions, but each time he was soon lost again in the tangle of streets, alleyways and covered markets. Some time after the bells had rung the tenth hour he emerged into a larger square, face to face with the massive façade and dome of the church marking the burial place of Christ. The main entrance was right in front of him, flanked on one side by a massive bell-tower and on the other by a crowded flight of steps which, he would later learn, led up to the Rock of Golgotha, site of Christ's crucifixion. For now, he noticed only that Matthias was sitting on the bottom step, scanning the crowd. William waved and hurried across to him, and the two friends greeted one another with an embrace.

'One of us has waited for you here every day – we were beginning to think you weren't coming!' Matthias exclaimed.

'Oh, no, I wouldn't have missed this,' William replied, with a sweep of his arm to take in all the wonders of the city, 'but my business in Jaffa took a little longer than expected. It had quite an unexpected outcome, but a good one! That can wait, though, it's quite a long story. But what have you seen here, how are the others?'

'Oh, it's beyond imagining – all the sites from the Gospel stories brought to life! Yesterday we were on Mount Zion in the very hall where Christ ate the last supper, and such a throng of people, from all over the Christian world and far beyond. There are merchants from Cathay – that's six months' journey away across deserts and mountains, so they told us – staying at our lodgings at the moment. They come to trade wonderful cloths of silk, perfumes and spices from the east, wear heavy robes in rich, dark colours and have such strange smooth faces and narrow black eyes. But you'll soon see it all for yourself!'

'I certainly intend to,' William replied, reeling from his friend's excited outpouring, 'but how are the others?'

'Oh, they're fine. They went out early this morning to explore the Mount of Olives and the Garden of Gethsemane just outside the city, but they should be back by now and waiting for us in a little street of kahwa shops near our lodgings.'

'Fine, let's go! And, Matthias…'

'What?'

'It's wonderful to see a familiar face again after spending the last few days on my own.'

'Ha, ha! Well, it's good to see you too!' he replied, throwing a companionable arm round his friend's shoulder and leading him back into the maze which he seemed to have become quite familiar with already.

The welcome from Albrecht and Thomas was equally warm

and the friends sat together over glasses of kahwa for an hour or so, catching up with one another's experiences. They listened with interest to William's tale of his visits first to the woman he had come all this way to find, and then to meet her and her husband who, as it turned out, had also known William's old friend from England. Even now William omitted the most personal details of the story, relating as they did to a couple now happily married and living as respectable members of the community in Jaffa.

William's friends slapped him on the back and congratulated him on the success of his mission. Albrecht, who had known William the longest and tended him through his almost fatal illness on the journey from Rome, had watched his friend closely as he told his tale, and felt again that there were depths to him that he had not fathomed, and probably never would.

For now, they had spent enough time hunched over the rough wooden table, and decided to visit together the vast, and conveniently close, Church of the Holy Sepulchre and the adjoining *souks*, before finding a cool spot to doze away the heat of the day.

William circulated around this great monument of Christianity with the vast crowd of pilgrims and travellers, who were dressed in every style from rough hemp tunics, through heavy robes, to beautiful brocades and who seemed to be speaking all the languages of the world – the Tower of Babel brought to life once again! He drifted past chapels and carvings, holy relics of bone and of crimson blood in tiny vials, gaudily painted statues of the Virgin Mary and tombs of popes and bishops of the Church. Separated from his friends, he shuffled up for his turn at the most sacred spot of all, the shrine marking the crucifixion of Christ. As he squeezed into the dark, crowded space, a wizened old woman gestured to the crack in the Rock of Golgotha, created when the earth shook and the rocks split at the moment of Christ's death… The crone stretched out her wrinkled hand and stick-like arm for alms and William pressed a coin into her palm. But he could not feel the sort of reverence which seemed to move his fellow pilgrims, who crowded all around him, crossing themselves and praying noisily. Another image haunted him, of the armies of Christ breaking into the city of Beziers, mounted four abreast on their huge, snorting chargers, slaying the gentle and defenceless people…He followed the example of the throng around him and crossed himself, but as he did so he raised up a prayer for the souls of the simple people who had been slaughtered in Christ's name that day. Surely a loving God could not have condemned *them* to the flames of hell?

***

Back outside in the heat of the mid-afternoon, William sat quietly on a low wall in the shade and waited for his friends. They emerged not long after, spotted him and strolled across, full of chatter about the wonderful, glowing frescos and the realistic statues of the saints they had seen, compared to the simpler images and figures they knew from the churches in their homeland. They sat down alongside William but were too preoccupied to notice how distant he was. Finally they quietened down, and Albrecht turned to him and asked what he was thinking. He looked up distantly and, after a pause, said: 'It was very moving. It made me think of a dear friend I left behind in Rome and……and of some people I once knew.'

When he sank back into his own thoughts, Albrecht turned to the others, shrugged slightly and said:

'Well, how about if we all go up to the Mount of Olives? Matthias and William haven't been there yet, and there's a great view of the whole city! *And*, we noticed this morning that there should be enough shade under the larger trees to doze the afternoon away...'

Matthias expressed his enthusiasm for the idea at once, then William looked up and nodded his agreement.

***

The rest of the day passed pleasantly enough. Despite what Albrecht had said, the heat was still intense up on the Mount of Olives, but there was some shade and now and again a slight breeze coming up from the sea to the west. Hawkers with great pewter canisters strapped to their backs were selling kahwa in terracotta cups, and older peasant women came round offering baskets of fruit, mostly slices of water melon and small, bitter oranges.

William remained distracted, sitting quietly a little apart from the others. Albrecht, who knew him best, murmured to Thomas and Matthias that he'd heard scraps of William's story before, of a happy time in the distant Languedoc but which had come to a bitter end and of a close friend whom he had parted from in Rome. He assured them that it was better to leave William in peace when he needed it.

Thomas and Matthias were happy to follow their friend's advice. As far as all three Saxons were concerned, simply being in the Holy City was the experience of a lifetime and one they were determined to make the most of. One day they would tell stories to their own children and grandchildren of the long journey they had undertaken as young men, and of the wonders they had seen. They would conjure up for their rapt audience these same sights through their story-telling, and perhaps would even inspire them to make the same journey themselves. It did not cross their minds that, when their pilgrimage had been fulfilled, they would do anything other than return to their homelands, to the town of their birth, marry and raise a family.

William, listening quietly to their chatter about the sights they had seen, and the fund of tales they would have to tell, understood all this. For him, the choices about the future course of his life were not so simple. The connection to his upbringing in distant Rochester had been broken by all that had happened to him since he had left England on that distant stormy night, which seemed so long ago.

***

The four friends remained in Jerusalem for another week, visiting and revisiting the great sights and relaxing in quieter corners during the day, and offering advice to new arrivals as they flooded in every evening, weary after the journey up from Jaffa but wide-eyed at the wonders around them.

At the same time, the other three were starting to discuss their route home. They had come via the mountain passes through Helvetia, and then travelled by ship from Venice, the city of the lagoon, but the mountain crossing had been gruelling and they were now considering returning by the more westerly route, travelling by ship all the way to Marseille and then heading north through France and so back to their homeland through easier, flatter terrain. They would need to find work in Palestine before setting off, if they were to build up sufficient funds for the ship and at least part of the further land journey, and in any case it was already the ninth month and they did not want to be travelling north during the winter. So gradually a plan began to emerge, which suited three of the four friends. They would travel back down to the coast and find work in Jaffa or Acre for the winter, which apparently could get surprisingly cool and rainy, before seeking out a ship for the return journey across the Middle Sea in the spring.

William did not take part in these conversations, and his friends did not press him, recognising that he was struggling with choices, and maybe demons, they knew little about. But once, when they were asking him about the ease of finding work along the road in France, he mused that maybe he would come with them, at least as far as Marseille. They welcomed the idea with enthusiasm, though without pressing him further.

So, at first light on a surprisingly chilly morning two days later, the group of four young men found themselves once again being allocated camels at the departure point outside the city walls, for the journey down to Jaffa. The novelty had worn off and they felt like old hands as they clamped their legs firmly round their 'ships of the desert' as the friendly guides called the camels, and set off. For the first time on their travels, the sun was rising fiery-red directly behind them.

William passed the journey sunk in the thoughts which had preoccupied him for months, and which were now beginning to take shape into some kind of way forward. The happiness which he had known in Beziers two short years ago could never be recreated – the crusaders had seen to that and he was the least of their victims! The Beziers he had known was no more, of that there could be no doubt. But equally he knew that the Cathars had been a much wider community, spread across the lush and rolling countryside of the Languedoc and reaching up into the mountains to the south. Surely such good people and their generous and open-hearted faith could not have been totally wiped out? Surely God, if there was a God of loving kindness, could not have allowed that?

And so, he would return to the place where, for a few brief months, he had been happiest. He did not dare let the thought surface that he would also be seeking out the person who had made that happiness complete.

The first stage of the journey passed uneventfully, and that evening all four of them were safely installed in Mohsin's clean loft dormitory and feeling like old hands. The Syrian had greeted the returnees as friends and allocated them to bunks at the quieter far end of the loft. Over supper they discussed their next move. The three Saxons needed to restore their funds for the journey and were eager to move on to Acre where there would be more opportunities for work. William's funds were also running low, but he did not intend to leave Jaffa immediately, explaining that he wanted to spend more time with the long-lost acquaintances of his former travelling companion, who had indeed urged him to visit them again when he returned from Jerusalem.

The friends agreed that the advance party of three would continue the journey to Acre the next day, having already established that Mohsin would be able to send one of the errand-boys to book their places. When they got to Acre they would seek lodgings with William's old landlord and employer Aram, or leave a message there if he had no room for them. William grinned and said he hoped that his friends wouldn't have taken all the best jobs before he got there! He himself would stay in Jaffa for a few weeks, long enough to spend more time with Emilia and Dominique before making the journey to Acre himself. When they were all ready for the sea crossing, they would seek out a ship together to take them back to the west by whatever route was on offer.

Tired out by their long day in the saddle, and with two more similar days ahead for Albrecht, Thomas and Matthias, they were more than ready to turn in, and were soon all asleep. William slept soundly and dreamlessly that night, now that his return to the west was settled, and would be undertaken with reliable friends to share the inevitable highs and lows along the way.

***

When William awoke the next morning shards of dusty sunlight were shining through the cracks in the roof and the dormitory was almost deserted; only a couple of older men were still asleep, snoring heavily, at the far end. William guessed it was around the tenth hour, but there was no pressure to get up and he dozed for another hour before doing so, washing at the pump in the courtyard and strolling in for a chat with Mohsin. The landlord, who now felt like an old friend, greeted him and signalled that he should sit down.

'Well,' he said, 'your three companions left early and should be well into another long day's journey by now! These Saxons must be made of strong stuff; not many travellers have the stamina for three days on camel-back without a rest-day in Jaffa. Of course, the longer you travellers stop here the better it is for my business!'

'Yes, I hadn't thought of that. Well, you'll be pleased then that I'll be staying a few days longer before I catch up with my friends in Acre.'

'I'm glad to hear it! But then you have acquaintances here in Jaffa now.'

William smiled. 'Yes, of course, and I thank you again for having helped me to find and contact them. I shall go to their house today to say that I've returned and would be pleased to visit them again.'

'Ah, well, you can deliver your own messages now without fear of detection! It's good to know that our little intrigue has ended happily.'

William smiled gratefully and could tell that Mohsin was hoping to learn a little more, but he replied simply:

'Yes, sir, thanks to you and your daughter it has!'

***

The heat was already building in the narrow lanes by the time William found himself once again outside the now familiar sky-blue door; it felt like coming home. The servant-girl showed him in and signalled that he should wait in the narrow hallway. He sat down on a velvet settle placed along the wall, and cast an eye over the fine wood-carving which covered the opposite wall to waist-height with delicate branches and leaves based on the local vines. He didn't have long to admire the craftsmanship before Emilia herself appeared and greeted him warmly. He stood, smiling, and kissed her proffered hand with an elegant bow.

'Madam, it is a pleasure to see you again. I hope you will excuse the intrusion at this early hour.'

'Dear William, I am delighted to see you back with us so soon – I trust your visit to Jerusalem went well? But, please, do call me by my Christian name. Dominique and I have talked of little but your visit over the last few days, and we were both so glad you came. It was a long road for you, and yet you followed it to the end, to fulfil your promise to our mutual friend. Both Dominique and I have always hoped there would one day be news, but with no real hope that it would come after all this time...

'But what am I doing, chattering on, when I should be showing you some hospitality! Won't you come in and take a glass of tea and tell me something of your visit to the Holy City. It is several years since I have been there.'

'I would be honoured, Madam – that is, I mean, Emilia. I had expected only to leave a message.'

'Oh, you are like one of the family to us now, William. There is no need to stand on ceremony.'

Emilia turned and led the way with a rustle of her long, crimson gown into a small sitting room, which led off the main room where they had dined before. This was a more private space, with a clutter of ornaments and heavy tapestry hangings on the walls. William noticed that one featured Saint George slaying the dragon, and wondered if that was a subtle reminder of the couple's long-lost English acquaintance, but then reminded himself of something he had learnt from his travels: that Saint George was claimed by many other peoples than just the English. The maid reappeared with a silver jug of tea, a dish of honey and delicate crimson and turquoise drinking glasses. She filled a glass for each of them, leaving the jug on the low six-sided table. William waited for Emilia to stir a little honey into her glass, then smiled at his hostess and said:

'It is so kind of you to welcome me into your home like this. I was, after all, the bearer of bad news, which might have disrupted your household.'

'Dear William,' Emilia replied at once, almost interrupting, 'not at all! Dominique and I talked late into the night after you had left that evening, and we were so grateful that you had come. The news of Edwin's death was a bitter blow, of course, but it was so – so moving to hear from you that he had wanted to return, in middle age, to make his peace with the past. We felt he could have held out little hope of finding me still waiting for him. But if he had been able to complete his journey we would both have welcomed him back as a dear friend. We would like to think we could all have put the past behind us and found a different kind of friendship at this stage of our lives. You will learn soon enough, William, that life flies past like scudding clouds. You must reach out for happiness when it is at hand. It will not wait and it may not come again!'

William could feel the tears welling up in his eyes as Emilia spoke and when he looked up she could see the pain there, though she did not fully understand it.

'William, do not weep, you have your life before you. You

have already seen and experienced more than many men see in a lifetime, and now, I feel, you should return to your own people, find your own place in life, and if God looks kindly on you, your own true love.'

Then William's tears finally came, in great, heaving sobs. This woman he barely knew reached out to him, put her hand on his shoulder, and he leant forward, buried his head in her enfolding arm and wept. He wept for the brutal loss of his first real friend, but he wept too for the gentle people of Beziers, and he wept for having left Gilles to return alone to his stricken homeland. He was unaware that Emilia was weeping too, silently, for Edwin's death, but also for that of the only child she had ever carried to term, who had survived but a week, and who might have been his.

***

By the time William left the house he had regained his composure, apologised for his weeping and been earnestly reassured that there was no need. Emilia had invited him to return that very evening and to stay in their house for as long as he remained in Jaffa, and assured him that Dominique too would be delighted with the arrangement – indeed he had suggested it. She had not mentioned her own tears, which William had feigned not to notice.

Mohsin greeted the news that William would be staying with his new friends for the rest of his time in Jaffa philosophically, but was gratified when William insisted on paying for two more nights. He sent him on his way with a friendly embrace in the Moslem manner, and wished him God's protection on the long journey back to the west. William thanked him and promised to call on him again before his final departure from Jaffa.

He packed his bag, left it in Mohsin's office and strolled

through the market district for an hour or so, purchasing gifts for his hosts of Arabian figs and spices, and a silk scarf for Emilia. Then he found a shady spot to doze for an hour or so during the heat of the afternoon, before picking up his bag and returning to his new, grander lodgings. The maid-servant greeted him with a shy smile, explained in broken French that her master was out and her mistress was sleeping and showed him to his room. It was a simple, white-painted room but airy and more comfortable than anywhere he had slept for many months and he curled up contentedly on the bed to pass the time until the house came to life again. The pain he had felt during the earlier discussion with Emilia had dissipated, replaced by a sadness, mingled with increasing clarity about what he should do next. What was it that Emilia had said? *You should return to your own people, find your own place in life, and if God looks kindly on you, find your own true love...* She had no doubt meant England, but for William her words could have another meaning, of which she had been unaware.

The bed was soft and comfortable and the next thing he knew, the call for the Moslem evening prayer was ringing out over the city. He washed using the water-tank in an inner courtyard which the maid had shown him, smartened up his appearance as best he could and made his way back to the living rooms.

Emilia and Dominique were sitting on either side of the hearth, which was unused at this time of year and decorated with palm fronds, though William could imagine it was needed in the winter months. His new friends stood up at once and welcomed him warmly, Dominique slapping him on the back like an old acquaintance.

'Dear William, so good to see you again! How did you find the Holy City? Sit down and tell us all about it.'

A third chair was pulled up and William sat down, then

found the maid hovering at his shoulder with a tray.

'Help yourself William! There's the local red wine, or pomegranate juice if you prefer...'

'I've not drunk wine since I was in Rome...'

'Well, you won't find the local population drinking it, but since the Frankish Kingdom was established settlers have always grown some vines in the hills and supplied it privately to customers in the cities. Here, take a glass! You won't find it in Jerusalem, of course, which is under Moslem control, but here in Jaffa and in Acre too it's drunk behind closed doors. Relations between the two groups here are generally quite relaxed, as no doubt you've noticed, but there's no reason to risk upsetting that by drinking alcohol too openly. I understand there are bars in the back-streets that serve a pale imitation of beer to travellers.'

William felt himself blushing as he muttered: 'Indeed there are, sir!'

The older man laughed. 'Well, you would know more about that than me! But, please, call me Dominique – we are friends now! You must tell us more about your latest travels – is Jerusalem as crowded as ever?'

They moved to the dinner-table soon after, more wine was brought and the conversation flowed easily. William found himself recounting not just his traveller's tales and the adventures of his journey. As the evening proceeded he unburdened himself of much that he had not spoken of so openly since Gilles had been his confidant. He talked of his upbringing in Rochester, of his father's expectations and his own very different dreams of travel and adventure. He told the tale he had told round the dinner-table in Beziers to Gilles' family, of his secretly following Edwin down to Romney and joining him on his own quest to return to Palestine, which as his hosts already knew, had been so cruelly cut short. He talked of his journey south through France, into ever warmer climes, and so to Beziers. He described his arrival in the city and the chance meeting with Gilles, who would become a dear friend. He told of Gilles' kindly family who had taken him into their home and their hearts. He talked of the gentle Cathars, of their simplicity, generosity and kindness.

But he had to speak too of the crusaders who came from the north, some of them from his own land, bent on wiping out these simple people in the name of the Roman Church. He glossed over the worst of the destruction of the city, but he could not hide the pain in his voice and his eyes as he recalled it. He said that it seemed that no-one had survived, apart from himself and Gilles who had managed by pure chance to escape. He described the terrifying descent from the city, Gilles' agony at leaving behind all he had known, and the awful return which had left no doubt that there were no other survivors. Emilia leant forward and put an arm on William's shoulder as the tears welled up.

'Your friend's loss must have been terrible,' she said simply, 'but at least he had your love to comfort him in his time of need.'

'Yes,' William replied, and paused for some time fighting back the tears before he could continue.

Then he moved on. He recounted the journey down the coast to Marseille, the ship to Rome, and the time they had spent there. He told somewhat ruefully of his work for the Church, of which he was now ashamed, considering the destruction that that same institution had brought down on the simple and kindly people of Beziers. At the time it had seemed justified as the quickest way to earn money for the onward journey; now he looked back on it as a shameful episode.

Then he told of the last leg of his journey, and of the bitter decision of the two friends to separate, though with William's promise that he would return to the Languedoc and seek Gilles out when his quest in Palestine was fulfilled. He described the journey from Rome along the coasts of the Middle Sea and eventually to Acre, though he explained that he remembered little of the later stages himself because he had been struck down by fever. He owed his life to good Saxon friends, most of all Albrecht who had looked after him in his hour of need.

William and his hosts sat quietly for some time after he had finished the story of his life, and of the travels which had brought him from remote England to the Holy Land.

Finally, Emilia said: 'It is an extraordinary story that you have to tell, William. Thank you for sharing it so openly with us. You have already experienced so much in your young life.'

'Yes, Emilia, that is very true,' was all he could find to say.

There was another long pause before she spoke again.

'And now? You have fulfilled your pledge to poor Edwin – God rest his soul! – by telling us the rest of his story and bringing his keepsake back to me. You are free to go back and seek out your other dear friend, who is still alive, God willing! Maybe he is sitting even now, watching the sun go down in some safe refuge in the distant Languedoc, thinking of you.'

William bowed his head and there was another long pause. Then he looked up and said quietly but firmly:

'Yes, that is exactly what I intend to do.'

***

In the event William stayed in Jaffa with Dominique and Emilia for another two and a half weeks. He knew that his friends would need at least that long to replenish their funds by working in Acre, and he had no wish to leave Jaffa sooner than was necessary. He also wanted to spend as much time as possible with his new, dear friends here, whose happiness at having him as a guest in their house was evident.

Then, one evening after Emilia had gone early to bed, Dominique had asked William whether he needed funds for his journey. William had replied at once that he would be able to earn enough in a few weeks in Jaffa, but Dominique knew that it wouldn't be that easy. He had produced a heavy velvet pouch from a pocket of his tunic and pressed William to take it. William had refused, of course, saying that he was already in his hosts' debt for putting him up in their home. But Dominique had insisted.

'William, you must realise that I am a rich man, and Emilia and I have no children of our own on whom to lavish our money. We have a comfortable life, and we are both deeply grateful to you for having completed your long quest to find us and to tell us what had become of our dear friend Edwin of long ago – bitter though the news was. It is the least we can do to ease your return journey to the west, to enable *you* to find the friend you left behind, and the place where you will be most at home. We knew little of the Languedoc before you came, but your stories of its kindly community which has been so ill-treated will always be in our thoughts, as will you, dear boy.'

With that he stood up, prompting William to do the same, and embraced him warmly, like a father. As they moved apart he again pressed William to take the velvet pouch, saying:

'It is Emilia's fervent wish too!'

William, with tears in his eyes, thanked Dominique for his kindness, his generosity and his words, and saw his own emotion reflected in the older man's eyes. Then he murmured:

'I shall return to the Languedoc as you say, and seek out my own place in the world. But I shall never forget your and your wife's kindness to me during the last few weeks. I do not suppose we will meet again in this world, but if one day I hear of someone making the pilgrimage to Jerusalem I shall send you word of how I am faring!'

'And we would be delighted to receive such news. We will think of you often, you can be sure of that!'

***

In the days that remained, William rose early most mornings to stroll the now familiar streets of the town, or to walk out along the coast to swim and have time to himself. When the heat built up he would return to the city and the house, sometimes entertaining Emilia with more tales of his journey, the people he had met along the way and his time working for the Church in Rome. His hostess enjoyed hearing his tales, but noticed and respected his reticence about Gilles. She could only hope that his return to his past would turn out more happily than poor Edwin's similar quest. Emilia talked often of the happiness she had found with Dominique, but nothing about her own life before she had met him, and William similarly did not probe her about her past. The couple's childlessness was an unspoken sadness which hung over the house but was never referred to.

When neither of his hosts was at home, William read from the shelf of poetry and Chansons de Geste. There was even a copy of the Chanson de Roland, and he returned to the wonderful story which he had first known from the troubadours' performances in Rochester when he was a boy. Returning now to the tale of friendship and valour in the face of Saracen invasion, he would draw comparisons with the fate of the Cathars. Like them, the Frankish forces of the Chanson had fought an implacable foe to defend their home and their beliefs, though of course the Cathars by their very nature were not warriors, and all the military might had been on the other side. Life was not as simple as it is in the troubadours' tales.

The generous couple insisted that William should dine with them every evening of his stay, and the three of them never seemed to run out of conversation. His hosts talked of the crusade of twenty years ago, and of the relative success of the peace treaty which had followed. Christians and Moslems lived for the most part peaceably side by side in the crowded towns, though the residential districts were divided. The Frankish incomers brought their own trading links and connections to the west, and built on the existing trade routes to the east. They had also brought their own tongue, which was now a *lingua franca* across Palestine.

Dominique was a fine example of the Frankish settlers. Like many of the crusaders, he had joined up with the French contingent for the travel and the adventure, but by the time the fighting was over and most of the crusaders had trailed back to their homelands, he had fallen in love with Emilia and had proposed to her. She had no other family in Palestine, loved Dominique as much as he loved her, and had shyly but gladly accepted. William wondered how Emilia had found her way out to Palestine in the first place, but did not feel he could ask. Finally, though, one afternoon she told him her story.

She had grown up as the youngest of nine children in an impoverished family in the back streets of Marseille. Her father was a wheelwright by trade, but was drunk most of the time and never earned enough to keep the family fed and clothed. Emilia had no memories of her mother who had died soon after Emilia was born, worn out by the constant child-bearing. Her older brothers and sisters found casual work wherever they could as soon as they were old enough, some of them drifting into petty crime. Her two older sisters turned, inevitably, to prostitution in the back streets of the great port, and Emilia, the prettiest of the daughters, seemed destined for the same fate, though in the event hers would be rather different.

Her father had come home one day with another rough-looking man, and told her he had found work for her with 'this gentleman'. The man, who looked nothing like a gentleman, had inspected her closely, felt her arm, and said:

'She'll do!'

Then her father had told her to pack a change of clothes and had handed her over to the man there and then, amidst the wailing of her mother who was the only other person at home at the time and could not save her. It was only when she was on board the ship bound for Palestine that Emilia understood what had happened. In common with a dozen other girls on the ship, she had been sold to the man and was now being taken to Palestine and the same fate as her older sisters back in Marseille. 'You'll be doing your duty to your country with our brave young men who are fighting the infidel!' the man had said with a leer. She never found out how much he had paid her father.

William did not know if it would be proper, but he reached out and placed a hand on her shoulder.

'I'm so sorry,' was all he could find to say.

Emilia looked up with a weak smile. 'Oh, it is all a long time ago! I have never told anyone apart from Dominique – not even Edwin in the short time I knew him – but I wanted to tell you, dear William.'

'Of course,' she went on after a long pause, 'my story turned out happily in the end. I got to know Dominique, we fell in love and he rescued me from my cruel fate. I suspect he paid money to release me from my master in the brothel, though if he did he has never admitted it.'

Emilia had had no idea then that he would become such a successful merchant, and that she would end up living in such comfort. In the early years it had been hard; he was often away for long periods, sometimes travelling as far as Tartary, as great a distance to the east as England lay to the west. Nowadays he employed others to travel and trade on his behalf, providing the credit and the camels for the journey, employing reliable overseers and paying his men a fair wage. He had built up the love and the trust of those who worked for him and the business was evidently thriving.

On another afternoon Emilia, fighting back the tears, had told William of the still-born baby, and of the mid-wife telling her afterwards that she would most likely never be able to have another child. Dominique had embraced his wife tenderly and reassured her when she, in floods of tears, had passed on this news. He had told her that he loved her as much as ever, and that they would have good lives. Coming back to the present, she explained that they had a wide circle of friends in the Frankish community, some of whose sons were already involved in the business and were being groomed to take it over one day, when Dominique was too old for the heavy workload. As Dominique explained all this, William was observing Emilia out of the corner of his eye. There could be no doubt of the bond of love between husband and wife, but at the same time… The thought flitted across his mind that the lost child might have been Edwin's, but he pushed it away. Emilia might well not know herself and it was probably better that way.

Some days later William finally set the date of his departure for the following week, and booked his passage. He could not leave it any longer and be sure that his friends would still be waiting for him in Acre.

***

William's final week in Jaffa passed quickly. He followed his established daily routine of a long, solitary walk along the coast and a swim in the morning, and a retreat to his cool bedroom at his hosts' house during the heat of the day. Later he went out into the town, making a few purchases of practical items for the journey, together with a few souvenirs of Palestine. The finest of these, a small but beautiful engraved brass goblet, he secretly thought of as a gift for Gilles, if he should find him again. It struck him that there was a strange parallel with Edwin's last journey which he had undertaken in the opposite direction but which the older man had not been able to fulfil in person.

As William walked the bustling streets and haggled in the markets of the old city, he was also recording in his memory all the sights and sounds and smells of the city, which he would perhaps one day pass on to wide-eyed children of the next generation.

He had dinner with Emilia and Dominique most evenings, and with Emilia alone on the evenings when her husband was kept late by his business. He understood the respect and trust which Dominique showed in allowing his wife to dine alone with a man who was not a member of the family. When he thanked him for this honour he had only laughed and replied: 'Dear William, we think of you as one of the family now!'

With Dominique's presence or without, the dinners were relaxed and enjoyable occasions. The personal matters were left aside and all three of them were determined to make the most of their little time together, valuing the friendship they had built on the tragedies of the past. William had a fund of tales from his travels, and further back from his childhood in England. It was a land about which his hosts seem to have few ideas, except that it was cold and rain-swept, and he was pleased to give them a more balanced picture. From here, he recalled his homeland as a green and fertile place of dense forests, winding rivers and lush farmland, though he spoke also of his father's expectations, and of his secret departure to join Edwin.

In return, Dominique talked one evening of his own upbringing near the great river Rhone in the County of Burgundy, of his violent and drunken father, and of his spur-of-the-moment decision to join up when a party of would-be crusaders passed through his home town of Macon. Then he had sighed and said: 'I don't think I was ever cut out to be a soldier, but I was young then and I would have done anything to get away from my father.'

On other evenings the conversation centred on the couple's

present lives in Jaffa, and then William was pleased that they both talked happily of their acquaintances, and he could hear in their voices the warmth and respect in which they were held by the community. By the time he left, William had met quite a few of these friends, particularly the men who were also traders and would call on business, but once or twice the wives too, who came to drink mint tea and gossip with Emilia in the afternoons. They all greeted warmly the couple's young visitor from so far away, though William was never sure how far his connection to them had been explained. In his presence, Emilia had simply introduced him as 'a visitor from England', which can't have been a common expression.

And so William's final week in Jaffa passed all too quickly, and the packing and preparations for his departure began. As the day approached he felt sad that once again he would be leaving behind people whom he had quickly become so fond of, but he knew too that this exotic land could never be his home. His quest now was to find that home, and put down roots. He must return to the place where he belonged.

Part IV – Coming Home

Middle Sea: late Summer 1211

The journey had been slow and arduous, and the four friends longed now for it to be over. They longed to walk again on solid ground, to be free of the unnatural motion of the ship, and the monotonous diet which never filled their bellies. This particular ship was the fourth of a succession of similar leaky tubs which had brought them, stage by weary stage, from Acre to Cyprus, from there to a string of fishing ports along the southern coast of Asia Minor, and similar tiny settlements on the Greek island of Crete. They had passed through seas dotted with rocky outcrops and full of porpoises which seemed to leap for joy, until they had finally turned north and followed the mountainous western coast of Greece itself. Some nights the boat simply moored in a sheltered bay, sometimes they put into a fishing port, and the passengers were grateful to go ashore for an hour or so, though the harbours were all equally filthy and stinking of fish. Their enthusiasm for seeing new places had been sated, they were tired of the rootless existence, they longed for home. The three Saxons all had their minds set on a return to the place where they had been born, settling down, and bringing up families of their own, as people everywhere did, however varied their customs, their religion and their dress.

William, of course, also had a fresh goal, but his was a less certain future. He had shared some of his intentions with

Albrecht, whom he knew best, and though he had said little about the dear friend he had left behind and would now seek out, Albrecht had drawn his own conclusions. He did not really understand, but equally he did not wish to pry or undermine a friendship which had only deepened in the long weeks of the shared journey. There can be few secrets between those who have tended one another through the fevers, fluxes, vomiting sicknesses and delirium of long sea-travel and unclean food.

***

At Corfu they had boarded a ship which was a little larger and more stable than its predecessors, bound for the great port at Brindisi. From there they would make the land journey across the Italian peninsula to Rome, where they would all rest up for a while, no doubt with William acting as guide and seeking out old acquaintances. Then they would make one more sea journey, probably to Marseille. From there William would head west to the Languedoc, whilst the others made their way north up the great river and eventually back to the dense forests and lush farmland of their Saxon home. They put out of their minds the impending farewells, after which they would almost certainly never meet or hear news of one another again.

After Corfu they had left the mountainous coastline of Greece behind them, and headed west across open sea for two days. It was the roughest stretch of water they had encountered so far and almost everyone fell sick. But on the second morning there was great excitement as a fresh coastline appeared in the west, low on the horizon although a faint outline of pinkish mountains rose up inland. The ship docked briefly at a fishing settlement on the coast, where there were a couple of hours for the passengers to go ashore, buy fresh sardines wrapped in palm leaves and exercise their stiff legs on solid land. But they made sure they were back on board in good time; the inhabitants were surly and avaricious, and it wasn't the sort of place where you'd want to get left behind. The following day they were in Brindisi, a sizeable city with a great Norman fortress and plenty of accommodation for travellers.

Neither William nor his friends had any wish to tarry. They booked into a pilgrim hostel for a couple of nights, and immediately started to investigate the best way to get to Rome. They had no wish to walk, as William had done on his journey down through France, and soon established that their funds should suffice to pay for places in one of the bullock-drawn carts which plied the route to Rome. The road, the via Appia, which like the via Domitia in the Languedoc dated back to the days of the Roman emperors, was said to be in fair condition.

After some enquiries, they opened discussions about a price for the four of them with a lean, sharp-eyed man who promised to complete the journey in 'under seven nights' for what seemed a reasonable sum, though the garbled mixture of vulgate Latin and heavily accented French which he seemed to use with all travellers made the details hard to grasp. Matthias, naturally the most cautious of the group, was concerned about the man's honesty, but the others told him to relax; there were after all four of them and only one of him.

Two days later the travellers gathered at first light outside the city walls where the rough track of cobbles and infill was already visible. Leandro was already there, with the cart and two bullocks ready in harness; they looked as if they had been strong beasts in their day. Leandro twisted his face into a leering grin and demanded full payment there and then. Matthias pointed out at once that they had agreed half now, half on arrival, and after some argument they settled for three instalments, one third now, one third along the way to enable Leandro to purchase more fodder for the bullocks and pay for his own lodging, and one third on arrival. Matthias muttered darkly that this was no more than he had expected, but the others pointed out that wanting some money in advance to cover costs was not unreasonable.

There were half a dozen other passengers, and by the time they had all arrived and sorted out their payments, loaded their bags and were seated it was nearly the tenth hour. Several other carts had left before them and Matthias sat on the other side of the cart from his three companions, glowering.

In the event, the first day's journey passed well enough. Progress was slow but everyone could see that the road, though still paved with great Roman slabs, was in bad condition. Leandro cursed the lazy villagers along the way who were meant to be indented to their landlords to keep the road in passable condition, but who were worthless curs and did nothing; as a result the journey was harder every time. The countryside was dry and barren, with not much sign of cultivation beyond straggly olive trees, and here and there a better tended grove of lemons or limes. The coastal plain was flat and featureless, though by the end of the first day the road started to rise – and to become still more uneven – as they climbed slowly into the dry interior. The fresh sea air was soon a distant memory, and the only consolation was that, considering the appalling condition of the road, the heavy cart seemed to be making quite good progress.

At the beginning of the journey the dozen or so passengers had introduced themselves and shared more or less about their origins and the purpose of their journey. Most were from the French lands and the Low Countries, though there were also a couple of other Saxons who kept themselves to themselves and a mysterious older man who spoke no language anyone could understand but was dressed like a pilgrim and bore the new shell of Compostella on his lapel. At first they conversed about their various journeys, so far as they were able, but as the sun rose higher the conversation faltered and the journey passed mostly in dozing and in silence.

By the time they reached their overnight stop, an hour or two before nightfall, everyone was clearly exhausted, apart from Leandro, who seemed to have the same stolid constitution as his two bullocks. Even Matthias had to admit that both beasts and driver had done sterling service on the first day of the journey, and the others agreed that Leandro might be gruff and have a wily look, but he had turned out to be reliable. Everyone swallowed down the bowl of thin stew and mug of weak ale which was all that was on offer at the farmstead where they stopped for the night, before retiring gratefully to the straw-carpeted hay loft which served as sleeping quarters.

The following days passed in much the same way and uneventfully, apart from one broken axle and a few delays where the road surface was in particularly bad condition. On these occasions, some of the stronger young men – inevitably including William and his friends – had to carry out impromptu repairs. William was actually quite grateful for an hour's exercise after the endless uncomfortable jogging of the cart, though some of the other travellers were more impatient at the lost time.

Overall they seemed to be making quite good progress, on the third night Leandro collected the interim payment, and on the fourth day they crested a rocky ridge and were relieved to see the track levelling out and then dropping away before them. The following morning they caught their first sight of the sea since leaving the east coast. Leandro stretched out his scrawny arm and exclaimed: 'The western sea!' and the usually taciturn passengers broke out in a babble of excited chatter.

By the following evening they were on a better maintained stretch of road which ran through low farming land a few leagues from the coast, and the following day they passed amidst a boisterous throng under the great arch of the Appian Gate into the city of Rome.

***

Returning to Rome had a strange sense for William of coming home, or at least of returning to something which felt less exotic, less foreign after the six months he had spent in Palestine. The four friends put up in the same lodgings near the via Santa Catarina where he and Gilles had stayed on his first visit. It felt strange to be there in different company, and however close a bond he had developed with his new friends, the pain of the separation from Gilles came back in waves in these familiar surroundings. Lying awake in the stuffy, noisy dormitory on the first night, he resolved to move on soon.

His companions, in the Eternal City for the first time, were for the most part too swept up in the scale and bustle and excitement of it to notice William's sadness, though Albrecht had sensed something in the tavern where they had supped that evening. He had put an arm round his friend and whispered to him the one-word question:

'Memories?'

William had smiled ruefully and murmured back: 'Yes, happy ones, and sad ones too.'

'About the friend you left behind?'

'Yes.'

'I don't suppose you'll be staying in Rome for long,' he murmured, with a sad smile.

'No,' William replied, 'not long at all. I shall leave as soon as I can find a passage to Marseille.'

'I shall miss you, William, we all will.'

'I shall miss you and the others too, Albrecht. But I know what I must do.'

'Yes, I understand, dear William.'

The two of them had sat in a cocoon of contemplative silence amidst the noisy diners and drinkers around them, until Matthias swung round to them, slapped William on the back and exclaimed:

'Hey, why so gloomy – we are in Rome! I hope you will show us some of the sights and your old haunts tomorrow.'

William looked up with a half-smile.

'Oh, I can show you some sights all right! But if you'll excuse me, I'm dog tired now. I think I'll turn in.'

Albrecht watched the friend whose life he had probably saved on the journey out to Acre. He cut a lonely figure as he made his way across the crowded room.

***

It took William a few days to find and arrange a ship bound for Marseille, and it would not leave for another ten. So in the end he spent another two weeks in the city, and was happy to have this final time here with his friends, now that his departure was set. He also called at the Lateran Palace and met his old master Aldhelm from the scribes' office. Aldhelm had greeted him warmly, and listened with interest to his talk of the places he had seen in the Holy Land, Jerusalem above all, though he had been disappointed that the reliable young man was not staying long enough in Rome to resume his work. When William departed, it was after another almost certainly final farewell – at least in this life, as Aldhelm had added with a smile. It was the same thought which had hung, unspoken, over William's conversation with Albrecht in the tavern.

And yet, William felt strangely at ease in the city, and he concluded that there were several reasons. He had completed his quest on Edwin's behalf, finding his friend's long-lost love and returning to her the precious lock of hair. He had had enough travel to last him a lifetime, seen many wonders, lived and worked amongst other peoples, and made many friends along the way. He certainly had a great store of memories and traveller's tales.

But now the end of his travels was, perhaps, in sight. Now the unfinished business was reduced to one end: to return to the place and the people amongst whom he had been happiest. Not the same people he had known then, of course, but to their community, their world. Surely that could not have been totally wiped out, as the city and the people he had known there had been wiped out? Surely some of that kind and gentle community must still be living out their open-spirited and selfless lives in peace and contentment? And, unspoken, too precious to be examined in the cold light of day, he would make his own final quest. He would seek out the dear friend whom he had watched receding to a tiny red spot on the quayside just a few leagues from here, when he himself had sailed away to Palestine a little more than half a year ago.

A few days before his planned departure, William shared his plans with Albrecht, who was not greatly surprised, but was relieved that his friend had taken him into his confidence before the final parting of the ways. He still did not pry too closely, but he embraced his friend and assured him only that he hoped he would find the happiness he sought amongst these people he described so fondly. It all sounded rather strange to him, and he had no doubt that it was a heresy in the eyes of the Church, but he could see the light in William's eyes as he spoke of the place to which he was inexorably drawn to return.

And so, in the cold light of dawn on the quayside at Ostia, another parting. The four friends who had travelled so far together and seen so much, embraced one another and the tears welled up. Finally, as the shouts from the ship became more urgent, William was obliged to tear himself away, shoulder his pack and hurry up the gang-plank, glancing back as he did so. The ropes were already being released and the ship was edging away from the quayside as William shuffled along the deck to the rear gunwale. He elbowed his way to the rail towards the stern of the ship. The dock-hands cast off the ropes and the ship lurched as the warm southerly wind filled the first of the sails. Soon the gap between ship and shore was widening, the water churning below, the final shouted farewells becoming more urgent. The figures on the quayside redoubled their waving, then rapidly became smaller, as if they were already disappearing into the past. Now the mainsails were deployed, the ship moved faster and the faces amongst the waving crowds on the dockside rapidly became harder to distinguish. William stayed by the rail and waved until the crowd on the dock had dissolved into a mere smudge of brighter colours between the warm ochre of the warehouses and the harbour wall and was finally lost in the glare of the rising sun. Then he wiped the tears from his eyes, and went below to find and stake his claim to a stable berth in the centre of the ship for the long journey ahead.

***

The journey was indeed long, but for William it passed agreeably enough. The ship was rarely out of sight of land, and there were frequent stops. Many of these were brief stops in smaller settlements, where a handful of passengers came aboard or went ashore, some at larger cities where there was time to leave the ship for an hour or so. William generally did so when there was time, though it was risky to stray far from the port because the departure time was never clear and the ship would not wait for stragglers. Onboard he kept himself to himself most of the time, absorbed in his own memories, thoughts and secret hopes. He did not feel the need of other people, perhaps made wary by the knowledge that friends made on a journey were so often lost again at the next port or fork in the road.

Day by day the ship and its passengers made their way up the coast of the Italian peninsula, stopping at Civitavecchia, an outpost of papal power, then at Porto Pisano though the city of Pisa which it served was not to be seen, further inland in the marshy plain. There was a brief stop at La Spezia, and then an overnight stop at Genova. Here there was time to go ashore in the evening, and William enjoyed the tasty food and the sensation of eating at a table where the floor did not move. After filling his stomach he strolled round on his own and marvelled at the splendour of the great trading city: houses of three, four or even five storeys were constructed vertically up the cliffs behind the port, each vying with its neighbours in the opulence of its carved and sculpted facade. Even so, William was tired of new sights, and tired of being the gawping stranger in someone else's city, and he returned early to the ship to curl up in his bunk and sleep. The next day there was a long stretch of coastline with high cliffs and only tiny until settlements, until the ship reached Monaco where a great Norman stronghold towered over the settlement. Soon after they were at Niça, the first sizeable port in the County of Provence, and two days later the ship arrived in Marseille.

Languedoc – Autumn 1211

William descended the rough wooden gang-plank and stepped onto the solid ground of the dockside. It seemed such a long time since he and Gilles had left from this same port, heading in the other direction. The air felt fresher than he was used to, with a stiff breeze blowing up from the west. He heard more French spoken in the crowd around him than he had for a long time, alongside the Occitane language, and of course the usual background of other tongues which could be heard in any port on the Middle Sea. As he turned into the back streets, the fruit and vegetables piled high on the market-stalls looked reassuringly familiar, but the stall-holders' jute and hemp tunics and breeches looked drab after the colourful robes of Palestine. He bought a couple of crisp green apples, pocketing one and munching the other as he walked; it felt like a homecoming. Then he realised that there was something missing: there was no aroma of freshly brewed kahwa wafting on the morning air.

He booked into a large and impersonal hostel not far from the port but which seemed clean and honest. There were plenty of other travellers around, but for now he preferred to be alone with his thoughts. It struck him that this was the first time he had been truly alone since the long walk south across France which he had made from Rheims after the death of Edwin, to Beziers where he had happened to meet Gilles as he entered the city on that beautiful morning which seemed so long ago. For now it suited him to be alone with his memories, and with his secret kernel of hope.

***

The next morning William bought breakfast of soft white bread and ripe cheese in the market, washed down with a glass of diluted wine. He asked around about his options for travelling on to Beziers, and was immediately met with anxious or embarrassed expressions and mumbled explanations. Surely he must know that the city had been abandoned after the dreadful events which had occurred there two summers ago? It was said that a few people were starting to rebuild and re-establish the city, but after what had happened… well, who would want to go there?

'I want to go there,' William had replied, 'to see if anyone has returned who might know of survivors…' But the people had shaken their heads and said that, from what they had heard, there were no survivors. The city had been burnt and all the people killed. A terrible fate, but well, they had asked for it with their foul heresy, hadn't they?

William had at first tried to explain that he had been there, and had known only kind and gentle people, but he could see the fearful glances this provoked and quickly learnt that he should keep both his intentions and his thoughts about the Cathars to himself. He had at least learned that there were efforts to rebuild what had been lost.

It seemed that there were two main choices for onward travel. One was to seek out passage on the smaller ships which plied the coastal ports between Marseille and the Catalan border, stopping along the way at the fishing settlement of Agde, which was only a day's walk from Beziers, or what remained of it. Alternatively he could follow the via Domitia, the old Roman coastal road. There were occasional carts carrying produce which would take a traveller or two for a modest sum, but as one more kindly man had put it: 'It will be a slow and uncomfortable journey, and a fit young man like you could walk the distance in a week.'

William remembered the cobbled road which snaked past the city on the southern side: he and Gilles had crossed it every time they went out of the city to swim and make love on those long-lost afternoons. He decided that he would walk back to Beziers, taking the opportunity to ask any friendly fellow-travellers or local people what they knew of the aftermath of the disaster. He would spend the rest of the day putting together some food supplies for the journey, getting his worn and ragged shoes repaired for the long walk ahead, and gleaning whatever further information he could.

He decided not to ask further about the fate of the kindly community he remembered. The people here all seemed to believe the story, no doubt regularly repeated from the pulpit, of depraved infidels who had rightly been wiped out by the will of God before they could spread their foul heresy any further. Trying to persuade casual acquaintances whom he met along the road to see a different version would only get him into trouble. He wanted to return to whatever remained of the good Christians and their community, not to be a martyr to their cause.

***

So, the following morning, newly shod, with a bag of supplies for the first couple of days and with one luxury, a finely carved olive-wood stick, William set off alone and on foot for the final stage of his journey. The autumn was already advanced and even here, in the south, the morning air was cool. There were few people on the road, mostly farmers or local people taking produce into the next town or village to sell, or to purchase supplies for themselves. He chatted to some who were going in the same direction as he was, but taking care now not to be too precise about where he was going or his purpose. Instead he passed himself off as a simple English pilgrim returning from Rome and Jerusalem. Once he had said that, the time passed pleasantly enough as he recounted his tales of the marvels of those famous cities. He soon discovered that the stories of everyday life, of camel rides and eastern markets, of kahwa and the Moslem call to prayer, provoked the greatest interest. He developed a rather good impression of the latter.

At other times he walked alone, and used the time to reminisce about his previous long walk which had led him to Beziers, and what he had found there. He was prepared, of course, for the Beziers which he remembered to be utterly gone and its tolerant community broken up and dispersed. But secretly he nurtured the hope that there would still be kindly Roman Christians, who remembered the old times, restoring the city and its life. There could be no hope of Cathars living openly within the walls, as they had done before, but perhaps there would be sympathisers who could tell him more, and where he might find communities of those who still followed the simple faith. Of course, he would not say – he barely even dared think it – that he was hoping to find one person in particular.

On the sixth evening he slept in the hut of an elderly shepherd, who assured him that a strong young man like him would reach Beziers easily the following day; or at least he would reach what remained of it, he had added with a grimace. William had not enquired further; he would see for himself soon enough.

**

William set off early the following morning, with a pack of bread and cheese left for him by his host, who was long since out with his flock. The road was reasonably well-maintained, William was impatient to reach his destination, and it was still early afternoon when he rounded a low hill and saw the skyline of the city before him.

It was not as it had been. The most prominent feature was the ruined tower of the church of the Magdalene which still stood, though it was charred and stumpy from the inferno which had consumed the good people within. There were some signs of life in the city: smoke rose from a chimney here and there, wooden scaffolding surrounded some of the larger buildings, and from his vantage point William could see a few figures making their way across the ancient Roman bridge which led into the city through the Porte de Carcassonne. He shouldered his pack and made his way along the last stretch of the road, ruefully recalling his very different emotions on that long-lost morning when he had first seen the city from the other side, as he had walked down from the Minervois hills whose outline showed faintly even now on the northern horizon.

Half an hour later he crossed the bridge, which appeared unscathed, and made his way up the slope to enter the citadel through the Porte de Carcassonne.

***

Those first couple of hours back in the city were a bitter experience for William. Everything spoke of the dreadful destruction and massacre which had happened here two years earlier. The great Porte de Carcassonne still stood – it had perhaps been too solid to destroy – but the smooth blocks of the original structure had been hacked away and the great doors which had swung open to allow the Crusader horsemen to burst into the city had been removed. There was now a rough wooden screen which could be pulled into position overnight. The deeper William ventured into the once proud city, the further his heart sank. The great houses had had their ornament and insignia hacked away, and the streets were still piled with rubble from the orgy of destruction which must have followed the taking of the city. Glassy-eyed crows picked fitfully at the detritus.

In a few places there were signs of reconstruction in progress, though none was actually taking place. The few people he crossed in the street avoided his eye and showed no interest in who this tired and ragged stranger might be. It was all in such stark contrast to William's first arrival in the city when he had marvelled at the evident wealth and the throbbing life of the streets, and had already been befriended by Gilles by the time he had reached this point.

He walked all the way up to the Church of the Magdalene, which still showed signs of smoke damage above the few high windows, but was firmly boarded up. There was no clue as to the massacre which had transpired there and William passed on with a shudder. He had noticed one or two other churches which appeared to be still in use, though all were firmly locked. Here and there, peasant farmers had set up their stalls in the corners of squares or in side alleys, where they were selling basic produce – vegetables, fruit and cheese, along with a few rough-looking cuts of meat – to mostly elderly customers. The overall effect was of a city which had been blighted, cursed, and from which most of the survivors had fled to rebuild their lives elsewhere. Only the old, who had perhaps been most drawn to return, or least willing to leave, were left in possession of the ruins.

In what had been the main market square there was a little more life, though even that seemed to be winding up as the sun dropped behind the buildings. William had not eaten all day, and he bought half a loaf, some cheese and a couple of apples, and sat on a stone bench in the corner of the square to eat for the first time since his breakfast soon after the dawn. An elderly man wrapped in a ragged cloak sat down nearby and eyed him calmly, and William nodded to him and wished him good evening. The man looked up with tired eyes and returned the greeting, then added: 'though evening is no different from any other time of the day here, any more.'

The man didn't seem inclined to say any more, but no-one else had addressed William at all, so he looked the man in the eye and said:

'I was here on that terrible day.'

'I know you were, young man, I recognised you at once, you were Gilles' friend who was staying at the house of Gerald and Therese. William, isn't it? You obviously don't remember me, but then I have probably changed more than you, after the horror we lived through.'

William looked at the man more closely.

'But I do remember! You were one of the perfect who attended the meetings in their house ...Thomas, isn't it?'

'That's right, William. I am one of the survivors, God help me! The only one from those evenings apart from you, as far as I know. Did Gerald persuade you to leave in time?'

William looked up. 'No, I stayed, and I know that there was at least one other survivor: Gilles and I escaped together down the outer wall of the city, and...'

But Thomas's rheumy eyes opened wider and he murmured:

'Dear Gilles, he is alive?'

'Yes, Thomas, he survived. He showed me how to escape down the cliff on the south side of the city. We returned briefly the following day, but when it was clear that the massacre of those within the walls had been total we fled and travelled East. Gilles came with me as far as Rome, before deciding that he must return to his own people, to seek out other survivors. He cannot have returned here, or you would have known. I travelled on, all the way to the Holy Land, but this place, and the memory of Gilles, have brought me back now, to seek out the past. I hope against hope to find my dear friend again.'

Thomas did not comment, but instead asked:

'Do you have anywhere to stay tonight, William? No? Well, of course you don't, there are no lodging houses any more. You will be welcome to share the humble shelter I call my home now. You can tell me the rest of your story. It will make a change from brooding alone on all that has been lost.'

'That is very kind of you, Thomas. I have enough tales to tell!' William replied, with genuine gratitude, though he was already wondering how much of his story to share. For now he helped the old man to get up and took his arm as he led the way through the dark and rubble-strewn alleyways.

***

William spent the next three days and nights staying with Thomas in the ruined city. His home consisted of two intact rooms which had once formed the living-area of a larger house. He explained that the few residents of the city who had been elsewhere on the day of the massacre, as he had, spent their days restoring their homes, or the buildings they occupied, as best they could, or starting again with whatever materials they could scavenge. There was no particular sense of ownership, only a vague desire to restore some vestige of the once fine and thriving city.

During the day William walked the streets, lending a hand here and there with lifting heavy beams or clearing rubble. In that way he got to chat with a few of the other returners, though most seemed to prefer not to talk about what had happened but to concentrate on restoring some semblance of order to the chaos. People showed little interest in who he was or what he was doing in such a benighted place.

One morning when the clouds cleared he even walked down to the shore, to the spot which he and Gilles had made their own, but a chill wind was blowing off the sea when he got there and he was not even quite sure which was the creek where they had spent so many joyous hours. He sat, huddled in his thin jacket, looking out at the sea for a short while, then returned to the city. The past was not here.

He also paid for his keep by purchasing basic foodstuffs from the few local farmers who set up stalls inside the gates during the early morning, selling mostly fruit, vegetables and olive oil, and occasionally rough off-cuts of lamb or goat. They drove a hard bargain, and complained incessantly of how difficult it was to survive now that most of the people had left. If they seemed friendly, William tried asking if they had news of Gilles son of Gerald, who had survived the massacre and returned to the city the previous autumn, but they shrugged and shook their heads.

Later in the day William returned to Thomas's makeshift home, helping him with boarding up the gaps in the walls before the winter came. He also scavenged for firewood, which was not difficult in the lower quarters of the city. The upper parts around the cathedral had clearly been torched and only stone walls and charred remnants of wood remained.

In the evenings they ate a simple meal and talked of the way it had been before. Of the wondrous simplicity and kindness of the good Christians, and of the tolerance that had existed between them and their orthodox neighbours. How could such simple goodness have been damned as heresy? On the second or third occasion when this subject came up, Thomas had said to William:

'There is something you should know, but which is dangerous knowledge. You must not speak of it to anyone else; the spies of the Church are everywhere. Be careful how much you say to casual acquaintances.'

William nodded, and murmured: 'Of course!'

'Well, after the destruction of Beziers, the crusaders committed other massacres too horrible to speak of, and they took Carcassonne too, though that fine city fell through the treachery of Count Trencavel and without great loss of life. But there too the population were expelled and lost their homes and livelihoods.'

The old man shook his head sadly before continuing. 'So many people have been forced to abandon their homes and flee! Our Christian neighbours, of course, could seek sanctuary with friends and family in other towns – many went to Toulouse, others further afield – but for our people, for the good Christians who held to their faith, the choices were more limited.

'One option was to renounce the faith and swear allegiance to the Church of Rome, and I am sorry to say that some did this. That was the choice they made, and they must live and die with it. But others, it is said, have retreated to the southern mountains, and have founded communities in hidden valleys, or taken over mountain fortresses where the local Lord is sympathetic to our beliefs. They are said to farm the land and to be free to live, for now at least, according to the tenets of our faith.'

Thomas closed his eyes and fell silent and William wondered at first if the old man had fallen asleep. But then he opened them again and went on: 'I can see our people there even now, in my mind's eye, and I would join them if I were a younger man, and my eyesight were not so bad.'

William looked up and murmured: 'Perhaps Gilles has found his way to this place of sanctuary too. God willing.'

In the long silence which followed, William knew exactly what he was going to do.

***

When William first made his suggestion, Thomas thought for a moment and, politely but firmly, turned it down. He had lived in the city all his life, and was too old to leave it now. There were poor and needy people here who needed comfort and support; despite the disaster which had befallen the city it remained his home; and, finally, he was old and frail and lacked the stamina for such a journey. William must go and seek out the communities of survivors who would nurture and carry forward the flame of Cathar belief in their hidden places and hilltop eyries. Thomas gave him his blessing, but he himself would stay here to make his peace with God.

But William did not give up so easily, and over the next few days he worked to persuade the old man. He was a fount of Cathar wisdom and sanctity, which must not be lost, and his place now was not here amongst the ruins, but with the surviving communities in the hills. Most of all he would be able to teach the children the old beliefs and show them the beauty of the good Christian way of life, which they would teach to their children in their turn. Slowly, the old man came to see that what the young man said was true. He did not tell William, but he came to believe that God had sent this young traveller, who had arrived out of nowhere, to remind him of his duty to his people and his faith, and to help him make the journey.

The preparations did not take long. William had only the pack he had arrived with. Thomas seemed to have barely more worldly possessions, and most of those he left behind. They bought a few meagre supplies of food to last the first day or so of the journey. William had enough money to buy more along the road, though Thomas had held out his empty hands and said only: God will provide. The old man had warned William that his rheumatic legs would only allow him to go slowly, though he believed he could still walk a full day, but William had reassured him that he had enough money left to pay for a ride on bullock-carts when the chance arose.

And so, on the fourth morning after William's arrival in the city they left through the Porte de Carcassonne, following the via Domitia as it continued south-westwards towards Narbonne. Thomas did not know how many days it would take to reach the hills, or the exact location of the communities they sought, but the chain of southern mountains glistened faintly on the far horizon to show them the general direction they must follow. William could not resist looking back once or twice for a final view of the city which carried with it such a burden of memories. By mid-morning it had shrunk to a mere smudge on the horizon, and when they ate lunch of bread and cheese it was gone, and the mountains, though still very distant, had become clearer as the late sun had burnt off the morning mist.

Thomas knew the names of some of the main Cathar strongholds in the mountains: Queribus, Aguilar and Peyrepertuse, this last also known as 'Carcassonne celeste' for its location on a vertiginous ridge of craggy rock; these were said to be the most accessible in the first range of mountains beyond Narbonne. More remote and more secure, there were said to be others, including the fabled redoubt of Montsegur in the foothills of the high mountains further west. William's plan, with which Thomas willingly concurred, was to head for one of the nearer retreats initially. They could no doubt stay there, seek out more information and rest for a while, before deciding whether to settle or to move on.

The journey proceeded as planned, mostly on foot but a couple of times bouncing along for a few hours in the carts of taciturn local farmers. If they guessed where the odd couple were heading they didn't pry; in these times it was better not to know too much about other people's business. Thomas' legs held out, though William made sure they stopped walking well before sundown and slept undercover most nights. On the third day they reached Narbonne. The city was bustling and full of life, in sharp contrast to the ruined buildings, empty streets and despair of Beziers which still haunted William's sleep. It was a bitter reminder of what the city had been. They restocked with food, slept in comfortable bunks in a simple hostel and left again the next morning.

William had noticed Thomas deep in conversation with another greybeard when he had returned from the market after breakfast, and once they were on the road alone again, the older man explained that he had recognised the man from Cathar councils in "the days before", which was how he always referred to the time prior to the destruction of his city. The man was a fellow perfect – Thomas did not mention his name – and he had passed on what he knew of the communities in the mountains. He had warned them to pass by the nearest settlements, in particular Aguilar which was within a half day's walk of the via Appia as it continued south towards Perpignan and Catalonia, but was in the hands of the Termes family who were vassals and allies of Count Roger.

Instead they should seek sanctuary at the great fortress of Peyrepertuse, which was further from the main road and thought to be impregnable on its long, craggy outcrop with its mighty encircling walls. The fortress was in the hands of Lords of Aragon, who were known to give shelter to Cathars. The man had nodded politely to William as he returned with the supplies, and said to Thomas: 'Your young friend will be a useful addition to the men of fighting age there.' He had then given Thomas clear directions on how to reach Peyrepertuse, and reassured them that the journey should take them no longer than twice the time they had spent reaching Narbonne, perhaps a further week on foot. William agreed with this plan, already thinking that someone there might have heard news of Gilles or know of his whereabouts. He dared not think that Gilles himself might even have found his way there.

So, on the following morning they were on the road again, and almost immediately got a lift with a farmer returning to his village which was some three hours' ride away. William asked Thomas if he would like to rest there for the remainder of the day and sleep in the farmer's loft, but Thomas had said no, he still had some strength in his legs and that they should walk for a further hour or two. They followed this same pattern of some walking and some bumping along in farmers' carts for the next couple of days, sleeping twice in barns and only once in the open, and William was amazed at Thomas's stamina and good humour in the face of a journey which must have been a trial for him in his old age.

On the fourth morning Thomas pointed to a narrow valley climbing into the hills which now reached almost down to the road on the western side and said:

'This is the turning which leads to our destination; my old friend described the lie of the land precisely. We should pass by the smaller fortresses of Aguilar and Queribus, and if God smiles on us we should reach Peyrepertuse easily on the second day.'

Once they had turned off the via Appia, there was a rutted cart-track rather than the Roman flagstones of the main road, but on foot it was, if anything, easier going, and for long stretches they could walk alongside the track on smooth pasture dotted with wildflowers. There was very little sign now of other travellers or local people, though they noticed a few shepherds tending flocks on the green flanks of pasture which rose higher around them the further west they went along the valley. The countryside was glorious and raised the spirits of both the weary travellers.

William noticed that he was haunted less by his memories of Beziers the further and higher they travelled into this wonderful landscape. They did indeed pass the foursquare fortress at Aguilar that afternoon, but on the advice of Thomas's friend they did not turn off the track. It looked a forbidding place.

They slept in an abandoned shepherd's hut that night, with only the remains of their own supplies and water as sustenance. William marvelled again at Thomas's stamina, and at the gentleness and humility which seemed part of his very being.

The remainder of the journey took a little longer than Thomas had foreseen, in part because he was clearly tiring now, and William suspected that his companion's old joints were causing him considerable pain, though he never complained. Nonetheless, they continued to make steady progress, catching a distant glimpse of the precipitous fortress of Queribus on its pinnacle of rock. Again they followed the advice of Thomas's acquaintance and did not approach closer. In the early afternoon they caught their first glimpse of Peyrepertuse, a long ribbon of walls strung out along the length of a massive, sloping outcrop of the mountains, and defended by towers along the curtain wall and by redoubts at both ends. William could see tiny figures walking on the walls, though even his young eyes could not identify if they were soldiers keeping watch, or civilians relaxing from their labours or simply enjoying the view. As they approached, a long track led up the lower grassy slopes of the hill, disappearing round the extreme right-hand end of the ridge, and presumably leading to the main entrance, hidden from sight on the northern face. The two men looked at one another without a word. William hoisted his pack onto his back, Thomas picked up his stick once more, and they embarked on the final long climb to their destination.

Neither of them spoke, though their thoughts were similar as they ascended wearily to the castle in the sky: they were coming home.

***

A few hours later William and Thomas were sitting alongside one another in the middle of one of the long trestle tables which ran the full length of the vast and echoing refectory. They had been welcomed as new arrivals, the one as a strong young man to bolster the working and fighting strength of the community, the other as a respected elder to offer spiritual guidance and support to the substantial number of good Christians within the walls. The newcomers had already gathered that there were some two hundred residents, of all ages and backgrounds, of whom most but not all followed the Cathar belief. There were some twenty perfect, whose ranks Thomas now joined, and there were a larger number of Roman Christians, horrified by the excesses of the crusaders or simple refugees expelled from their homes by the fighting. It appeared that there were a fair number of sick and wounded, who were cared for as well as possible in a makeshift infirmary. In the warm and friendly surroundings of the refectory, and with a steaming plate of vegetable broth and a hunk of bread in front of him, William was already relaxing. He had no doubt that he had returned to the place and the community where he belonged. He scanned the room, noting Thomas deep in conversation with another of the perfect, then running his eyes over the long rows of other diners who filled the room, seeking, but not finding, one particular face.

As the meal drew to an end, and the diners began to return their plates and knives to the servery and drifted away in smaller groups to relax for an hour or so before bed, William noticed Thomas get up from his bench and make his way across the room towards him. The kindly old man looked more at peace with the world than ever and caught William's eye with a broad smile as he approached. He leant down and whispered in William's ear:

'You should go through to the kitchens. I understand there's someone working there who...'

William could feel his eyes filling up. Thomas touched his arm, pointed and said:

'Go!'

William nodded and crossed the rapidly emptying room towards the door through which the food had been brought. He entered the cavernous, arched kitchens, and scanned the room. There were twenty or thirty kitchen staff, dressed in white aprons, clearing and washing plates and knives, but his eyes stopped on one particular figure with an untidy mop of light-brown hair, bent over a basin of steaming water. As if aware that he was being watched, the figure looked up and their eyes met across the echoing space. His heart beating in his chest, the tears welling up, William rushed across the room and he and Gilles threw their arms around one another, unaware of their surroundings or of the surprised expressions of the other kitchen staff, unaware of anything except that they were together again. When they finally separated and looked into one another's eyes, it was Gilles who spoke first.

'I have longed for this moment.'

'So have I, Gilles, so have I!'

Then Gilles threw his arm round William's shoulder, and said:

'Let's take a walk around the walls – there's so much I want to tell you!'

Gilles' colleagues smiled to see the reunion, and no-one pointed out that there was still work to be done in the kitchen.

***

They walked the walls in contented silence for a while, then found a quiet spot where they could sit together and share their most pressing news. Gilles asked William at once about the outcome of his quest to find Edwin's lost love and to fulfil his promise to his dead friend, and William recounted the story of the successful outcome and of the welcome and generosity he had received from Emilia and Dominique. William then said that he had seen many marvels and had much to share, but that the rest of his traveller's tales could wait. For now he longed to hear how Gilles had fared since their separation.

Tears came to William's eyes again as Gilles told of his loneliness and despair on the ship home from Rome, and of the dreadful reports he had heard on his return to the land of his birth. Before continuing, Gilles put his arms around him and told him not to weep; they were together again now.

Gilles repeated what William already knew: that Carcassonne had been the next target after Beziers and had eventually been taken the following summer, though without a massacre this time. The civilian population had, however, been forced to flee, leaving behind their homes and all but the few possessions they could carry. Bloody reprisals had been exacted elsewhere across the Languedoc: blindings, burning of villages suspected of harbouring heretics and summary executions. Terror had stalked the land, much of it at the hands of William's countryman, Simon de Montfort, who had been appointed Count of Beziers and Carcassonne after the imprisonment and suspicious death in his own dungeons of the erstwhile leader of the southern forces, Raymond Roger Trancavel.

When he heard all this, William had shaken his head, laid a hand on Gilles' shoulder and said: 'I should have come back with you, not gone off to the East on my own. My first duty was to you, my dearest friend, at such a time.'

Gilles looked into his eyes and was silent for a long time before he replied. Then, quietly, he said:

'I missed you terribly of course, and longed for you, but

I reminded myself that your first loyalty was to Edwin. You fulfilled your promise despite all the difficulties and challenges, and that is a fine thing. Yes, I missed you more than I can tell, but I found my way here as soon as I had seen enough elsewhere, and was taken in and welcomed. I always believed you would return and find your way here, and now you have. I have longed for the day when I would see your smiling face again, and today – today, you have come!'

He stopped, took William's hands in his and looked him straight in the eye for a long time. Finally he spoke again.

'But I have done a lot of thinking too. My place is here, with my people, fighting for our cause, defending our beliefs and our way of life. You must find your own course. If you decide to stay here, with us, I would be overjoyed, but if you were to decide that your future lies with your own people, in the place where you were born and grew up, then I would understand and respect that too.'

Gilles could see that William was about to speak, but he put a finger up to his lips to silence him.

'No, dear friend, do not answer now. You must think it over in the coming days and weeks, *then* tell me your decision. It must be yours and yours alone, and it must not be taken in haste – least of all on such a day as today has been!'

William bowed his head and realised that his friend had changed over the period of their separation. He had done some hard thinking and reached some wise conclusions. He had, in short, become a man.

William looked into Gilles' enquiring eyes and replied:

'You speak wisely and I will do as you say.' Then he grinned, and took out of his pocket a package wrapped in fine muslin which he shyly handed to Gilles.

'It's just something I brought back from Palestine, for you.'

Gilles took the package, unwrapped it carefully and took out the brass goblet.

'Thank you, William, it's beautiful! I shall treasure it always,' he said, and they embraced again.

***

The next few days confirmed both Thomas's and William's expectations of this place of sanctuary. The older man was quickly absorbed by his own people: he spent part of the day performing routine duties, but was also occupied in discussing the spiritual needs of the credentes with his fellow perfect, and offering support and guidance to individuals. William learned from Thomas that there were many amongst the credentes who had suffered terrible losses during the period when the crusaders had raged across the land, killing, raping and burning. There were a smaller number of Christian survivors from Beziers, who had left before the destruction of the city, but virtually no others. Gilles himself, and William also of course, were the only people known to have escaped the city after the attack. William was surprised and gratified to learn that they were welcomed and respected as survivors, not least because they could pass on for future generations the dreadful details of what had happened that day.

William was quickly assigned to work in the carpentry shop, and found himself renovating worn-down or decayed parts of the defences, as well as undertaking more mundane work repairing furniture and making more for the constant flow of new arrivals. When the enticing smell of baking bread wafted across on the morning air from the great ovens, he savoured the aroma which reminded him that Gilles was nearby, deploying in the kitchens the skills he had learnt in his father's bakery.

Thomas's work included devoting a couple of hours three mornings a week performing lighter tasks in the vast kitchen-garden which covered a good quarter of the ground-space within the walls and was expanding all the time. It provided most of the supplies for the community, though parties also went out during the hours of daylight to forage for wild fruit, nuts and berries, and for herbs, and to barter with local farmers for wheat and other supplies. It seemed that most of the local people were sympathetic to the community at Peyrepertuse, and indeed saw it as a potential place of refuge for themselves in times of danger.

William soon realised that the community was growing steadily in numbers: every few days there seemed to be new arrivals, many of them with harrowing stories to tell of the torture and killing of Cathar believers or sympathisers, and even the torching of whole villages where the people were suspected of heretical leanings. It struck William that the community would soon outgrow the available space for accommodating and feeding everyone, but he kept the thought to himself for now. There was an inner council which held regular meetings and presumably addressed such matters. And so the days passed quickly, and William was amazed when Thomas remarked to him one evening at supper that they had already been here for three weeks. His days were fully occupied in rewarding work and this warm and supportive community, formed in the face of tragedy and adversity, had quickly come to feel like home.

***

October came, and with it a noticeable chill in the air, though there was still some warmth in the sun on clear days. The clouds started to roll in from the sea, the leaves turned to ochre and gold and then to brown. The community in Peyrepertuse made their preparations for the winter, laying down stocks of pickled vegetables, of apples and potatoes, and filling the granaries. Some of the livestock were slaughtered and the meat salted, others were brought in to closer pastures or even into the wide precincts of the fortress. The women participated in this work, but they also span and sewed and repaired the winter clothes. Parties were sent out now to forage for firewood, and to barter with local farmers and villagers for blankets and straw to provide extra bedding for the sick and the elderly. William sometimes went on these excursions, and despite the problems and dangers facing the community he was struck again by the beauty of the countryside as the lushness of summer faded into the muted shades of autumn. Surely God would protect these good people now, after all they had suffered? Stories and rumours of further round-ups and killings still circulated, though for now at least Peyrepertuse seemed a safe haven, a mountain-top eyrie protected from the brutalities of the wider world. William always felt a renewed sense of homecoming when the foraging parties returned, making their way up the long ascent and passing through the narrow and half-hidden gate in the encircling walls.

The bond of friendship between William and Gilles was as strong as ever, but there was little privacy in Peyrepertuse and seemingly few opportunities for a return to the intimacy they had once shared. They talked of everything else, but not of that. Then one morning Gilles asked William if he thought he could get a few hours' leave from work the following day, to go outside the walls, explaining that he was due a half-day away from the kitchens. William saw the gleam in his friend's eye, nodded and said yes, he would like that. He spoke to the elder who organised the carpentry rota and he agreed to allow William the same half-day. He put a hand on the young man's shoulder and said: 'You work well and hard, William; you deserve some time off with your long-lost friend.' It seemed everyone in the fortress knew the story of the two friends who had been tearfully reunited in the kitchens of Peyrepertuse after a long separation.

The next day, after lunch, the two of them walked out of the great gate and down the rough stone track amidst green meadows, which Thomas and William had ascended a month before. Short excursions beyond the walls were permitted during the hours of daylight, though everyone was advised not to go too far afield; in these times it was always better to be cautious. Gilles suggested that they should simply take a circular walk along the north side of the fortress; that way they would never be far from the entrance which was in the north-east corner. He had been out on regular foraging trips and seemed to know the paths quite well, leading the way through dense undergrowth to a tiny clearing adjoining the base of the fortifications. In the clearing there was a small stone building, presumably intended for storage, but now empty. Gilles led the way inside and pointed to the pile of dry straw with a flourish.

'There's no sandy beach or rippling sea, but it's clean and dry and it's off the foraging routes.'

He didn't need to say any more, William was already taking Gilles in his arms and kissing him urgently. They rolled down onto the straw, holding one another tight, revelling in the closeness, their long separation over and their reunion complete. It felt so good.

The sun had dropped behind the castle by the time they reached and entered the great gate of the fortress. William felt a sense of calm and contentment which he had never imagined possible. The community might be in danger, but he would fight to defend it. He had lost Gilles once but now, against all the odds, he had found him again. He was ready to return to the great question which Gilles had posed but left to him to resolve.

***

That evening, at the end of supper, William murmured to Gilles that he was ready to tell him what he had decided. Gilles nodded, and they sat in companionable silence until most people had left the refectory, then moved closer to the remaining warmth from the dying embers of the great fire.

'Well, William,' Gilles said, laying a hand on his friend's shoulder, 'what is your decision?' William looked down for a moment, gathering his thoughts, then he spoke, in a calm and serious tone.

'Gilles, it has not been easy. In the last four years I have travelled further and seen more of the world than I could ever have imagined. During that time I have seen wonders, known great joys… and experienced unspeakable horrors. The senseless death of Edwin was a terrible blow, but in the weeks and months that followed I started to learn that I could survive on my own; I started to become a man, maybe.

'Then my path took me to Beziers, and to you, and I like to think that that did not happen by chance, that God smiled on me. And so the happiest time of my life began.'

William, who had been gazing into the glowing embers as he spoke, looked up at this point, and Gilles could see the emotion glistening in his eyes.

'And for me, too!' he said.

'I am glad to hear you say that, though I have seen it in your eyes too,' William continued. 'But then, of course, the evil came and we were cast adrift. All we had was one another, and we carried on, preoccupied with the journey. But even before we reached Rome I knew that you would be drawn to return, and when you made your decision I would have come too, were it not for my promise to Edwin. That separation tore at my heart.'

'You are right, William,' Gilles replied, 'I cared for you more than I can say, but the thought that I had abandoned my people tormented me and my sleep was filled with nightmares of death and mutilation. It tore me in two, but in the end I knew I must return to my people. I did not regret my decision, but every day, from the day I watched your ship disappearing over the horizon to the day you walked in here, I thought of you and longed to see your face again.'

'It is so good to be with you again and to hear you say that,' William said, and the two friends embraced and held one another for a long time. Then they sat back again and William continued.

'But I had my promise to Edwin to fulfil, and I knew I could not abandon that. So I went on, alone, saw many wondrous sights and found the person I was seeking and succeeded in my mission, as you know. Indeed, it fills me with joy that my arrival brought some relief to both Emilia and Dominique. I brought sad news, but freed them from never knowing what had happened to a man whom they both remembered so fondly.'

'You did your duty by your friend; nothing is more important than that!' Gilles said.

'Yes, yes I hope I did,' William replied, and they sat quietly again for a while. Another of the candles guttered and went out, so that they could barely see more than the outline of one another's faces in the surrounding darkness.

'And that brings me to the here and now, and to the future,' he went on finally. 'Of course, I have thought of my family and my birthplace and my childhood in Rochester, and the separation from them will always be a sadness in my heart. But I have seen so much and been away so long that it all seems very distant now. If I returned, I would have little in common with the people I grew up alongside. To be honest, I feel more fellow-feeling with the people of the Languedoc, with the kind and gentle Cathars, and with their Christian neighbours who – before the crusaders came at least – lived alongside one another in friendship and in peace. I like to believe that the present is a time of strife which will pass, and that peace will return to the land. And I want to be part of it.

'Life will never be quite the same as it was before – how

could it be after all that has happened? But we will have one another, and I realise now that that is the most important thing in the world. I have thought long and hard, yet in the end it is simple. I love this land and these people, and I love you. This is where I want to settle and live my life, whatever it may bring.'

Gilles' eyes filled with tears. He rose to his feet, pulled William up too, and there, in front of the great fireplace in the dark and echoing chamber the two young men embraced tightly, and swore the closest bond of love and friendship until death.

Acknowledgements

Special thanks are due to Michael Coates for his invaluable proof reading of the final text, to Roger Hinton and the other members of the writing group where it all began, and of course to Alan.

About the Author

Steve Whittington was born and grew up in Poole, Dorset. He was educated at Poole Grammar School and Exeter College, Oxford, where he studied French and German, travelling widely in Europe during summer vacations. Those early experiences of the wider world would later contribute to the idea for Quest.

Later in life, Steve honed his writing technique through evening classes and with the support of a writing group of other first time authors. Quest is the result, and his first full length novel.

After a career in London, and a short period in France, Steve lives in Brighton with his partner, Alan, and continues to enjoy regular travel and creative writing.